I0691266

Quid Est Veritas
The Tynemouth Werewolves

Martin Clephane

A Wild Wolf Publication

Published by Wild Wolf Publishing in 2017

Copyright © 2017 Martin Clephane

All rights reserved. No part of this book may be reproduced, stored in a retrieval system or transmitted in any form or by any means without the prior written permission of the publishers, except by a reviewer who may quote brief passages in a review to be printed by a newspaper, magazine or journal.

First print

All Characters appearing in this work are fictitious. Any resemblance to real persons, living or dead, is purely coincidental.

ISBN: 978-1-907954-62-7
Also available in e-book edition

www.wildwolfpublishing.com

For my beautiful wife Justine…
…four letters inside a heart, drawn in the sand.

Introduction: Quid est veritas? (What is truth?)
John 18

37 And so Pilate said to him "You are a king, then?"

Jesus answered,"You are saying that I am a king. For this I was born, and for this I came into the world: so that I may offer testimony to the truth. Everyone who is of the truth hears my voice."

38 Pilate said to him, "What is truth?"

Chapter 1
The 1ˢᵗ Incident

Seafield View, Tynemouth, on the North East coast of England. A January evening, full moon:

Rose Stearman turned off the TV. She got up with a sigh and went to the kitchen to do her final job for the evening; washing the dishes. As she watched the sink fill, she regretted the row with her husband Bob. "Why do I fly off the handle like that? It never solves anything. Bob just storms out to the pub. God knows when he'll be back."

Rose was in many respects a typical Geordie housewife, a real "Mrs. Cannybody" people would say, meaning she was down to earth and one of us. Although her youthful prettiness had gone, she still retained a noble stature that set her apart from other women of her age. She cut a fine figure; even in her apron, which hung from a slender neck and pinched in to her narrow waist. She was now in her late forties and had been married to Bob for 20 of those years.

She hadn't been her "canny" self the past few days. She had been snappy and emotional; she knew it was her time of the month. Normally sweetness and light, she had struggled with PMT since her teens.

She thought to herself, "Isn't it amazing how a person can change just because of the time of the month?"

She looked out at the sea. The moon marked a straight path of silver from the horizon to the beach. She watched the white water break against the shore then draw back. She thought of the power of the moon controlling the tide, controlling the months, controlling her.

She heard the door open and felt an icy gush of wind against her exposed calves. "So you're back then?" She shouted, over her shoulder towards the hall, which led from the kitchen to the front door.

She ascertained that Bob really had, had a skin full tonight, as the door was left open behind him.

She wanted to talk about their earlier argument, but thought it would have to wait until the morning. The icy draft was

7

accompanied by an unpleasant smell, a smell that Rose seemed to recall; wet dogs. Wet dogs that had been rolling in something nasty, that strange territorial thing she remembered her dog Bonnie doing, all those years ago. How she'd loved that puppy…

She could hear heavy breathing. How she wished Bob would kick the fags and ease up on his drinking. He said it was his defence mechanism when she was "in one of her moods".

The smell grew stronger, "Oh for God's sake Bob, what ever you've fallen in don't get it on the sofa!"

She grabbed the carpet cleaner spray from under the sink, just to be on the safe side, and turned and walked down the hall, but only a few steps. She tried to scream but fear paralysed her.

The creature stood filling the doorway; the smell was unbearable; sickening. Rose gagged. Its eyes, yellow and soulless yet strangely familiar, pinned her where she stood. Rain dripped from matted, muddy hair onto the laminate flooring. Rose instinctively wanted to call for her husband, "Bo…" She never finished the word.

Growling, fur, teeth, blood.

In a second it was over.

The feasting began.

8

Chapter 2
Sly McConait

Dr. Sylvester McConait Phd Strode across the sun lit courtyard of Trinity College, Cambridge. Beautiful 16th Century architecture towered above him everywhere he looked: a wall of academia; a protection against an uneducated world. This was where he belonged. The first place he had really felt at home. Surrounded by the enlightened, the wise, the understanding. Qualities he had rarely found in the people of his native North East. Oh they were friendly enough "Canny Folk." His mother used to say, but "canny" wasn't enough for Sly McConait, it never had been; even when he was a child.

He had never liked his nickname, but it was better than Sylvester (for God's sake) an old family name on his father's side. It sounded even worse in Geordie, full blast across the school playground; "Slvestaaa!!"

The arrival of Sly Stalone as Rocky and Rambo changed all that, although the name seemed to be all McConait and Stalone had in common.

McConait had blazed a trail at Cambridge from his early 20s. He had studied Human Psychology and turned his expertise into best-selling books:

"The Profile of the Ripper." and "The profile of the Wearside Ripper: the great Hoax."

His reputation and celebrity resulted in him working on some high profile murder and kidnapping cases. If the press were to be believed, McConait had, single handed: profiled, tracked down, arrested, judged and sentenced the perpetrators. The police and judiciary seemingly not involved.

Amongst fellow academics this earned Sly a certain amount of kudos and lighthearted mockery. He got away with his 'public hero' status because they knew he had the intellect to back it up. He was the genuine article.

Physically he was no Rocky or Rambo. The quintessential boffin: wavy, wiry, mousy brown hair, brutally parted to his right by fierce combing straight from the shower, 5 am every morning. His puny physique was a testimony to no exercise and plain food.

9

No spice, no sauce and often no flavour. A dose of multi-vitamins was his nod towards a healthy lifestyle. These, however, were not the only pills he popped religiously. He was a prozac addict, and completely in denial about it. A failed relationship with an undergraduate two years earlier had pushed him over the edge and the prozac was the only thing keeping him this side of sane.

The girl he had fallen for was completely wrong for him. Maria was not the quiet mousy bookworm, which would have suited, but a glamorous tease with a reputation around campus, she had calculatedly constructed and enjoyed. She would never have looked twice at a geek like Sly but his relationship with the Great British tabloids seemed an opportunity for personal advancement.

She used him and then the inevitable happened, she sold her story, and not just about McConait, she boasted bedding several other noted Dons and Professors at Trinity and other Colleges. Not all the stories were true (a creation of the gutter press and her own cruel imagination) but safe to say… many were.

McConait was embarrassed, humiliated and heart-broken; his own faults had led to his ultimate downfall.

McConait, hit the bottle, hit rock bottom and the worst of all… he hit her; a rage that the conservative Don had spent a lifetime suppressing. Turning the other cheek, keeping a stiff upper lip and looking on the bright side were the clichés that had governed his emotions since childhood, bottled up for years until the lid blew off; a single lashing out in frustration, but enough to leave a mark; a mark on her face but a bigger one on his reputation.

Maria's beautiful olive skin was a spectrum of bruises. Her beautiful green eyes, bloodshot; her left swollen out of recognition.

The proceeds of his previous best seller, his house and all his savings were just enough to buy her silence. Cambridge itself could ill afford the shame and the Old School tie network did what it does best, it pulled together, kept 'shtum' and gracefully swept this unfortunate and uncharacteristic lack of control under the carpet.

10

As he reached the other side of the quadrangle, he contemplated how lucky he was to have had a second chance. He had avoided losing his position at Cambridge, further public disgrace and most importantly criminal charges. He comforted himself with the fact that he had been under extreme stress and that's what had transformed him into a monster, and anyway that wasn't the real Sylvester McConait, but he would keep taking the Prozac… just in case.

"Dr. McConait!" beckoned a voice, which to McConait was Cockney, but to this Northern son, could have been from anywhere South of Watford. Sly turned round from where he had just come from, to see a red-faced, sandy-haired man with his hands on his knees panting.

"Thank God I caught you! I've been running all over this blessed place. Don't they have sign posts round here?"

It was Detective Sergeant Charlie Peel of Scotland Yard. It had tickled McConait that there was a policeman who bore the name of their founding father, Robert Peel. To his fellow coppers he was known as Agent Orange an uncompromising policeman who had gained his reputation by doing things his own way, and not always to the letter of the law.

"What can I do for you, Sergeant?" McConait had helped the police profile a serial killer, who had struck five times the previous year in the East End of London. McConait had been courted by the press once again, with headlines like:

"Jack's Back" and "The Ripper Returns"

The killings were finally pinned on a loner in his thirties with an interest in the occult, which matched perfectly with McConait's profile.

Peel drew close and lowered his voice. "Just had Northumbria Police on the blower it's happened again, the killings, just like last year. We suspect a copy-cat. This is literally up your street Dr… it's in Tynemouth. You're from there aren't you?"

"So what have they got in common?" Recoiled McConait almost defensively, disturbed that his home town had now fallen victim.

"Brutal. Bloody. No weapon. No motive. And …"

11

McConait finished the sentence for him. "A full moon?"

That was the part the police had kept from the press. They didn't want crazed cult members, devil worshipers and the Goth youth of Britain jumping on this bandwagon. They had gotten away with it so far but it wouldn't take a genius to spot the connection, on the contrary, there were already conspiracy theory websites springing up citing connections to ancient myths and occult practices.

And another thing, the full moon connection meant the police knew exactly when the killer would strike again and it hadn't helped in the slightest; that wouldn't look good in the papers.

"We could do with your help Doctor. Fancy a trip back home?"

The truth of the matter was he most certainly didn't fancy a trip home one little bit. He hadn't set foot in Tyneside since his mother's funeral, twenty five years ago. And particularly under these circumstances, it was not something he relished.

"Can I say no?"

"England expects!"

"Thank you Horatio." said McConait Sarcastically

Peel looked confused.

Chapter 3
Ergot Tale

A dark haired Irish gentleman dressed in black, sat at a desk in his hotel room overlooking the sea. In front of him was an ancient parchment covered in beautiful copperplate writing; all of it in French. Liam Price, the well-travelled man from Mayo, spoke several languages fluently; he made himself comfortable in a velvet covered chair and began to translate:

La Malédiction d'Avignon; the Curse of Avignon...

September 1st 1601, the Avignon area in the South of France. Jean-Claude Deloir looked across the valley, as teams of people made the most of the few minutes of remaining sun to get the last of the rye into sheaves. Jean-Claude's family had farmed and hunted in this area of France for centuries, but in the low final rays of the sun the valley looked more beautiful than ever; a land drenched in final sunlight, as if created by a master goldsmith. The unforgiving heat of the day had relented and a gentle breeze made the rye ripple below him and breathed new life into the young Frenchman. Tonight he was going to ask Brigitte to marry him.

He skipped down the valley. It was 200 metres above sea level, but the fields below him were like a golden beach. As he drew closer to the bottom of the valley he tried to identify the faces of the gathering huddle of workers; Brigitte would be one of them, and the very chance of catching sight of her made his heart race. But as he joined the weary swarm he could not see her. He pushed against the flow and desperately looked around for his love. He looked for her flowing blonde hair, which stood out in a village of brunettes. He longed for the flash of blue eyes and cherry red lips, which were unmistakably Brigitte, but she was not there.

Jean-Claude sighed and turned to join the flow when a hand tapped him on the shoulder, he spun round hoping it was her but it was his friend Jules. "I know who you're looking for." He said cheekily, "Sorry my friend she left a couple of hours ago, complaining of feeling dizzy."

"Oh my God is she alright?" Gasped Jean-Claude.

13

"Oh I'm sure it's just the sun, these blondes aren't made for it you know. What you need my friend is a dusky maiden." Jules pointed to Matilde, the fattest girl in the village who's love of sweet things had not only increased her weight but turned her teeth as black as her hair.

"Very funny Jules but you are sure Brigitte was OK?"

"Well I'm sure you'll be going round to check anyway so let's walk together. Hungry?" Jules pulled out a small loaf of bread from his sackcloth shoulder bag, the local rye bread, which made up the staple diet of the valley.

"Yes just a little." Jean-Claude tore off a chunk and the two friends followed the dusty trail to the village. The banter was light-hearted and bawdy as it always was between the two of them and as the sun finally disappeared behind the hills laughter filled the air of what seemed a perfect evening.

After a twenty minute walk the two companions turned into the humble French village of San Hubert, and, as always made a sign of the cross as they passed the church that stood flooded in the light from the Harvest Moon which had now taken control of the sky.

Five steps later they stood in front of the cottage where Brigitte's family lived. As Jean-Claude bristled with excitement a blood-curdling scream pierced the September night and froze the two friends with fear. The scream came from inside the cottage and was followed by panicked roars and yells.

Jean-Claude ran to the door and began beating on it frantically. "Let me in...let me in... Brigitte...are you alright?"

The screaming and yelling continued, Jean-Claude now accompanied by Jules beat the door even louder, but no one was coming. Jean-Claude ceased his pounding and ran to the back of the house where Brigitte slept. He grabbed the old ladders that he knew Brigitte's father kept there and slammed them against the wall

"I've got them, up you go." as always Jules was by his side and was now supporting the creaking ladders as Jean-Claude climbed the first few rungs.

"CRACK!!" one of the rungs gave way and Jean-Claude's ankle scraped against splintered wood; drawing blood. He winced

14

but ascended again this time with more urgency, not trusting how long the ladders were going to withstand his weight.

He was at the top but to his dismay the curtains had been drawn. He shuffled precariously at the top of the creaking ladders until he could glimpse the interior through a gap where the curtain material had folded against itself. As his eyes squinted and focused on what was inside his jaw fell open and he gasped.

Screams still emanated from inside Brigitte's house, but were now joined by a sickening wining sound of groaning wood. One of the uprights split and swayed and twisted under the weight of Jean-Claude, in succession rung after rung popped from its fixture or snapped with the strain. Jean-Claude held on to the remaining vertical like a poll vaulter but then this too gave way, sending the young man flailing in the air, then with a wicked thud Jean-Claude felt his ribs crack and his shoulder pop as he hit the dusty floor and passed into unconsciousness.

*   *   *   *   *

It was three days before Jean-Claude awoke for any length of time. In his delirium he had called out Brigitte's name on several occasions but now he was at last able to speak coherently. His mother sat beside him and welled up with tears when she realised that her son had finally come round. "Ahh, Jean-Claude you're awake, thank God."

The memories of the accident came back to him with a stomach churning jolt. But were then overrun by what had happened just before it. He sat bolt upright and instantly regretted it. He let out a whimper as if even the breath leaving his lungs pained him. Managing only a whisper he said, "Brigitte." And then fell back on his bed now sweating as waves of agony swept up and down his broken body.

His mother quickly tried to comfort him with a cold flannel against his forehead. "Shh, mon petit, you must rest. I'll fetch Doctor Morin." She stood up to go, but Jean-Claude grabbed her arm tightly. She turned to find Jean-Claude's eyes burning into her.

"Brigitte, what happened to Brigitte…I must know!"

15

His mother knew he would not be appeased and sat down again and turned to face him directly. " It may be for the best if you forget about Brigitte my son. I am afraid to say that she has not been seen for three days. Every night however when the moon rises the screaming begins. Doctor Morin has been back and forward, but will say nothing. Most people feared sunstroke, but it's more than that. Many are now saying that she is ...possessed... by the devil."

Jean-Claude closed his eyes in anguish, how could it be that Brigitte, his beautiful innocent Brigitte, the purest of souls, could be possessed? How unfair it seemed when there were so many wrong doers in the village who would have made an easier target for the Devil's intentions. His mother leaned closer and placed a calming hand on his fevered brow. "What did you see when you looked in the window that night? Is it true what they are saying?"

Jean-Claude opened his eyes wide as if he were back at the window staring in. "They had her tied to the bed; thick coarse rope that you would tie an animal in the field with. She had pulled and twisted against it until the skin was torn from her arms and blood ran freely from her fingers. Her hair was matted and looked shades darker than normal. It hung lank in front of her face but blood red eyes peered through it. She had sores, oozing and weeping all over her body, and she foamed at the mouth. It was horrible. Then with the loudest of screams she pulled once more against the ropes that held her fast and one snapped. A rope that would hold a bull, she snapped it, like a thread. With her arm free she grabbed at one of the women attending her and flung her across the room. Her strength, it was incredible, almost...unhuman." With the effort of retelling his tale Jean-Claude fell back into unconsciousness. As he drifted away he heard his mother's voice.

"Poor Brigitte, just like the other poor souls, just like the others..."

     *   *   *   *   *

It was many days later when Jean-Claude regained a lucid state. He was awoken by the clanging of the bell at the Church of

16

San Hubert's. He took it that, from the ringing, it must be seven a.m. Sunday morning, but as he rose shakily from his bed and gained his first peak outside his room for over a week, he could see that the sun was beginning to set, perhaps 5:30 in the evening. But the bells continued their solemn toll.

Restricted by his bandages Jean-Claude struggled to pull on his boots. The pain that had swept his body was still there but had now died down to a dull throb. Slowly, one step at a time he descended the steep wooden stairs down to the single room that made up the ground floor. The fire smouldered in the grate. Everything was tidied away. The house was lifeless, his Mother, father and two sisters were nowhere to be seen. Jean-Claude looked out at the other cottages, up one way and then down the other: not a lantern flickered; not a dog barked; not a baby cried; the only sound was the ringing of the church bells.

Jean-Claude ventured out onto the dusty street and turned to face the direction of the sound. The steeple of San Hubert's loomed from its place at the highest point of the village; a steep climb for the aching Jean-Claude. He recalled how usually he could leave the house at three minutes to seven and still make morning Mass on time, now every step made him huff and puff as if he had been walking for miles.

As he passed the other cottages up the road he peered in to check for life but no-one was there. As he passed the village square he saw the boules had been abandoned by the old men who played there. The café was closed and locked. Which only ever happened at Christmas and Easter.

Jean-Claude continued shuffling up the hill, and the bells rang louder and sharper in his ears, when suddenly the ringing stopped. Jean-Claude paused as if time itself had been frozen. The bells had led him here, now they had stopped he was unsure what to do. Then there was movement, a solitary figure dressed in black appeared from the church yard and walked down the hill towards him. Even from a distance Jean-Claude knew it was his mother.

As she drew closer there was no welcoming smile as one would expect from a loving mother to her son but her face stayed grim and solemn. "Jean-Claude you should not have risen,

17

this steep climb will have done you no good. Let's turn and go back."

"No, what's going on? Where is everyone? Why are you dressed in black?"

"Never mind all that, we must go home immediately, you are not well. I came away quickly to make sure you were alright. I knew I shouldn't have left you."

"Came away quickly from what? Left me for what?"

This time his mother was prepared to use force, she tugged at his arm but even in his weakened state her strength was no match for his. Then there was a bustle up ahead. The rest of the village, every man, woman, child and dog appeared round the side of the church and began marching down the hill. No one spoke a word.

His mother pulled again, frantically, "Please Jean-Claude let's go back, everyone's going back, look here's your father and sisters let's join them."

If Jean-Claude could get no sense from his mother then perhaps he could from his father, who appeared in view holding his seven and eight year old daughters by the hand. They clutched their rag dolls and as they drew closer Jean-Claude could see they were crying, in fact so were most people; all of the women and girls of the village, and many of the men. People brushed past Jean-Claude but none wanted to catch his eye, as if ashamed.

As his father caught sight of Jean-Claude struggling with his mother he stopped and let go of the girls' hands, and ushered them homeward. Then he turned to two of his friends and began to talk to them while gesturing towards Jean-Claude. His father and the two burly men marched towards him. His father pointed at him and commanded the men. "Get him home!"

"But Father I..." With little respect to his injuries the two of his father's friends each grabbed an arm and began dragging him back down the hill. Jean-Claude dug his heels in but to no avail. Adrenaline brought on by fear, panic and anger dampened much of the pain. Enraged and confused he began to yell, " Let me go, what in God's name is going on? Father... Mother... help me, just tell me... what's going on?"

18

Next there was a scuffle and one of the men let go which sent Jean-Claude spiralling to the ground. As he looked up at what was going on he could see that Jules had arrived on the scene and swung at one of the men knocking him to the ground. The other man now let go of Jean-Claude to join in, but Jules was already turning, and his elbow smashed into the man's face sending a spray of blood across his white shirt.

Jean-Claude saw his opportunity; he got to his feet and waded through the thickening crowd. By now his Father had lost sight of him as he was pushed backwards down the hill by people trying to see the ensuing fight. Jean-Claude hobbled as fast as he could away from the villagers, back up the hill towards San Hubert's Church.

He heard his mother calling after him; she could see him but was still struggling to break free of the crowd.

As he got to the church he could see that the door was in fact locked. There had been no service, no requiem Mass, which would have explained why the villagers were all in black and coming from church.

The din that broke out behind him faded as he rounded the corner to the right of the church. He staggered through the gravestones and turned left to the very rear of the church grounds.

There he saw a large black cross, perhaps eight feet tall. At first the cross in the church yard did not seem too unusual, apart from the fact he had never seen it there before, but as he walked towards it he could see that the black wood was in fact charred, and still smouldering, some edges had turned white with ash, and there was a low hissing sound as the heat withdrew from the wood.

It was then that he realised with horror that he was looking at the back of the huge cross; he could see something was attached not by ropes but by iron chains to the horizontal arms. He held his breath and moved round to face the cross.

His nightmares were confirmed. There hung the lifeless body of his beloved Brigitte; burned black and wizened up to the waist, raw and blistered and sooty up to her breasts, where the flames had licked but not devoured. Her face was almost

19

untouched apart from a blackening around the nose and mouth where she had inhaled a lungful of smoke, from her own burning flesh. Her hair, singed at the ends, still had a golden shine in places. Her arms chained and spread out, so that she resembled Christ himself.

As he took a breath he realised he was breathing in the stench of her burnt flesh. He immediately fell to his knees and vomited.

*   *   *   *   *

Jean-Claude stumbled away from the charred remains of his beloved, and sobbed uncontrollably in front of the church door. His Mother was waiting there for him and made to hug him but he pulled away.

"I know you are angry Jean-Claude, but you saw her with your own eyes, you saw her possessed by the devil. Her body had to be cleansed by fire until the demon left her. Now her soul can go to heaven. Don't you see she has been saved from damnation?"

"Couldn't anything be done for her?" he sobbed. "What about Doctor Morin?"

"He has fled, he said it was a disease called St. Anthony's Fire, he said she had been poisoned by the rye, that it was some kind of fungus, he called it Ergot, caused by the cold winter we had. Well his treatments came to nothing and Brigitte's family got angry. They knew, as did we all, that this was no disease. It was the devil's work; all the signs were there. So they turned to Father Victoir. He performed an exorcism that lasted for two days without a break. But to no avail. So she had to go the way of so many others; she had to be cleansed with fire."

Jean-Claude remembered his mother saying this before, "The others; what others? And you said 'all the signs were there' what signs?"

Jean-Claude's mother sat on the church steps with a look of resignation on her face. I suppose you'll have to understand, or you'll never find peace in your life. "She paused and wiped a tear

20

from her eye with a delicate lace handkerchief. "Your family has worked the rye fields and hunted in these hills for generations, and the stories have been passed down. Every now and then, the devil visits our beautiful valley, the sign he has arrived is the sign of a black or purple club shaped growth on the rye. It appeared a month ago in the southern most field and worked its way to us. On the eve of the Harvest moon, the devil possesses people, as he did Brigitte. They howl and bay at the moon, and follow their master's call to kill and mutilate those they hold most dear. Some say they transform into a wolf, others that it is their spirits that transform. Either way, when the moon comes up they begin their savagery. Brigitte is one of five taken this time, one was cleansed by exorcism and survived, but the rest were burned. We must take comfort from the fact that we read the signs quickly, before the beast could run wild and devastate the village, like he has done in other parts of the valley."

She took her son's hand and gazed into his tear stained face. "We did what we had to do for the village and Brigitte's immortal soul. I'm just glad you weren't awake to witness it."

Jean-Claude succumbed to his mother's warmth and they sat and wept in each other's embrace at the foot of the steps of the church of San Hubert.

21

Chapter 4
The Meeting Of Liam Price And Sly McConait

The train stopped on the Rail Bridge crossing the River Tyne and passengers knew it would only be minutes before they arrived at Central Station. McConait jumped up. Having done this journey so many times as a student, he knew how to get a step ahead. He had been sitting on the train long enough, so he decided he would spend the last few minutes of the journey pressed against the door ready to alight at the first opportunity.

It had been three days since the meeting with Peel. He had been briefed, debriefed, filled in, interviewed and generally prodded and poked by all concerned. As little as he wanted to make the journey north, he was relieved to escape the madness and bureaucracy for the three hours it took to get from London Kings Cross to Newcastle Central.

A lot had gone on in three days. What they dreaded had happened. The press got wind of the full moon connection and "Werewolves of London" had become "Werewolves of Tynemouth" or "Tyne and Wear Wolves". Even on the train McConait couldn't escape it, every newspaper bore the headlines. People fluttered from the front pages to get more gory details inside. All the weirdoes had crawled out from under their stones like cockroaches. Séances had been held, and the Tynemouth Priory (an ancient Christian ruin) had strangely been taken over by Goths and Druids. McConait had even been described as a 'modern day Van Helsing', which as to any pure academic made McConait very uncomfortable. He had upped his dose of Prozac.

Scotland Yard had put him in contact with a fellow Phd who also had a reputation of some standing. Not to the tabloids and the Great British public's knowledge, but to those involved with Psychology, he was a byword for serious empirical study. Dr Liam Price had used experiment and case study to demonstrate the relationship between natural occurrences and the effect on the psyche of individuals and communities. He cared for theory but used evidence, hard earned and meticulous, to justify any opinion.

22

Price was meeting him at the station and McConait looked forward to working with such a respected brain. McConait stepped off the train looking round for someone who looked like they might have a Phd, his jaw fell open as Price, dressed in black, put out his hand and introduced himself. "Sylvester McConait I presume? Liam Price; although if this Werewolf carry-on gets any worse I may change my name to Vincent." Price's levity had no impact on the serious Dr. McConait, "Or if it's easier, you can just call me…Father."

McConait knew of his reputation but little of the man. He didn't know for example, that Liam Price was a man of the cloth, a Roman Catholic Priest!

Price was a dashing Irishman, who really did possess the gift of the Blarney. He could charm the birds from the trees; he had a real charismatic presence. Tall, with a thick head of black hair and sparkling blue eyes, his charm, as well as vast expertise, made him invaluable to the church. Although his outspoken views had, at times, put him at odds with Bishops, Cardinals and even the Pope, Price's political 'nouse' and silver tongue soon ingratiated him back with the powers that be.

He worked from London, directly under Cardinal Cormack Murphy O'Connor (the Pope's representative and head of the Church in England), but was often summoned to Rome, and then dispatched on Papal investigations.

Price drove a black BMW and travelled from one stately, church owned, dwelling to another. He slept on crisp white linen sheets prepared by nuns. He drank the finest wines and had travelled the world several times over.

Price was a one-off; there was no other priest like him. His role in the Church was as a Postulator; an Assessor of Miraculous Occurrences. If someone wanted to claim an event to be a miracle, they would have to prove it to Price. He had discredited many respected grottos and places of worship as being nothing out of the ordinary. However unusual, Price could find genuinely scientific reason for it: from weeping statues (often of Mary the mother of Jesus that would appear to shed tears) to stigmata (the wounds which appeared on the body of believers which resembled those of the crucified Christ) he found physical or

23

medical causes for them all. In certain church circles he was known as "The Miracle Buster".

His most celebrated work was an investigation into Ergot poisoning, as a cause of hallucination and psychosis; ergot being a fungus that grows on rye and other cereal crops in damp conditions. His biggest break-through came in 1986 when he showed that accounts of bewitchment in Salem were similar to those of acid trips. Rye bread was a staple food in Salem and Ergot and LSD were discovered to be chemically similar. The history of witchcraft, the trials and executions were blown open.

He made the link between a flood in 1951 in 'Pont St. Esprit', (a rye producing area 25 Miles north of Avignon in the South of France), and a subsequent outbreak of mental illness which the church had put down to possession by the devil and performed exorcisms. He then found other similar cases that went back to the Middle Ages. In effect Price had debunked centuries of so called 'possession' and made the ritual of Exorcism nonsense; this made him very unpopular with a lot of people in the church.

It seemed like hours of awkward silence before McConait replied. It was too late for manners; he jumped in with both feet,

"You're a priest?" The disgust was palpable.

"How observant, you can tell you're a scientist." Price's deep blue eyes sparkled warmly; he had obviously experienced this reaction before.

"What kind of priest are you?"

"A good one I hope."

"No I mean what denomination?"

"Oh I see, the biggest and the best in my opinion, Roman Catholic."

"But didn't you debunk the whole Salem witchcraft trials and the whole Catholic Exorcism thing from the 50s?"

"I just sought the truth. Isn't that what religion does?"

"I beg to differ!" McConait, a confirmed atheist, blew a disgusted breath like a bull getting ready to charge. "That's the jurisdiction of science I think you'll find!"

"And need the two differ in that respect?" replied Liam Price, with a wisdom and serenity that McConait found

24

particularly annoying. He had come across this in priests before. They never challenged or blasted forth like a Presbyterian, Calvinist or Baptist minister. They would simply pose a question and leave you to go away and feel thoroughly bad about yourself. From a psychologist's point of view this was classic 'passive aggressive', but McConait knew there was another expression for it: Catholic guilt.

"Look Dr... Fr...whatever, I'm not here on a jolly; this is bloody murder, and the solving of it is already seriously hampered by a lot of ... "mumbo jumbo" Druids, Werewolves, Vampires all sorts."

Price placed a calming hand on McConait's shoulder (which was totally unappreciated) and interrupted what was becoming a rant "And that's why I'm here; to help."

"I'm sorry but they've already got me down as a modern day Van Helsing! What good is a priest?" McConait pulled his shoulder away from the hand of Price, and turned away in frustration.

"Why does my being a priest cause you such a problem?" another, conscience probing, Catholic question. McConait resisted the temptation to say, "Where do I bloody start?"

"Look, your dog collar, your get up, your religion; it's exactly the kind of "mumbo jumbo" I'm talking about. If the press see me with you they'll have a bloody field day. What do you think we're going to do together? Shall I get the steaks nice and sharp and you can throw the Holy Water?" McConait had never spoken so irreverently to a priest before, although he had often wanted to.

McConait picked up his bags, which he had dropped in disgust to free up his hands to gesticulate his anger. Price returned his hand to his shoulder and guided McConait towards the exit; he spoke softly as they walked.

"Look, if it helps, this collar does come off. But actually I think you may have a point, if I am a "mumbo jumbo" merchant then maybe that's exactly the area in which I can help you." This time he did not give McConait an opportunity to interject. "You have to appreciate that, even in the 21st Century, superstition still

25

runs deep. I've been in Tynemouth since the killing. It's a changed place Dr. McConait. I'm afraid it's returned to the dark ages in many ways. People are frightened; really frightened. As you know Tynemouth is a fairly well heeled place, these are educated reasonable people but they are really stirred up and I think I know who's doing the stirring."

"Is it the press?" asked McConait more willing to listen.

"No… This is really going to upset you…it's a priest."

For the second time in a few minutes the thought of a priest made McConait drop his bags and his jaw fall open.

Chapter 5
The 2nd Incident

Outside the Tynemouth Priory Clinic Mark Pembridge stood in pyjamas and dressing gown, gazing vacantly over the fence into the school field which lay beyond. He had been in rehab for six months this time. He had been in and out over the past seven years; it was a cycle: He got out; fell into the same old crowd; started smoking dope and drinking; then taking acid or LSD; that would kick off his psychosis and then the TV would start talking to him, telling him to burn things.

He had done time for arson: each stretch only a few months, and recovered from serious burns a couple of times. At least now he knew the signs and when the TV started talking to him he would admit himself straight away.

He stepped outside; it was a cold February night and clouds were blown quickly over a full moon, by merciless gusts whipping across from the North Sea. He thought about what it would be like to be clean. Even in the home he was on anti-psychotic drugs, and tranquillisers.

He looked back over a wasted seven years. He used to have a job in PC World, perhaps he could have gone further but on reflection he remembered the job was purely a way to fund a developing drug habit. It was when the flat screen PC monitors began to speak to him that his life began to unravel. He shuddered, partly due to the cold, but also at the thought of him arguing the toss with a 15inch Dell monitor which, was telling him to trash all the HP printers (Hewlett Packard, a cover up for Hell's Prince). The police were called and although, not charged, he was dismissed from PC World leaving the Prince of Darkness to continue the production of computer hardware.

"It's amazing what a chemical in the brain could make you do." He thought. The Acid he had put into himself had made him happy, see things in amazing colours, expanded his consciousness, but his brain had reacted by producing its own psychotic chemicals which were never pleasant; they had very much narrowed his consciousness and turned him into someone

27

or something, he (standing calmly at the quiet back door of the clinic) could barely recognise.

Mark took a final drag on his cigarette and was about to turn back when something caught his eye. A hunched shadowy figure crouched at the side of the large wheelie bins. The only movement was the rising and falling of its back as it breathed. As the wind died slightly the breaths became audible.

"Well this is a new one," quipped Mark to himself. "They must have got my dosage wrong." He stepped forwards towards the shadowy figure. " Look, I know you're not real and you can fuck off if you think I'm doing any more of that burning shit. Even if you are the Prince of Darkness, even if you were the Prince of fuckin' Wales there's no way I'm listenin' to your shite!"

Mark was, for the first time in years, proud of himself. He felt he could now face his demons, even challenge them with what sounded like authority, rather than succumb to them; which was his usual response.

The figure slowly began to rise. Although still shadowy black, its eyes now reflected the moonlight they were yellow and soulless. Its breathing stopped… then it pounced.

Chapter 6
Father Dan Tuthie

McConait had quickly dropped off his bags at the Grand Hotel on the seafront in Tynemouth. It was an impressive Victorian building, which lived up to its name; this was going to be his new home for a while. He popped a pill; he was now adding bluies to the prozac and felt his latest wave of anxiety begin to numb. He was quiet on the short walk from the hotel, around the beautiful sea front, to St. Oswin's Church. He couldn't believe that he was back home and was actually going to Mass; even under the influence of drugs, an unbelievable act for this confirmed atheist.

Fr. Price accompanied McConait. He was not saying the Mass that evening. He convinced McConait to go with him, however, by explaining, "As a priest you understand that I must attend, and I think you'll get a better idea of where Father Tuthie, the parish priest, is coming from, if you see him on home ground, so to speak. You see I'm here to help him as much as I'm here to help you."

"I'm sure I'll feel right at home." These words were the only words McConait spoke on the walk to the church, and they took Price by surprise; they were not as full of sarcasm as he would have expected.

St.Oswin's was a few yards from Tynemouth Priory, an imposing ruin at the end of Front Street (the high street in Tynemouth). The Priory had been a powerful institution when Northumbria was run by the church centuries ago, and administrated by monks in abbeys and priories. The Priory had lost its power when the monks were banished or even killed during the reformation. Its status as a place of worship was dissolved, but was picked up again by the small church of St.Oswin's when it was consecrated in 1851. Father Tuthie was trying to heal the historical rift, between parish and priory, by conducting open air Masses in the ancient ruins. English Heritage, the organisation that owned the site, were fine about the arrangement and Tuthie even had a set of keys, so he could come and go as he pleased.

29

A provincial Catholic Church service had taken on a new significance. Press photographers and journalists were gathering to pedal more ridiculous headlines to a hungry readership; many from down South laughed at the daft Geordies and their werewolf stories.

As they entered a rapidly filling St.Oswin's, McConait instinctively dipped his fingers in the holy water at the door, crossed himself then proceeded to the pew nearest the entrance, where he bent one knee and genuflected, before kneeling down.

Price raised his eyebrows impressed and rather surprised. "I see you've done this before Doctor."

"I was an altar boy here." McConait looked at Price and they couldn't help see the absurd humour in the situation. Despite everything, these were McConait's people, and he knew what was called for.

"Nothing's what it seems." grinned Price. And the sniggering continued as a tuneless organist piped up.

Father Dan Tuthie was as different a priest to Liam Price as could be imagined. He was now in his sixties short and white haired. Despite his stature he still managed to look down his nose over the top of his spectacles, and he was a giant at the lectern. He was strictly old school, in a strictly old school church.

The meeting of all the Catholic Bishops, the Second Vatican Council, in the 1950s had opened much of the Mass and church practices to the public, but Tuthie would gladly have set the clock back sixty years to return things to what he called, " The proper Mass."

He was a local man who had attended the local Catholic school then the Catholic Grammar School. He had only left the area when he trained to become a priest in Rome. There he studied under the Jesuits and excelled in Latin. He had served in the parish of St.Oswin's for thirty years.

He approached the altar, which had emblazoned across it:

"Introibo ad altare dei." (Walk into the altar of God.)

The organist at the rear of the packed church blasted out a hymn called, "Here I am Lord", and the congregation did their best to keep up. She was much stronger on Chords than she was on melody, but the main weakness was rhythm.

30

Tuthie had said Mass at St. Oswins countless times but this was different. This was a Mass in memory of the victims of the brutal attacks, and for the general welfare of the parish. It was Thursday evening but the Church was packed. Every inch of sitting, kneeling or standing space was spoken for and the congregation was now overflowing outside the church.

The Mass proceeded pretty much as McConait remembered it. There seemed to be even more Latin than he recalled but the format hadn't changed. What did stand out was the deliberate choice of readings. The first reading was from the book of Daniel and described King Nebuchadnezzar as suffering from depression that deteriorated over a seven-year period into, what McConait would have described as, psychosis at which time the Old Testament king, imagined himself ...a beast.

"Let him be drenched with the dew of heaven, and let him live with the animals among the plants of the earth. Let his mind be changed from that of a man and let him be given the mind of an animal, until seven times pass by for him."

McConait and Price looked at each other. Price's eyes saying, "See what I mean?" And McConait nodded back.

The reading continued, "He was driven away from people and ate grass like cattle. His body was drenched with the dew of heaven until his hair grew like the feathers of an eagle and his nails like the claws of a bird."

McConait could have predicted where the second reading was going; Acts of the Apostles giving an account of them driving out demons. And the Gospel followed suit with Jesus doing a similar trick. Then came the moment the audience were waiting for. It had ceased to be a congregation; it was now definitely an audience. There were more than mere parishioners there: the press were represented; the police; the Council and with McConait and Price, the world of science.

The old priest bowed slowly in front of the altar, with a frailty that surprised McConait, and stepped up to the lectern.

"As you have heard from scripture, strange occurrences, bizarre behaviour and transformations, are nothing new. In the Holy Bible there are many interesting characters. We could

31

perhaps dismiss some of the Old Testament ones as being used allegorically, as an example, not actually real; Adam and Eve perhaps, or Noah and all the animals."

At this point Tuthie's gaze fell firmly on Fr. Price. "But as Christians we must hold what the Gospel says to be a genuine account of Christ's conception... birth... mission... passion...and ...resurrection." He had made that point frighteningly clear. "If the Gospel tells us that the Lord Jesus himself was faced and tempted by the devil in person, then how vulnerable must we be? If the Lord Jesus came face to face with people possessed by demons!" At this he brought the palm of his hand onto the Gospel page he had just read and again locked his eyes on Price. "Then how vulnerable must we be?"

Price inhaled and raised his eyes to the ceiling away from Tuthie's gaze. It certainly appeared that the old priest had come well prepared for his meeting with the eminent Liam Price. " And if, through the grace of God and the power of the Holy Spirit, the Apostles, the followers of Christ, were given the power to cast out those demons in Jesus' name..." his voice reduced in volume making everyone's ears prick up. " ...then why not we?"

McConait was appalled yet impressed that the crowd were getting what they came for. The media and general onlookers were getting their devil/wolf mumbo jumbo and the genuine believers were given the answer to their fears. McConait put his head in his hands. He had heard this all before. If you have a problem, have Faith in Jesus, and if that fails it's because your faith is weak, so you probably deserve it.

Tuthie continued, "In Pope John Paul II's book he writes of 'mysterium iniquitatis', the coexistence of good and evil, he talks of the forces of evil he saw in his time: Fascism, war, Communism, and of his own attempted assassination. He also explains how good triumphs in such a way that we come out of the experience more fulfilled and closer to God."

Tuthie put his hands either side of the lectern and gripped tight, as if bracing himself for what he was about to say, "Evil walks among us. And evil works within us. So let us remain vigilant."

32

As if not dramatic enough, Tuthie had saved his best until last. The dictum of, that famous medieval theologian, Thomas Aquinus. He closed his eyes as if he had the words tattooed on the inside of his eyelids, (which wouldn't have surprised McConait): "Omnes angeli, boni et mali, ex virtute naturali habent potestatem transmutandi corpora nostra. All angels, good and bad have the power of transmutating our bodies"

McConait sat up; arms folded in indignation. There; he'd covered the whole spectrum of ghoulish fancy and used theology to back it up: Wolves, demons, evil, the devil and to cap it all transmutation. It could have come straight out of a Harry Potter book. McConait had tried his tolerant best but had had enough; he was about to walk out when Price grabbed his arm. He nodded towards the front two pews in the church. He couldn't hear but he could see the unmistakable movement of people sobbing. "It's the victims' families, stay for them if no-one else." whispered Price.

As if sensing their gaze, Bob, the first victim's husband, turned round and fixed McConait with tear-filled, bloodshot eyes. McConait felt a chill run down his spine. Bob turned back round.

McConait knew that Father Price was right. No matter how much contempt he had for Tuthie, he should not disrespect the families. He sat back down resigned to suffer the rest of this medieval ritual, but he couldn't wait to escape and breathe the fresh sea air of the 21st Century.

33

Chapter 7
Sly McConait And Liam Price Talk With Father Dan Tuthie

It seemed to take an age for the congregation to file out of the narrow aisle of St.Oswins. Small groups of people gathered outside on Front Street, discussing the Mass, or intrigued by the News cameras that had now appeared. The poe-faced presenters trying their best to remain sincere and sombre on the fifth take.

McConait and Price stayed at their pew. McConait looked around the walls of the old church at the Stations of the Cross; gory scenes depicting Jesus' Passion and death. The images spinning in his mind with the many bloody images he had seen in his work, followed by images of Maria's bruised face and the blood on his hands. He felt sick.

Price knelt and prayed; eyes tight shut, face in his hands, as if blocking out the physical world to make his discussion with his God all the clearer.

McConait did not want to interrupt but he had to get some air, before he threw up.

He rose and slipped out. Following the rituals that had been drummed into him from childhood, he genuflected as he had on entering and blessed himself once again with Holy water.

He felt claustrophobic and he was sure he would feel better as soon as he stepped out of the church, instead he bumped into a small huddle of teenagers; Goths, who had the pentacle, the five-pointed star, famously associated with the occult, printed in white on black baggy t-shirts. This image now joined the others, swirling around McConait's dazed mind. The teenagers never spoke but looked coldly at McConait with distain. Did they know why he was here? Was it because he looked like he was about to vomit? Or was it just because they were teenagers? Either way McConait barged through them, up the church path and onto Front Street, a wide street, lined with attractive old buildings; now mainly trendy pubs and restaurants.

At last the spinning stopped and the world returned to some sort of equilibrium.

34

"Are you alright son?" It was Father Tuthie. "I saw you run out. Aren't you Mary McConait's boy?"

It was only a matter of time before someone recognised him. "Yes Father. Last time we met was at the Requiem Mass you said for her, 25 years ago. I'm Sylvester."

"Yes of course. It was such a shame about your mother. She was a martyr to that cursed illness. Indeed, a sad loss to the parish, a more devout woman I never came across. And you, I see you are still practising the faith. In these times we'll need it more than ever." Tuthie peered over his specs deep into McConait's eyes. This was a warning.

McConait's indignation, rage disgust and cynicism since he arrived had climaxed during the sermon. Now he felt warmed to Tuthie, and slightly embarrassed at the old priest's mistake.

"Are you alright Dr. McConait? I didn't realise you'd left." It was Fr. Price, his prayers had left him oblivious to McConait's plight.

"Yes, I think it's all been a lot to take in. And there are so many memories too; my mum's funeral and stuff." McConait felt a pang of guilt that he'd used his own sainted mother as an excuse. He knew it was something else that had made him so uncomfortable, but he couldn't say what. His reason made perfect psychological sense, but he knew it wasn't true, but for now it worked to appease the gathered priests.

Tuthie looked back and forward between McConait and Price, as if in amazement that they were together. "So I take it you know each other!" he said, disappointedly.

"Yes," said McConait, almost ashamed, "This is Father Liam Price."

"Oh I know who this is. I've been expecting him. The Bishop is concerned I may be guiding my flock in the wrong direction, so he sent in …the marines."

"Pleased to meet you Father. And I take it you've met Dr. Sylvester McConait already.", Price characteristically unruffled at his reception.

"Oh thirty years too late for introductions. I remember when he was an altar boy. He was always a good lad, what a shame he's fallen in with such a rough crowd." There was more

35

humour than malice in his remarks, but the malice was there all the same.

"Father perhaps we can talk in the Presbytery, perhaps over a cup of tea, like civilised gentlemen." Price's diplomacy was obviously a strength the Bishop was relying on.

"Oh for God's sake if we're going to be civilised we'd better make it a whisky." With that Tuthie turned back to the now deserted church; pulling out a large bunch of keys ready to lock up.

On the way to the presbytery, conversation was polite, how one would imagine it to be. Each talking about acquaintances they shared and how they were doing. But as the first sips of whiskey sank and they offered each other a "cheers", or a "slange!" from Price, they realised that some straight talking was imminent.

"Look Father," began Price, leaning forward gazing at the golden liquid in his glass. " We are all here for the same purpose. To help the people of Tynemouth, the families of the victims and the police, where we can. Dr McConait is a leader in the field of psychological profiling."

Tuthie interrupted. "And what the blazes is that when it's at home?"

McConait joined the conversation, " Well Father, I have studied how people react to certain situations. I have studied what motivates or effects people's behaviour. From looking at crime scenes and evidence, I can start to build up a profile, a picture, if you like, of the murderer or murderers, and in that way guide the police towards the type of person they are looking for." He thought he'd explained it in the simplest way he could.

"Well isn't that just grand." Said Tuthie in a sarcastic tone; it appeared that he was still unimpressed. "I've done a bit of studying myself in my time... laddo. And I've got a profile of the killer myself don't you know?"

McConait saw this as a waste of time, but thought it could only help to humour the old man. " Oh really Father, well I'm sure your views would be very useful."

"I'll tell you who you're looking for." Tuthie grew deadly serious. He raised his pointed finger and glared over his glasses at

36

McConait. "It's the devil himself. Lucifer. Working his evil; changing good, God fearing souls into his black hearted demons. Transforming their immortal souls and their own physical bodies into that of the monster." Tuthie built up to a crescendo. "That's who you're here to profile, Sylvester McConait, Satan and his lackeys. Not man... but beast!" The very words seemed to take their toll on the old priest. He slumped back in his chair clutching his chest; his eyes watery and distressed.

"My God he actually believes this stuff!" thought McConait to himself.

Price knelt on one knee by Tuthie's side and placed his hand on the Old man's arm to comfort him. "Take it easy now Father." Price picked up Tuthie's glass and handed it to him. "Come on now, the water of life." Price was remarkably comforting. McConait thought of him administering the last rights to deluded people like his mother, and what a consolation that delusion would be. He had only been back home a short while but already he found himself softening towards the trappings of a faith he had rejected years ago.

McConait struggled for a reply to break the silence. He didn't want to give the old guy a heart attack, but he knew within himself that Tuthie was wrong and that he had to make his own point of view.

"Father if there is a devil, then I can vouch for his handy work. I've worked on many horrific cases. They all conjure up our natural feelings of disgust and repulsion, fear, hate and, yes, the word evil does spring to mind. We do use the word monster to describe these sort of murderers, but as you said, quite rightly in your sermon," McConait was pleased to be able to flatter the man, even if he did fundamentally disagree with him. "Evil works within us; within man. And when the police catch the perpetrator of these heinous crimes, you find that they are just men. Like you or me."

"Surely not?" argued Tuthie insulted by the implication that he could have anything in common with such evil.

"Like you or me. But something is broken in their mind, that is why they are able to do terrible things and we aren't."

37

again the image of Maria's bruised face pierced McConait's consciousness; he hoped the hypocrisy in his words didn't show.

Tuthie didn't reply, whether he was convinced or simply had no energy left, McConait was happy the old man didn't retaliate. Especially as his guilt around Maria was making him feel less sure of his own argument.

Price now saw his opportunity to interject. "Father, I am not here to criticise the core, or the intention of what you have to say. There is no greater lover of the Gospels than myself, but we are dealing with 21st century people, we must speak to them in 21st century language, using all the tools and information at our discretion. We must be rational and calm at this time of crisis. We are the leaders of our spiritual communities. We mustn't generate false hope or false fear, everything we say must be with the eternal in one hand and the present in the other."

"Oh I've no doubt you are a lover of the Gospels, you are a good and kind man Father Price, and don't think that you are the first to give me a slap on the wrist. But destroying the miraculous, taking away God's divine work from the faithful and from the Gospels you yourself hold so dear. This cannot stand. If you take away the miraculous you are left with only the mundane. If you take away God then we are left only with man. And if mankind is all that's left, with all its cruelty and contempt for one another, then we are as well leaving the world to the devil." Again that word seemed to prick something inside Tuthie. "All your intellectual banter, publications, and letters after your name are all fine and well, but I know the truth. I know the truth!"

Had Tuthie been a younger man in better health they may have taken the conversation further. As it was, they left and walked back to the Grand Hotel. To McConait's surprise Price was now an ally and he regretted his reaction at their first meeting.

"Well one of these days someone will be pleased to see me", joked Price. "and I hadn't counted on you already knowing him. The thing is he's a devout man and a wonderful priest; he would give his life to his parish. He's right in a way, it's one thing me writing books and travelling the world passing judgement, but he's here doing the work Jesus wants us to do. He lives, laughs and suffers for his people in a way that I don't think I ever will."

"What was that about you taking away the miraculous, is that something to do with the Exorcism /Ergot thing?" asked a now intrigued, as well as confused McConait.

"Well one of my roles is as "postulator", an assessor of miraculous occurrences. That is to say that, every now and then, people see things that they claim to be miracles."

"Weeping statues, stigmata, potatoes in the shape of Mother Teresa?" McConait liked the way this conversation was going, any opportunity for cynicism.

"That kind of thing" replied Price graciously. "Well, as a scientist, I don't just take things on people's faith, which is in no doubt. And when you have seen people walk 200 miles to kneel before a piece of old tea chest that some fraudster claims to be a part of the true Cross, well then you know what faith is. Tuthie's point is that some feel that it is better for the church to leave people believing the lie, with their faith in tact, rather than seek the truth and lose their faith"

"And you obviously feel differently."

"Obviously. You see a lot of people have no problem with Jesus. What he stands for, what he did, what he achieved through his struggle. He was a real revolutionary of his time. His peaceful revolution, his sacrifice is still radical today. What turns people off is all the smoke and mirrors stuff. Making powerful claims without using modern scientific methods to back them up." Price's normally calm voice showed the first sign of passion.

"And you think you can?" McConait would need a lot of convincing.

"Well, take Lazarus; the raising of the dead for example. We know how common a coma can be. We have heard of people, even these days, wrongly pronounced dead. Well it's no less of a miracle to me if Jesus' voice and presence brought someone out of a coma." Price was beginning to make some sense.

"A bit like when footballers or pop stars visit children in comas because the child really admired them, in the hope that they will come back." added McConait.

"Exactly! Or consider another example, the feeding of the 5000. There is evidence that 'the 5000' was a name given to a respected sect of elders in Jerusalem. It might not actually refer to 5000 individuals, merely a group perhaps eight or nine, who were known as 'the 5000.'"

"Yes but then it's no big deal; feeding eight or nine people is it?" McConait was still no more impressed by this interpretation than the literal one.

"It's not any less a miracle to me if Jesus got a group of important people to listen to him. In fact even more importantly in the culture of the time to eat with him." Price stopped walking to look McConait in the face. "Don't get me wrong, I don't do this because of a lack of faith. On the contrary, my faith is as strong or as blind as the people going to see the piece of true cross, or the weeping Madonna. I believe that Jesus is so good and so strong and mighty, that any revelation of the truth would not even put a dent in His work in our world."

McConait was impressed by Price's conviction even if he didn't buy it all, he had read similar treaties along this theme before, "What you're talking about here is 'Science Deism. The belief that science explains what happens in the physical world but is guided by God's hand, and these two views are not conflicted."

"You can call it 'Science Deism' if you like, but it's all in line with the teachings of the Catholic Church.", said Price, toying with his dog collar with a sense of pride.

Chapter 8
McConait Visits The Crime Scene

Automatic glass doors slid open to reveal a classy modern entrance. A smart young girl sat behind an oak counter. To the right of her a splendid staircase curled upwards. "There's a gentlemen to see you Dr. McConait." The receptionist of the Grand Hotel pointed to the bar through a doorway on her left.

McConait, with Price still in tow, followed the direction indicated by a beautifully manicured finger, into a large, elegant bar resplendent with a baby grand piano in the corner. There, in front of the window, hands in pockets, gazing out at a wonderful sea view, was Sergeant Peel.

"Hello Doc. I don't believe they actually have surfers up here. You wouldn't catch me in the North Sea it would freeze your bollocks off." Peel stopped and realised he was appearing, not for the first time in his life, a little inappropriate. "I know you've not been back long but err... there's been another one. Thought we'd get you right on it. And you must be Father Price. I can see you two have got yourselves acquainted then."

When Peel had first come to see McConait there had only been one murder. After a few weeks of going through the motions, nothing turned up. Now McConait was back in Tynemouth there was a fresh crime right on cue. It was time to get to work.

It was a quick journey in Peel's Volvo and when they arrived at the clinic the tell tale signs of blue and white police tape cordoned off the entrance. It was an impressive Victorian building, set back from the road by a large picturesque garden which sloped upwards to the entrance, which was a good ten feet higher than the road. The front of the home had three floors with eight windows and a large white door; a polished brass name plate glinted to its right.

Peel briefed them as they climbed the path to the front door. "The scene is through the back. He was a resident so we're going through the whole place. Not letting anyone in or out until they've been checked." Now in work mode, Peel no longer seemed uncouth. He was a professional; and very good at what he did.

Going through the blue and white striped tape into the home, McConait enquired, "Any suspects?"

Peel stopped and gestured with a nod of his head towards a communal TV room with floral wallpaper, which would have been better suited to an old people's home; all the residents had been rounded up. "Take your pick." The three of them stopped and looked at about twenty people, most of them men, all in pyjamas and dressing gowns. "They've all got history of narcotic involvement, all got history for violent or destructive behaviour, and all got history of psychosis. Mind you, whether any of these characters would have the physical strength to have done this I don't know."

"What do you mean physical strength?" asked Father Price. McConait knew exactly what he meant.

"This way gentlemen." Peel opened the door to the back of the home.

A scene that, over the past year had become all too familiar, presented itself to McConait; lots more police tape. Scene Of Crime Officers (SOCOs) in blue hooded, all-in-one overalls, with latex gloves and shoe covers, dusted and scraped at every surface and crevice. Before them was a metal fence which was the boundary of Priory Primary School. A crowd had obviously got wind of the events and were gathering on the school field beyond looking over the fence. Two Bobbies in helmets and luminous yellow jackets struggled to pin them back.

"Here he is, Mark Pembridge, age twenty five, lives with his mum on Percy Park... no sorry Percy Street." Peel was very matter of fact.

Father Price recoiled; "Oh Dear Lord Jesus!" an exclamation of shock and horror as much of a prayer. The priest blessed himself, and then the remains of Mark Pembridge.

The body, or what was left of it, lay on its back in between the care home wall and a wheelie bin. The arms and legs were in tact, apart from long random claw marks. The lower jaw was missing but the upper part of the face, eyes open, gazing skyward, was unmarked; the rest was a bloody mess.

42

Peel collared a small, slight man who looked nothing like a policeman. "Are you the Pathologist?"

"Yes, Dr. Andrew Boe. Can I help?"

"What do we have here?"

"Well, it looks like the attacker went for the throat first. That would silence the victim, if not kill him. But I don't think it did …kill him that is."

Peel looked at the body and nodded, "Why not?"

"Well it's the spray marks from the blood. The direction substantiates that the victim was facing the wheelie bin. The distance of the spray was in the normal range for the jugular. Its quite a powerful force you know; from the jugular. But then there's this."

Boe gestured behind him at the door, where there was a smeared handprint, "He must have escaped the killer's clutches and made a desperate grab towards the door. But…" Boe went over to the body. He bent down and, in a way that suggested he had done this a thousand times, placed his hands firmly on the corpse's shoulders and in one clean movement flipped it over. "There you see; here."

Down the back were deep claw marks. "And you see here?" Boe pointed at a big bloody smear mark along the ground, from the door. "That's where the killer dragged him back. Flipped him over…" Boe flipped the corpse back to the way he had found it, "…and" he didn't need to go on, the horrific body told its own tale, but the pathologist continued, "As you can see, the organs of the thorax are missing. The rib cage has been pulled apart splitting the sternum; the heart has also gone. Moving up, the larynx, trachea and lower mandible are missing." Boe flicked off his latex gloves, nonchalantly, "We've sent samples to the lab, it could be a couple of days before we have any further information for you."

"Anything else?" asked Peel not expecting an answer.

"Yes, the part about the rib cage being ripped open. It would have required incredible strength."

McConait snapped into gear. He had one hand on his hip, the other he waved as he spoke, "So someone with access to the home, or more likely, someone who came over the fence. He was

43

waiting here by the bins. He was waiting for Pembridge," McConait paused looking at the body, he felt that 'it' rather than 'he' might have been more appropriate. "Or at least he was waiting for someone anyway; either that, or he was hiding and Pembridge was unlucky enough to come across him."

McConait squinted his eyes as if trying to conjure up a vision of the killer. "Someone very strong, incredible upper body strength, large build. Access to tools, perhaps specialised, but it's too early to tell."

"Tools?" Price, still uncomfortable, had gained control of his logical mind and was now able to start thinking.

"Tools, yes. Jack the Ripper used surgeons' tools, which may have meant he had medical connections. Peter Sutcliffe the Yorkshire Ripper was a lorry driver; he used tools from his garage or lorry. Identify the tools and you may identify what the man does for a living."

"And you would definitely need tools for…this?"

"Oh goodness you couldn't do this by hand. Getting through the fat and muscle of a body quickly requires a precision-sharp cutting blade. Then separating the ribs would require some sort of leverage, and cutting through the sternum…"

Boe interrupted, "No the sternum was not cut; it's split, we'll look in more detail back at the lab, but it's definitely ragged. A saw blade, and that's what you'd need, would leave a straighter edge."

"So even greater leverage in that case." Price was starting to get the hang of this now. "Well that would have to be extremely specialised equipment, I mean to do something like that."

"It depends what you call specialised." Sly McConait was in full flow now. " You all got a car jack?" He looked around.

"Who hasn't?" Peel the only one to reply.

"Exactly, a common piece of machinery, place that inside the ribs, turn the handle and…" he stopped himself there, with his hands, fingers spread, he formed a rib cage in front of him and acted out the two sides parting.

44

It seemed to make sense but Price wasn't satisfied. "And why are you relating this murder with the Rippers and not other killers?"

Peel and Boe knew the answer, but they let the Cambridge Don do the explaining.

"It's the organs. In both Ripper cases, the organs are systematically, methodically removed. They were sexually motivated, the victims predominately prostitutes, so it was the reproductive, genital organs that were given particular attention. The organs would be laid out in a line. Piece by piece." As comfortable as McConait was to talk about this subject matter, Price was as uncomfortable to hear it.

Peel checked with Boe. "But as yet none of the organs have been found?"

"All gone. He was very, meticulous."

This sparked off another connection in McConait's brain and off he went. "Meticulous. Picking up every last drop. No spills. He put the organs in sealed containers. He's keeping them. Trophies. Classic!" Pre-empting the priest's confusion McConait continued. "It's classic serial killer behaviour. Jeffrey Dammer, Dr.Crippen they didn't dispose of the bodies, they weren't ashamed of what they'd done. They kept parts of the bodies around; as trophies or souvenirs; Dammer in his fridge, Crippen under the stairs. This killer doesn't feel remorse he wants to show off."

"A psychopath." Price knew enough psychology to identify that type.

"Psychopath, they have no remorse, they glory in what they do, in fact they want to be caught, eventually, so they can take the credit publicly."

Peel who had heard this explanation before put his hands in his pockets and took one more look at the carcass that was once Mark Pembridge. "Well I hope he wants to be caught sooner rather than later."

"And the full moon?" asked Price.

"Oh this person isn't horrified by death, they're fascinated by it. I imagine he's very much involved in the occult; ritual sacrifice, ceremonies, artefacts, pictures."

45

"Almost religious you might say?" said Price rubbing his chin as he saw the connections between these activities and the activities of his own church. He thought again of Tuthie and those who would set the Church back a thousand years. He shook his head.

Out of respect no one answered his question. McConait continued. "The internet is proliferated by these kinds of sites. I imagine that the killer spends a lot of his time on the web, perhaps in chat rooms, maybe even boasting about these things."

"So that might be a good way to catch him?" Price again showed his inexperience.

"Like a needle in a haystack. There's a whole world of people out there. There's probably a thousand websites with people saying they did it. We've got people looking into it but it doesn't narrow down what we're looking for. It expands it."

Something had been bothering Price since the conversation and explanations had begun. "Sorry gentlemen, but this looks like the work of an animal. A savage dog, you know; like these fighting dogs."

McConait and Peel looked at each other. They'd had this discussion before. They knew that what Price said was exactly right, it did look like the work of a savage dog, but more like a pack of animals rather than one.

"A natural conclusion we've thought of. If it was an animal, there would be traces; droppings around, urine to mark territory. We might expect to find animal hair under the fingernails of the victim where he tried to fend off the attack. If it was an animal there would be no tools of course. There would be saliva from the animal's mouth, and we'd be able to trace animal rather than human DNA. It's just too clean to be a dog. It would have to rip and chew and drag." Price closed his eyes for a second, trying to stop the graphic images, presented by McConait, appearing in his mind. "And there's the most obvious thing…"

Price did know the answer to this one. "The full moon; a dog wouldn't wait for exactly the night of the full moon."

"No, the timing is key. This is a choice; a choice related to occult practices, made by a trophy-collecting psychopath, using

46

tools, perhaps ceremonial in design." He paused and scanned the remains top to bottom. "How tall was Pembridge?"

"Six four" replied Boe instantly.

McConait continued, "Our man must be incredibly powerful, a big man, very secretive. Probably lives on his own, internet access, occult artefacts in his house. And he's local, or at least he's been here a while, not a visitor; he slipped in and out and blended into the background. The victims may have even known him. Someone without an alibi for the nights in question, that narrows it down a bit." He turned to Peel for affirmation and got it.

"And that's what you're here for Doc. I think I'll be making a few enquiries, if you're done here I'll show you where we're basing the investigation. Turning to the pathologist he offered a hand shake, "Thanks Dr. Boe, good work. Ready gents?" with that Peel gestured towards the blood-smeared door, and Price was first to react, he couldn't wait to escape this scene of horror.

McConait started and then turned again to Boe. "The car jack idea, you will check for any traces of motor oil on the victim?"

It was the first time he'd really made eye contact with Boe, and as he did a familiar feeling returned. "I'm very meticulous Dr McConait.", he said and continued an unblinking gaze at McConait who had gone decidedly pale. The feeling in the church had returned, images flashing. The body that had hardly made him flinch, suddenly horrified him. In his imagination the staring eyes of the victim blinked then looked at him. Savage fighting dogs barked and snarled in his mind, saliva drooling from their jaws. Hands grasping in defence, fur clogging under their fingernails. The face of Maria appeared again, along with the sickening guilt that went with it. The world was swirling once more.

McConait dashed through the clinic. A few doped up faces flashed before him, an angry nurse bellowed at him. Then he was out the front door and through the police tape. He thrust his hand in his pocket and swallowed a prozac, with no water at hand he let his mouth fill with saliva before swallowing. At last the madness subsided.

47

He caught his breath and as the torrent in his head gave way, he finally got his bearings. On the other side of the road was the picturesque village green. A gravel path worked its way symmetrically through pretty flowerbeds and lawns. At one end was a war memorial, and, at the other, a statue of Queen Victoria. A more tranquil English scene McConait couldn't have hoped for, what a contrast from what lay at the back door, just yards behind him.

Peel got to him first." Are you OK Doc? It's terribly gruesome; this one."

"Sorry, I thought I'd be used to it by now." McConait knew it had nothing to do with the murder scene; it was that same, strange, inexplicable reaction from the church.

"I couldn't get used to sights like that. I don't think you should either. If you do I think it's time to quit."

Price's kind hand on his shoulder, and gentle voice soothed McConait further. "Now you take it easy, you've nothing to prove. I was fighting the nausea the whole time I was in there. It's natural to get spooked; even if you are a Cambridge whiz."

The understanding of Price impressed McConait again. Spooked: That's exactly what he felt like; spooked, frightened.

Peel was in a hurry to get the investigation moving so he needed to get formalities out of the way. It was time to get McConait set up ready for work. They got in the car and sped round the corner heading towards the sea front. On the left was a triangle of grass and on the far corner nearest the sea was a small two roomed building with the word "POLICE" on the side. McConait recognised it. It made him smile. It had been there for years, since the old station was knocked down, this prefab hut was all that was required in a town that, until recently, enjoyed very low crime rates.

"The main station is North Shields, a couple of miles away, this is all that Tynemouth's got. But we're getting two mobile units in the morning. I think it's important there's a presence on site at all times for this one." explained Peel.

The police hut was a retreat for officers patrolling the sea front; a beat that went in a straight line from Tynemouth to Cullercoats, then curved round to Whitley Bay. The Community

Beat Officers were on foot or mountain bikes, and a more attractive beat wasn't to be had on Tyneside.

Inside; the hut consisted of a room, with a kettle in one corner, a telephone, police radio and a laptop in the other, the back of this room was a smaller room with a toilet and sink. In the middle was a rectangular table with four chairs around it, which looked like they'd been there since the 1970s. There were two small windows with a protective metal mesh over them. The walls had white boards, with miscellaneous bits of paper blue-tacked on; resembling timetables or government guidelines and the obligatory 'Health and Safety at Work' poster.

Peel quickly conjured up cups of tea for McConait and Price and poured himself a glass of water.

McConait enjoyed his tea but his mind was already back on the job. "These boards, can I use them?"

"Help yourself. I'm to give you Carte Blanche, according to the Yard." said Peel who'd used his investigative powers to track down a packet of ginger nut biscuits and waved the packet around the room in offering.

"I'll take a couple." said Price, in an effort to appear relaxed; more to put McConait at ease than anything else. McConait declined the biscuits and began pulling pieces of paper from a whiteboard. He then picked up a dry wipe marker and began to produce what resembled a spider's web on the board.

"Here he goes; the artist at work." Peel smiled and Price reciprocated.

On the board McConait was not scrawling. He took his time to write neatly. Lines were drawn with the aid of a wooden metre rule. In the centre it said 'Mark Pembridge', a line went out to the right and at the end of the line McConait started to write down the few details he knew about the victim: height, age, address, family history.

Going straight up a line ended with the words 'circumstances of death'. Around it McConait penned in details, listing the organs missing, the claw marks, the ruptured sternum, the smeared handprint.

49

To the left, the line ended with the words 'possible causes', where McConait began to list the possible tools, the car jack theory, the direction of the attack.

A line drawn southward, contained details of symbolic significance. The missing organs, the lack of blood trails from the incident, the full moon. "I'll need detailed plans of the murder scene, street maps of Tynemouth, the victim's movements and known associates and detailed photographs of the corpse."

"Anything you say, but remember it's corpses. I'll take you to the scene of the first crime tomorrow, we've got all the stuff you'll need in North Shields, I'll have it sent over." Peel rinsed his glass and walked to the door. "Right gentlemen I'm off to the main station; I think it's going to be a late one but thanks for your help. See you in the morning; I'll give you a call. Goodnight."

McConait and Price nodded, Price smiling, McConait itching to return to his white boards. On a separate board he had already written the word killer in the middle and was doing what he was here to do. Various lines eminating from the centre profiled the character and habits of the killer as McConait saw them:

Into the occult
lives alone
surfs the net
big powerful male
no alibis
tools
psychopathic tendencies
trophy collector
history of cruelty towards animals as a child
intelligent
clean
meticulous.

Price sat and watched as the diagram grew as if it had a life of its own. A visual representation of the thought processes going on in McConait's mind, each line connecting one word to another like connections in the brain; firing electric impulses across the synaptic gaps to produce an idea.

50

It was impressive to watch and Price could see why McConait had such a reputation with the police, but he couldn't help think that McConait was missing something. He made his excuses and left.

Chapter 9
Andrea Swan

Andrea Swan of Forensics pulled off the obligatory hair net then flicked off her rubber gloves and looked at her hands. Her left hand still bore the groove from her wedding ring. She gave it a rub as if to rub out the unpleasant memories of her failed marriage. The loss of a once perfect youthful romance still smarted after a year of separation. She ran her hands through her bobbed blonde hair and gave it a shake, then tucked it behind her ears. At forty-three her hair still retained its youthful bounce. She wasn't permitted to wear makeup in the lab but even in its raw state, and despite a few laughter lines, Andrea still had a shiny schoolgirl's complexion. Her toned physique from her gym addiction added to a reclaimed vitality.

There was a new package on the desk marked urgent. Andrea let out a sigh; it was half an hour until she finished her shift and although she hadn't opened the package, processing a new batch of samples could take hours. She could always do with the overtime, but she was hoping to get home and have dinner with her teenage son and daughter like a proper family for a change. It looked like the pizza delivery would be getting another call.

She flopped into a swivel chair and stared at the bulky paper package on the desk. She knew what was in it by the shape; blood and tissue samples in plastic vials held in a rack. The package was no more than six inches square but it symbolised much more to Andrea, a waste of hours on end and at times a real bind, but at the end of the day it was her job and her obsession. Delving into the blood cells and DNA was Andrea Swan's world. The world at the end of the microscope was an escape, where everything made sense and where the truth could be found; nothing could be hidden from her trained eye.

She flipped open her mobile, and clicked one then hash and the speed dial function called home. "Hiya Libby darling, I'm going to be late again…"

A teenage tut came down the phone, "What again?"

"Sorry pet but you know how important this is at the moment, what with all the killings. Be a love and phone for a pizza."

"Alright."

"Good girl. Oh, have you done your homework?"

"Yeh."

"Well done, and make sure your brother does his. And no arguing tonight."

"Yeh."

"See you later love."

"Yeh."

Andrea Swan flipped her phone shut, and ripped open the package.

Chapter 10
Royal Madness

Back at the Grand Hotel, Price said a silent prayer, then placed an expensive leather briefcase on a table. He opened it and pulled out a tattered and faded old book, dating from 1768, which at one time had been bound in a beautiful purple cover and embossed with gilt lettering all of which was now illegible. A piece of paper with a Vatican header was attached to the cover by an elastic band. Price scanned the information on it which detailed the books origins and how it had been banned by the church for its erotic and heretical content. He flipped open the book to a page marked with a Vatican book mark and began reading.

...then came the bang on the door. Hard and relentless banging. The door to Lady Matilda's bedchamber was thrown open. The dishevelled figure of Charles filled the doorframe. His shirt was open and filthy. His chest was bare and sweaty, rising up and down in deep passionate breaths. The ribbon had gone from his hair and thick dark chestnut curls coiled over broad strong shoulders.

Matilda was defenceless against his advances. Charles needed only one arm wrapped around her tiny pinched and corseted waist to lift her off the ground leaving her legs flailing beneath yards of petticoat, silk and lace. His mouth pressed against hers so the only sound she could make was a muffled whimper; it was the rustling sound of her dress that filled the room, as her tiny frame writhed against his unmoving stature. His free hand now lifted her skirts and ripped at her undergarments then pushed up between her legs. She felt herself falling as he threw her onto the four-poster bed. Before she could gather her senses he was on her, his full body weight, his groin pressing down between her legs that were thrown apart. Then he entered her. She felt like she had never felt before. It was animal, savage and primal. The two bodies melded into one writhing mass. She clawed at his back and tore at his hair as he ground deeper into her.

Carnal groans burst from inside her lungs and filled the air, which was humid and clammy. Sunlight streamed in rays from

54

tall, grand windows whipping the bodies with lashes of light; beads of sweat glistened on naked flesh like glass. With a final thrust Charles arched his back and with face contorted, turned his grimace towards the ceiling, his strong bold jaw tilted up and away from Matilda who lay beneath. His exposed throat revealed four diagonal scars, only days old. Then with one final shudder Charles let all the air out of his lungs and collapsed on top of the glowing Matilda.

Earl Charles Deveraux was the second cousin to the king. He had come into his inheritance at the age of twenty-two after the death of his father and mother in an outbreak of typhoid. The loss made him wealthy but sent him off the rails for quite some time. He was left Deveraux Manor in the heart of Somerset, in the South West of England, and one hundred acres of land. The village of Shepton Mallet were his tenants, they paid him rent and worked the land. The Deveraux family had been fair in comparison with other landed gentry but the new young master had a wild streak about him which made men wary but women found irresistible. The beautiful Lady Matilda Marsh was no exception. The Marsh family were close friends to the Deveraux and just as wealthy; they owned lead mines and considerable swaths of farmland.

Lady Matilda saw Charles' wild reputation, as an expression of the poet that lay within him, she thought she understood him and therefore could tame and cage the beast. But that afternoon, after all they had been through, she got more than she bargained for; their relationship had grown out of her control.

  *   *   *   *   *

It all started only two days before; Charles had been hunting with friends in the forest. He was the best and most daring huntsman anyone had ever seen. He seemed to have an understanding of the beast he chased and would not give up without a kill. Some say that if the prey eluded him he would turn on one of the hounds and beat it to death; not satiated until blood had been spilled.

This time, in the deep forest they came upon the rarest of prey, which had at one time been common in England but was now approaching extinction, a wolf; a she-wolf, split up from the pack to look for its pup, unusually caught out in the daylight. One of the horses became startled and threw its rider to the ground; the hunt was in an uproar: dogs barking and snarling; horses rearing; men yelling. The she-wolf snapped and snarled at the horses before turning and vanishing into thick undergrowth.

Without a thought Charles cut through the group of disarrayed huntsmen and spurred on his horse to make chase. Dodging branches, jumping toppled tree and brook, over fence and under bow, horse and rider ploughed forward, chasing the darting white tip on the tail of the she-wolf. Then the wood gave way to pasture and the wolf was in open ground. Charles could sense the kill was imminent as his thoroughbred made up the ground on the wolf. Charles drew his sword and leaned from the saddle still at full speed. Sensing the hunter behind her, the wolf changed direction, which sent her rolling over in the dirt. With a look in Charles' direction the wolf was on her feet again and running back towards the wood. With the horse rearing up on its hind legs, Charles turned the powerful charger about and again began closing in on his quarry.

As they reached the edge of the wood there was a fence. The wolf had no option but go under and the hunter and horse had no option but go over. Almost simultaneously they took the fence. The horse cleared it but the landing sent the daring Charles crashing to the ground and into the path of the on coming she-wolf. Man and wolf collided and hurtled down the banks into the brook below. Fur and flesh, claw and blade, tumbled over and over until they entered the shallow water.

Disorientated, man and beast parted. When Charles got to his feet again he was standing at one side of the stream staring at the she-wolf on the other. She had a sword wound on her neck and blood was matting in her silvery coat. Her cold grey eyes gazed at Charles as she puffed for breath. As Charles too gasped for breath he felt a piercing pain. He placed his hand to his neck to find he was bleeding. The she-wolf had inflicted a slashing claw wound in the tumble. Man and animal were even. The wolf

56

licked her lips, turned away and disappeared into the forest. Charles had gained an amazing respect for this noble creature, he was exhilarated and felt at one with the she-wolf.

When he returned to his friends he was so invigorated; near death had brought him to absolute life. They caroused in the tavern that night and all was well. Charles fondled and laughed with a local wench and quaffed flagons of ale, but as the moon rose above, the village the girl suddenly leapt from his lap. Charles began to shudder uncontrollably; eyes glazed. The shudder grew more violent throwing him from his stool onto the straw covered floor. His muscles locked and as the drunken gathering formed a distraught circle around him, he frothed at the mouth; the shudder now so bad that his head clashed against the floor in an unearthly rhythm.

$$* \qquad * \qquad * \qquad * \qquad *$$

When he awoke he was in his bed back at Deveraux Manor. His head throbbed and the room spun. A chambermaid entered; seeing he was at last awake she went to open the curtains. As the light entered he winced in pain and dragged the bedclothes over his head. "No!" he shouted, "Close those blasted curtains!" The light pained him; his head, injured from the banging on the floor pounded relentlessly. His muscles felt like they had been pulled apart and the wound on his neck burned into him.

It didn't take long for the rumours of Charles' fight with the she-wolf and subsequent strange behaviour to sweep through the village and stir up the locals. One of his fellow huntsmen that day was Sir Harry Marsh, the second richest landowner in the area and brother of Matilda. He knew how Matilda had carried a flame for the dashing Charles for years and tried to play down what had happened; hoping to protect her feelings, but the staff at the Marsh family home were fuelled by superstition and fear. The morning after the hunt Matilda overheard two maids whispering; she snapped at them, "What are you girls saying about the Earl?" The girls fell silent, "If you value your jobs you'll tell me right now!"

57

Emily, the younger of the two, gazed up at Matilda with big brown eyes, "He's taken with a spirit so they say."

Matilda stepped to Charles' defence, "The Earl has had a traumatic experience, he's not well that's all."

The other maid, Fanny, now piped up, "He's been bitten, Ma'am. He's been baying at the moon, changin' with it. And I hears that now he won't come out in the daylight, creeps out in the night, lives in the woods. It's a terrible thing, a terrible thing for the whole village if you ask me."

These rumours troubled Matilda as much as anyone but she kept her controlled demeanour as was expected of a lady of her position, and waved a hand dismissively at the maids. "This is preposterous! I'll go to him myself, the poor man needs help not rumour mongering."

The two girls looked at each other as if their Lady's suggestion was insanity. As Matilda turned to leave, Emily broke with maids' decorum and shouted after her, "Don't go me Ladyship, don't you see ...he's a werewolf!!" but Matilda was walking briskly down the long corridor to the hall, heart pounding, pretending not to hear

Within the hour she had ridden to the Manor only to be met by her brother Harry who was not pleased to see her there. "You shouldn't be here Matilda."

Her brother's reaction gave Matilda more cause for concern but she continued to put on a brave face, and gave Harry a peck on the cheek; as was customary. "But I want to help him; poor Charles, have you heard what they are saying about him?"

The protective brother held her firmly by the shoulders, "There's nothing you can do. Doctor Willis has been sent for from London. He's the Royal physician, the best there is; we just have to wait until he gets here."

"And how long will that be?" said Matilda now raising her voice; exposing her real emotions.

Harry looked solemn, "It may be a day or so."

Matilda's pleading continued but Harry was not going to budge and finally he dismissed her. Harry went into the Manor and the frustrated Matilda began to walk back to where a maid of

58

the household was talking to the stable boy attending Matilda's horse; it was Charles' chambermaid. The gossip of her own two maids had given her an idea. Matilda took a locket from her neck and pressed it into the maid's hand. "You know who I am, don't you? Please make sure the Earl gets this. Let him know I'm thinking of him." The maid nodded anxiously, clearly worried about being an accomplice and scurried inside.

Charles had given Matilda the locket two years before when they had first started meeting for clandestine moonlight walks. She had loved the way he would talk about travelling to exotic places and having great adventures and how he would write it all down and dedicate it to her one day. How her heart would beat, how the hairs on the back of her neck would stand on end, how every part of her being came alive in his presence. She knew that their relationship was special and in this time of need, she felt she might be the only one who could help him.

Matilda had galloped to the manor as quick as her steed would carry her, but now, going away from her true love, she plodded along desolate, in a daydream thinking of better times with Charles.

The sun was setting and only weak rays of light filtered through the trees in the woods. Matilda's horse needed no prompting; it trod the same path it had trodden a hundred times, bearing its mistress to and from her romantic liaisons with the Earl.

A crack broke the silence, and the horse whinnied anxiously. Matilda patted its neck and brought it to a halt; she was not anxious. She stepped down and looked into the gloomy forest; there in the half-light he stood. The message from the maid had worked. Charles had come into the woods where they had met so many times; even as children it had been a favourite place to play.

As Matilda drew near the same excitement she always felt in his presence returned. Her stomach churned and a skip came to her step. Looking at the handsome Charles he seemed more magnificent than ever. Not the Earl in splendid robes, but something more natural, more earthy. Somehow he belonged here in the forest, he had never been comfortable in the Manor with its finery, now in a way that Matilda had never realised,

Charles was part of the forest. Even in the gloom, his eyes seemed to shine as if he could see into the dark. His dishevelled, rugged state gave him the demeanour of Pan but his toned physique, which was shrouded by a loose thin cotton shirt, was that of Adonis.

As Matilda grew closer, Charles raised his hand, "Stop, Matilda, you must come no further."

This baffled Matilda, who wanted nothing more than to run into his embrace. "But why my love, can't you see I'm desperate to see you?"

In the free and rebellious way that he always spoke when alone with Matilda he began, "Matilda remember how we talked of escaping our lives, our responsibilities, breaking free of the shackles by which we are bound: society, church, family, privilege?" Matilda nodded clutching her hands together excitedly, "Well now I'm free. I have changed. I have become one with the forest; one with the night. Now I understand what it's all about." He held his arms wide apart gesturing to the forest, "It's what you see, hear, touch, smell and taste. That's all there is. All the decisions we have to make, what we do, where we go, who we talk to, what we wear, what is appropriate, ... it's all nonsense. There are only two choices, live or die." Charles was now at his most poetic; most radical. Everything that excited her about him had been accentuated; reduced into its essence. At this moment she would have done anything, gone anywhere with him. But his next sentence sent a shiver down her spine.

"Live or die, or in a more beautiful, more pure sense ...kill or be killed."

In this darkness, after all that had gone on, Matilda's excitement had, for the first time, boiled over...into fear.

"That's why you must come no further, Matilda. I don't ask any more; I take. It's nature's way, if I have a need I act on it. And I shall." Again the shuddering in Charles' body began. Matilda was horrified to see her beloved Charles behave so strangely. As his muscles contorted and sent him spiralling in pain to the ground, Matilda, now in tears, reached out to help him. With the last rational breath in his twisted body, Charles let out a roar to his Matilda, "Go!!!"

60

Seeing the snarling writhing mass, that had been her beloved, now foaming at the mouth, Matilda turned and ran to her horse. With a swift kick in its side, the trusty animal raced its mistress back home away from Charles.

*   *   *   *   *

Dr. Francis Willis was the most respected doctor in the land; Royal Physician and personal friend to the March family. A thin and willowy man with an immaculate appearance and fastidious manner, he was the only man in England with the medical knowledge to tackle a case such as this.

On receiving the letter that Earl Charles had, like others before him, succumbed to such a disorder, Dr.Willis dashed to his hypothicary and, with expert hands, gathered a collection of glass vials labelled in Latin, containing all manner of oils and powders, herbs and minerals and hurried them into a stout leather bag; he then dashed to the coach that had been sent for him. He sat beside the messenger that had come from Sir Harry Marsh and wasted no time getting aquainted with the case, "What state is he in? Has the fitting begun? And the sensitivity to light?"

The messenger turned gloomily to the Doctor, "Yes Dr.Willis, he has all the symptoms already."

Willis sat back in his seat, "Then I hope we're not too late." He called forward towards the driver, "Don't spare the whip man, to Deveraux Manor. Godspeed!"

*   *   *   *   *

Charles ran through the woods; every sense prickled as he flittered left and right. More alive than he had ever felt, part of the wood, part of the night, he had taken on the spirit of the she-wolf he had confronted that day. He was part of her pack now, part of her family, and he wanted to run and to kill with them.

*   *   *   *   *

61

In her chambers, the distraught Matilda fell to her knees, in tears. The two maids rushed to her side; they already knew what was the matter. Emily spoke first, "Oh mistress, we tried to warn ye'. Well ye' must 've seen for yerself now. Oh and him bein' so 'ansome and you bein' so in love an' all."

Matilda was suddenly, for the first time, impressed with the wisdom of the people who served her; people she had always held in such low esteem. "You knew about our love?"

Fanny smiled at her mistress, "Oh your Ladyship, the smile in your eye, well it was catchin' like. We was 'appy when you was 'appy. We're all women, we know what it feels like, don't we?" She said turning to Emily, as if it was something they had talked about many times. Matilda felt as if she was with sisters not servants; and in her sisters arms she wept.

$$* \qquad * \qquad * \qquad * \qquad *$$

Charles sensed that dawn was upon him: birds became restless; insects crept back to their hiding places; he could even feel the flowers readying themselves to greet the first rays of the sun, in a phototropic dance. Charles knew it was time to retreat back from his nocturnal kingdom back to the torture that was day time; hiding in his bedroom at the Manor, servants and friends fussing over him, cowering from the day light, his skin turning waxy and pale, his gums bleeding, the fits, the head aches, the confusion. He had to find another place to hide.

$$* \qquad * \qquad * \qquad * \qquad *$$

Matilda looked up into the eyes of her newfound sisters. "You understand, you know of these things. What can be done?"

The two maids looked at each other. The roles had been changed, they were now in charge and they knew what tradition said had to be done. Emily turned and said, "Ma'am there's a woman in the village. She knows of these things, she says that she can make a potion of sorts. A mixture of a plant called Wolfbane and Garlic Flowers. If this mixture were spread in an unbroken circle around the Earl, the demon that possesses him

62

would not be able to stand it and leave his body. The circle would protect him through the night until he was able to leave it in the safety of daylight."

The Lady looked up with hopeful eyes and the other maid spoke, "Then you would 'ave 'im back, your love, your Charles."

Matilda sat up and wiped the last of her tears from her eyes with a new conviction. "This woman you speak of, take me to her, after I sleep."

The two maids left. Matilda felt a new hope in her heart she felt that soon she would see her Charles back to his old self, and she was to see her Charles sooner than she had expected.

Then came the bang on the door. Hard relentless banging…

*　　　*　　　*　　　*　　　*

By the time Dr. Willis arrived the following day, it was all over. There had been a whirlwind of cataclysmic events. Sir Harry Marsh's discovery that his sister had been deflowered by his friend made him fly into a fury; a vindictive, destructive rage that can only be dished out by the ruling classes. The two maids were flogged as witches for trying to bring Matilda and Charles together. A mock trial was set about, where various people stepped forth to denounce the Earl as a beast, and finally a magistrate, who was a relative of the Marsh's, condemned Charles officially as a Werewolf. Matilda was deemed not emotionally fit to testify and, within an hour, Charles was hung by the neck until dead.

A bewildered and outraged Willis expressed condemnation of the events that had taken place but was given short shrift by the angry Sir Harry. "Doctors aren't what are needed here, if you must be of help then attend to my sister who has taken on such a melancholy because of this whole affair."

Willis sought out the grieving Matilda. Although his presence was not going to be any comfort to her. She grabbed his hands in desperation, "He came to me as Charles: Charles the wild; Charles the daring; Charles the strange perhaps but still my Charles; he was not a monster. Doctor tell me, my poor Charles

63

could we have saved him, with wolfbane and garlic, could we have set the demon free?"

The wise and enlightened old doctor looked into her watery blue eyes, "I am a man of medicine, a man of science. I know not the remedies of which you speak. Charles was not, as you rightly said, a monster, but he was ill. He suffered as many of his relatives have from Porphyria 'the Royal Disease' also known as 'Werewolf disease'; it causes fits, light phobia, waxiness of the skin, bleeding gums and delirium. King George himself suffers from the same ailment. I think that, if they had their way, perhaps certain 'friends' of the king would afford him the same punishment as the poor Earl."

Doctor Willis bid farewell with a gentle hand on Matilda's shoulder and left with his bag of medicines still unopened. The grieving Matilda would never recover from the loss of her Pan/Adonis.

Chapter 11
Rose's House

It was a month since the first incident and the house of Mr. and Mrs Stearman had returned to the respectable 1930s semi, it was meant to be: The laminate flooring; designer rug; 32 inch flat screen TV; family photos in stylish silver frames and pictures with a sea theme reflecting the views from the window; nothing looked out of place, as if nothing had happened. But something definitely had. McConait held the photos of Rose Brown's corpse. It was in a similar condition to Mark Pembridge but it seemed even more gruesome seeing her surrounded by all her possessions. The body was face up and the mid-section... gone, just a huge red/black stain between her chin and her legs. McConait compared the photo with the room and pictured her lying there.

"So fill me in Peel." asked McConait, bracing himself.

"Well Bob Stearman had been out for some time. Apparently they'd been arguing all day. He was in the pub until 1 a.m; he has plenty alibis. The neighbours heard screaming at about 1-1:30 pm; they took it they were still rowing and left it. Bob says he went for a kebab, Ali the shop owner says he recognised him as a regular but can't recall if he was in on that particular night; it was a really busy one. Bob said he found his dead wife at about 3am but he's not too sure; he was plastered. He couldn't accept that his wife was dead and actually tried to give her the kiss of life."

"My God that's awful." The desperation of a husband trying, even under these circumstances, to do something, anything, to help the woman he loved; he pictured his own father and mother and McConait was unable to utter a word.

Peel broke the painful silence, but spoke only in hushed tones, "He didn't report the death until 5 am; two hours later. He'd walked up and down the beach in a state. When we got him he was drenched and talking gibberish. We didn't get a statement until 8 that evening; he was a real space cadet, but you can't blame him, if he hadn't gone for a kebab he might have been back in time to protect her."

"You said they were arguing; what about?"

"We don't know but Rose's doctor said she had a hormonal problem; severe PMT. She was on pills; she'd had it for years and recently it had been getting worse; more tears, more arguing, depression. The doctor was going to try her on some new drug but never got the chance."

McConait's sympathy took a cynical shift from the distraught husband to the dead wife. "Maybe it wasn't her that was getting worse."

"What do you mean?" Peel felt as if McConait hadn't been listening.

"I mean it takes two to have an argument. Maybe he wasn't the best husband in the world." McConait's own guilt was getting the better of him.

"Whatever, it doesn't change the outcome. We've ruled him out as a suspect. He's a million miles away from your profile. He has a few hours unaccounted for but unless his mates are lying, he has an alibi for most of the evening." Peel was confident in the process.

"Yes but not the time of the screams. What about the other murder, how does the alibi check out for that one." McConait didn't want to leave this avenue unexplored.

"Water tight. Earlier that evening Stearman was at the church service; you can vouch for him there. After that he was whisked off to BBC Newcastle studios to record an interview, appeal thing, that finished at about 9 pm. Then he caught an evening train to Edinburgh at 10 pm to visit his sister, and he's been there ever since."

"OK I just had a feeling."

"Come on Doc. We don't work on feelings any more. You're doing a good job; we've got a group of suspects, thanks to your profile, and Bob Stearman isn't one of them."

"You've got suspects?" McConait felt relieved, nothing seemed to have gone right for ages; suspects were good news.

"Come on we'll walk back to the hut and I'll fill you in."

At that moment they both glanced to the right. Out of the window in their peripheral vision they had spotted movement in the front garden.

66

"Someone's outside, in the garden." Peel stating what they both already knew. He went to the door, dragged it open and stepped authoritatively into the garden. McConait followed; it was a familiar face.

On his knees, arms aloft, clutching something in his right hand and with his eyes tight shut, muttering, over and over, was Father Tuthie. Peel put his hands on his hips and looked to McConait for inspiration. Peel would have been more comfortable if it was a 15 stone thug trying to nick something; he'd know exactly what to do then. Unfortunately for Peel, there was no law against people praying in public, especially priests. But this was in front of a dead woman's house, and already people were crossing the road to see what the commotion was.

McConait was uncomfortable with what he saw as some form of dementia in the old man. Turning to Peel he asked, "What are you going to do with him?"

"I'd like to lock him up but, lifting an old priest for acting like a fool won't win the hearts and minds of the good people of Tynemouth. You have a word Doctor. You're the Psych."

Peel was right McConait was the right person to confront Tuthie, all the same he wished Father Liam Price was with them; he had the Bishop's backing to sort out the old trouble maker.

As he drew closer McConait saw that the thing in Tuthie's hand was a crucifix, which didn't surprise him. What he did find unusual was the style of the crucifix; he'd seen plenty in his time but not one like this. It was wooden with a silver metal Jesus nailed to it as one would expect. But behind the drooping head of Christ, where the vertical and horizontal met, was a metal disc with what appeared to be writing on it. McConait was now close enough to hear what Tuthie was saying.

"Crux Sancti Patris Benedicti
Crux Sancta Sit Mihi Lux
Non Draco Sit Mihi Dux
Vade Retro Satana
Numquam Saude Mihi Vana
Sunt Mala Quae Libas
Ipae Venena Bibas"

67

Although McConait picked up a few words, his Latin wasn't up to a translation. But then Tuthie began repeating a phrase that McConait did recognise.

"Agnus dei, qui tolis pecata mundi, Miserere nobis,

Agnus dei, qui tolis pecata mundi, Miserere nobis,

McConait knew what the words meant; they were from the Latin Mass.

(Lamb of God you take away the sins of the world, have mercy on us,

Lamb of God you take away the sins of the world, have mercy on us)

The chant continued without let up. Still on his knees, his arms trembling as they struggled to stay aloft in prayer, Tuthie repeated over and over:

"Agnus dei, qui tolis pecata mundi, Miserere nobis,

Agnus dei, qui tolis pecata mundi, Miserere nobis,"

McConait had to do something so he simply spoke, "Father." The old man continued chanting, "Father Tuthie." Still no let up. "It's me Mary McConait's boy." Again Sly used his mother to con the priest, but to no effect. McConait looked back at Peel, who was keeping a safe distance and then at the small gathering of onlookers who were congregating on the path at the end of the garden.

McConait took a deep breath and decided to try something. He knelt down face to face with Tuthie and joined the chant:

"Agnus dei, qui tolis pecata mundi, Miserere nobis,

Agnus dei, qui tolis pecata mundi, Miserere nobis,"

McConait couldn't see Peel's face but he knew it would be a picture, the chanting continued:

"Agnus dei, qui tolis pecata mundi, Miserere nobis,

Agnus dei, qui tolis pecata mundi..."

McConait made his move, before the priest could say Miserere nobis, Sly cut in with:

"donna nostrum pacem." (Grant us peace)

ending the verse.

And peace was granted. Tuthie stopped and opened his eyes. Despite the madness of the last few minutes, McConait couldn't

68

help warm to the man. They looked at each other for a minute, strangely bonded by the bizarre experience. McConait got to his feet; his knees sodden from the wet earth. He took Tuthie by his arms, which were still raised to heaven, and gently lifted the frail old man to his feet.

"You'll catch your death out here father, it's the middle of February." Let's get you inside out of the cold."

"I'll not enter the house of the devil son, and neither should you. The beast entered this home and his stench is still upon it; it must be cleansed, and so must this whole village. The Lamb of God alone is our salvation, don't you see? The lamb will overcome the wolf, the lamb will overcome the wolf!" Tuthie's eyes were bulging out of their sockets as if trying to fix the idea into McConait's brain.

"Shall we talk about this down at the police hut, at the end of the green." Peel had decided to join them but Tuthie never took his eyes from Sly McConait.

"Ah, you have your mother's eyes son, she'd be glad to think you were back home; fighting the fight, the good fight. He pressed the crucifix into McConait's hand. "Take this, you'll need it; keep it near you, it will help. God Bless you." The show was over. Tuthie shuffled off up the street, back towards the presbytery.

McConait looked at the crucifix and the series of apparently random letters on the disc behind the lifeless body of Christ, then slipped it into the inside pocket of his jacket.

Seeing the old priest leave, Peel now drew closer, "You alright Doc? I thought you'd really flipped there. Give me some warning next time will you?

"I didn't know I was going to do it myself."

"And what was all that malarkey you two were chanting. Who exactly is Agnes?" Peel was at his cheekiest and most likable.

"Agnes Dei, Lamb of God, it's Latin; I remembered it from years ago."

"Latin indeed, mind you it's easier to understand than Geordie."

69

They both looked at each other and grinned, partly at the surreal events that had unfolded, but mainly because of the relief of tension. The two men walked, not really knowing what to make of it all, across the triangular green back to the police hut. Peel unlocked the door and walked in to the chilly profile room. McConait wasted no time in flicking on the electric fire. After rubbing and blowing on his cold hands, Peel went through the files of the suspects; nine in all. They were pretty close to the profile but none matched anywhere near enough for McConait's liking.

All large men with links to the occult, ranging from devil worship down to being seen in a Marilyn Manson T-shirt. Some had alibis to one of the killings but not to both. They all lived on their own. A couple were bikers with their own garage. All but one was born and grew up within 10 miles of Tynemouth and that was the one that McConait was drawn to.

"Well he's definitely not a local. Rufus Infareño, from …" McConait perused the file for more information, "…Mexico?"

"Yeh that's right. 'Johnny Foreigner' here is a surfer who moved to England in…" Peel checked the details on a photocopy, "1998; started in London working in hotels, then bars… got in with some Aussie surf types and ended up travelling about…in Newquay in Cornwall for 3 years, that's a big surfer place, then they got the itch again, Manchester, Liverpool then Newcastle in 2004…lived in Heaton, worked in a pub in town, then they moved to Tynemouth in 2006. The Ausies left in 2009 leaving Rufus in Tynemouth where he works in…" Peel paused to lick his fingers and turn over the piece of paper. " Where else? The Surf Shop."

McConait flicked through a couple of pictures and stopped on a shot of the suspect in surfing gear; a wet suit stripped off to the waist; his long black hair slicked back with seawater. White teeth beamed from a swarthy complexion. His tattooed right arm and surfboard decorated with the same design; the 5 pointed star, the symbol associated with witchcraft, the devil and werewolves, also known as the pentacle.

Peel's phone chimed into life. "Hello Peel here…ah forensics about time, what have you got for me?" Peel put his

70

hand on his hip and stared at his feet as Andrea Swan explained her findings. "What do you mean you need a second opinion?" Peel frowned trying to make sense of technical jargon coming through the phone until one word made him raise his eyebrows, "A vet? What the bloody hell's a vet going to … no I can't come now I'm with Dr. McConait he's a … Oh you know who he is do you?… OK, I see, well let me know if you find anything else."

McConait looked at the confused policeman, "Well what was that all about?"

That was the girl from forensics. She says she's looked at the blood and there's something unusual but it's a bit vague. She says it's nothing she can pin point so she's consulting a specialist… a vet."

McConait was as taken aback as Peel "A vet, but we'd ruled out an animal."

"Well the forensics say the samples weren't found on the victims but in the victims' blood streams; the blood is pretty much normal apart from this thing which she can't explain so she's going to ask a bloody vet, I can't help but feel this is an error. What a waste of time."

McConait felt, as Peel did, that this was a distraction they could do without. Peel's expression lightened a little, "Oh she reckons she knows you; went to school with you."

McConait was unnerved with someone knowing him as a geeky teenager and shuffled uncomfortably, "Really what's her name?"

"Andrea Swan…blonde…so high." Peel indicated 5' 2" with an outstretched hand.

Peel wracked his memory and with relief shook his head, "No, I definitely don't know an Andrea Swan."

71

Chapter 12
The 3rd Incident

Three weeks had passed. Press conferences had been held; the media, especially the local press, were building up the "local boy made good". Everyone was sure that the Tynemouth lad would solve the crimes. But the fact was the investigation was getting nowhere. Even with warrants to search the main suspects' houses, all that had been turned up was some marijuana and some occult jewellery, nothing to link them to the crimes. Even delving into their past showed no history of violence, on the contrary, they were a pretty harmless bunch; the two bikers had done a lot of work for charity. The killer seemed to have vanished into the night, and once again the full moon cast an eerie shimmer over Tynemouth.

Police patrols were visible to increase public confidence; they were going to be there throughout the night. The druids and travellers camped out on the beach, the Priory kept securely off limits, and the whole thing had been cleverly orchestrated by Father Liam Price; this was his area of expertise. He knew the social dynamics needed to create a cult, a mass belief, and how to pull it to pieces.

The ancient significance of the Priory as a Holy place of worship would only give validity to any occult worship there. The druid faith was gaining respect; their link to nature and history had turned a lot of heads in their direction. They had of course claimed that the cliff, where the Priory stood, was a place of Pagan worship long before a Christian one. It sounded feasible but, without a scrap of evidence, Price wasn't buying it.

As an English Heritage site the police were totally within their rights to move on any trespassers from the Priory or even prosecute. This required a sizable police presence. The front entrance was of course locked but there were several points around the cliff where anyone, fit enough, could scramble onto the site.

Peel had taken some convincing but Price had explained what an astute move this would be to dent the growing "Wolf" cult. With the serious worshipers driven away from the Priory,

72

they could be rallied onto the beach at King Edward's Bay, a small stretch of beach immediately to the left of the Priory; the high cliffs that surrounded making an excellent holding area. There the Druids would be joined by gangs of Goths, rockers and ravers, the police actively funnelling the crowds down to the beach. Any serious, legitimate pagan worship and promotion of the werewolf myth, would be undermined by an unholy piss up. And any sign of trouble could be easily controlled by the police in the confined area. If there was any trouble it wouldn't do Price's cause (to dispel the "mumbo-jumbo") any harm.

Barbeques glowed in the dark. Outlandishly dressed travellers with dreads juggled with flaming torches. Pounding dance music blared from stereos around the beach and wide-eyed, spaced out youths danced in the moonlight. Druids in long white gowns prayed to the moon. They looked like something from Star Wars apart from their footwear; mainly designer trainers. It was turning into a festival of death. It was difficult to tell if the revellers were trying to ward off the killings or encourage them.

Of course Father Tuthie wasn't about to miss out, he held an all night prayer vigil, in which rosary beads were being worn out by devout fingers, as one Hail Mary followed another. Price had no problem with prayer, and that's where he intended on spending the night. When it came between Pagan and Christian, Price knew fine well what side his bread was buttered, and tonight, at least, Price would stand (or kneel) shoulder to shoulder with the old Parish Priest of St.Oswin's.

It was as if no one would sleep tonight, and certainly not Detective Peel. He toured Tynemouth on foot. Checking everyone was where he or she was meant to be. On the way past the Priory Primary School field he looked across towards the back door of the rehab clinic; the scene of the last killing. To his surprise the field was alive with activity. Four teen-age boys were having a game of football; in the dark. Peel knew that someone had screwed up here. The school field was generally out of bounds, and especially after the killing, and especially on a full moon.

73

"You lads shouldn't be there. Get off the field and get home!" shouted Peel.

The youths didn't know Peel from Adam and his Cockney accent was not doing him any favours.

"Fuck off man!"

"Aye, piss of ye soft twat!"

"This is all I need." mumbled Peel to himself and got on his police radio. "Peel to base, Peel to base."

In a scratchy, airy tone the police radio came to life, "Base here, evening Sarge."

"Never mind all that. Where's the patrol on Queensway? We've got the bloody FA cup final going on here; without flood lights. And what's more I'm getting dogs abuse. I want two officers here, SHARPISH!" He'd put too many hours in for some lightweight to mess it up.

Base certainly got the message and two officers came scurrying up Queensway as Peel reached the bottom of the road.

"Sorry Sarge, an old dear had us talking; just making the public feel safe. You know hearts and minds stuff."

"Well I've got no heart, and I'm going out of my mind, so do your bloody job and get those kids off the school field!" Even in his worst mood Peel could be a real character.

"Right away Sarge!" said the two officers in unison.

Peel continued, but turned back after a few yards, "And make sure they go home!"

The officers didn't reply but gave an acknowledging wave, and began to walk up Queensway.

On the field the youths caroused noisily, there was no game as such. The thrill was avoiding a ball kicked at you full blast in the dark. It was only a matter of time before the ball went astray, and, with a hoof from an Adidas trainer a bright silver Nike football went crashing into the bushes which lined the north edge of the field.

"Ye can gan and get it, Ye kicked it!" said one boy in broad Geordie; not wanting to search in the blackness.

"Ye can gan, I didn't even see where it went, anyway it's dark." the second boy making his fears more obvious.

74

"Aw man ah'll get it, ye soft shites." boasted Jamie Spence, a belligerent 15 year old. He had been that way since reaching puberty at 13. Once the apple of his mother's eye, altar boy and school prefect, he had changed into a sullen, awkward and at times aggressive youth. Suspended from school, and at odds with his parents, Jamie was a real candidate for an ASBO (Anti Social Behaviour Order). He had a 20 a day cigarette habit, and, most nights, 3 or 4 cans of lager were consumed in a variety of locations: bus stops; supermarket car parks; and tonight the Priory Primary School field. An acne marked face, visual proof, if proof were needed, of the hormones racing through his skinny adolescent body.

Jamie saw an opening and stepped into the hedge. He pushed through some stubborn twigs, and then he was through to the other side; into someone's garden. The ball was only a yard away and he stepped towards it. As he bent down he heard a rustling and a rasping breathing sound.

"Aw fuck off man ah na its one o ye' pissin' aboot." His words were sheer bravado. He felt a chill down his spine and he wished he'd never entered the garden. Slowly, feet frozen to the spot, he looked all the way around the garden, first to his right, then to his left from where he had come. There was something in the bush. He must have pushed right past it.

The light filtering from the clinic, the scene of the last killing, on the other side of the field, created a shadowy outline. It was moving ever so slowly. He could hear the voices of the others beyond.

"Haway man hurry up with that fuckin' ball!"

He wanted to shout back but he was rigid with terror. The creature in the hedge leaned forward so that its face was exposed. The boy saw a curl of a drooling lip and the glint of white teeth.

"Right lads off this field right away. It's not safe.'

It was the police, Jamie, still behind the hedge felt a little safer, and the beast withdrew its face back into dense leaves.

"We cannit gan yet our mates in that hedge."

"What is it, Narnia?" asked the second copper.

"Naw honest he is. Haway man Jamie it's the police, we have te shift!"

75

Jamie desperately wanted to yell, but something told him he wouldn't get the words out of his mouth. The beast seemed to be disturbed by the police, perhaps it would slink away; if he just kept still.

"Lads off the field or we're taking you in. Shift!"

The boys walked off the field remonstrating with the police and intermittently shouting back for Jamie.

As the voices of his friends faded, Jamie began to shake uncontrollably and sob through chattering teeth. The beast took its cue. The face was back. Foul smelling breath reeked from it mouth. Dead flesh rotted between its teeth. It sniffed the air, the scent of the boy drawing it on. The beast stepped forward and the hedge cracked and snapped under it's weight.

"Wait! I heard something there." It was the first policeman who sensed that perhaps the boys weren't wind up merchants after all.

"See Ah Fuckin telt ye, it's Jamie."

"Well why doesn't he come out?" asked the second policemen suspiciously.

"Well cause you two are here and he thinks he'll get in bother for gannin in that garden like."

"You look after this lot I'll have a look." And with that the first policeman, the larger of the two, was over the fence heading back across the field towards the hedge.

This time the creature did not retreat back, but the full length of its body was now exposed. Powerful shoulders covered in matted hair tapered down to a slender waist, then shaggy hind quarters. With the policemen 10 yards away, Jamie gave out a desperate yell and hurled the football in his hands towards the creature.

The policeman recognised the terror in the boy's voice, this was not a prank, and he burst into a sprint towards the hedge.

The beast pinned the boy by the throat. The weight of its body cracking his ribs as he hit the ground. A hind leg stamped down and clawed at the boy's groin.

The policeman thrust his full weight at the opening in the hedge. Twigs scratched at his hands and face, jabbing his eyes, so he had to thrash his head from side to side to find a space. He

76

opened his stinging eyes to see a hair-covered mass writhing over the boy.

The policemen couldn't breath, astonished at what he was witnessing but with one more shove his bulky frame, which had been hampered, by a stab jacket, epilates, radio, truncheon and pepper spray (all the paraphernalia of the modern policemen) lunged through the hedge, and landed in a heap at the twitching feet of the boy.

A light went on in the house of the garden where they lay. The policemen pushed himself up onto his knees, the beast had gone. The light from the house illuminated an awful scene, the boy's mid-section was gouged and spewing blood and his throat was torn away. As the door to the house flew open, to reveal a startled middle age woman in her nightie, the policeman looked down at the boy's feet... They stopped twitching.

Chapter 13
Queensway

All the efforts of the first night of full moon had come to nothing. Another victim, and this time a child.

Peel arrived at the scene. Inside the house, he found a burly policeman with his head in his hands, on the sofa. A middle-aged woman was trying to get him to take a cup of tea. Peel recognised him as one of the coppers he'd sent to clear the teenagers from the field.

Even in his shocked state, the officer straightened his back at the sight of a ranking officer. Peel knew he had to get facts fast before the officer's adrenaline decreased and conscience, guilt and regret took over.

"Let's walk the scene, explain everything then you can get away home."

"Yes Sarge." replied the jittery policeman.

They retraced the steps of the past hour. Starting with the bottom of Queensway and walked up the street, back towards the house and the school.

The policeman stopped at the fence, "Well after we saw you, we got to the school and told the two lads to get off the field, they wouldn't, so…"

Peels analytical brain was at full speed, he wasn't going to miss a trick. "Two lads, you said two?"

"Yeah Sarge the other one…" The officer gulped hard, "the victim, was already through the hedge into the garden."

Peel looked at the bobby face to face. "Well that makes three boys in total."

"Three altogether, that's right Sarge."

"But there were four boys on the field when I walked past. What happened to the other one?" Peel feared that there may be two dead boys tonight not just one.

"He must have already left, gone home."

Peel collared a CID officer going past. "Where's the lads who were on the field?"

The CID thought then replied, "They're with that WPC down there Sarge." The CID pointed towards the field beside the

78

hedge, where a policewoman was questioning two teenage boys. Peel strode over and interrupted; an act of urgency rather than arrogance.

"I'm Detective Seargent Peel. Where's the other lad, the one who left earlier?"

The boys recognised Peel as the 'soft bastard' who had spoken to them earlier. "He went home, after you telt us to get off the field like. He said he was in enough botha' with his mam, so he was just gannin' home."

Peel looked at the WPC, "Find out who he is, where he lives and that he got home safe; then get him back here, I want him questioned as soon as possible." With that, Peel turned back to the dazed, bulk of a policeman, whose grey complexion was a testimony to the night's events. "Come on let's go back through the house and you can tell me what happened in the garden.

The officer didn't answer, but nodded and braced himself to re-live the worst few minutes of his life.

*　　　*　　　*　　　*　　　*

McConait got a rude awakening at 5 o'clock in the morning. Not a phone call, but a bang on his hotel door by one of the many police officers present on the sea front, who then accompanied the Doctor through the black March morning with knots in their stomachs.

After entering through the middle-aged woman's front door (the 1930's semi, not dissimilar to that of Rose Brown) they went straight through to the back of the house. Sly braced himself at the kitchen door, which led out to the garden, knowing what to expect.

Price was already there, the vigil finishing at about 4 am. He was, as he had been most of the night, on his knees, carrying on where he left off, praying, this time for the soul of the young lad splayed out in front of him. Peel was to the left looking into the hedge, a burly PC next to him, with scratches on his face, gazed in a state of shock at the hole in the hedge; the same hole the boy, the creature and then he had passed through.

79

Peel put a sympathetic hand, copper to copper, on the policeman's shoulder, and led him back to the kitchen, keeping himself between the policeman and the cause of his distress.

McConait appeared from the house to complete the triangle of Priest, Academic and Detective. They all gazed down at the mutilated boy in silence.

"God it's London all over again." McConait the first to break the silence. "Only worse. London was bigger, more anonymous, less of an obvious pattern, less connections. Here it's smaller, tightly knit, everyone's affected. It's personal." The pressure was getting to McConait. The press had made him a star but now a boy was dead; after the biggest police action in Tynemouth's history. McConait's lustre was starting to fade. He wanted someone to blame. "How the blazes did this happen? The place was crawling with police."

"Quite literally," replied Peel, "that officer you just saw, was inches away. He heard the victim, came through the hedge and ended up on his hands and knees at the boy's feet; seconds too late."

"Well didn't he chase him? A big copper like that could take on anyone." McConait was finding his scapegoat.

"Take on anyone, what about anything?" Peel was on the defensive; he knew what trauma the officer had been through.

"What's that supposed to mean?" asked McConait, quite confrontational.

"I mean he saw the thing that did it."

"He saw the thing that did it, you mean the person who did it?" McConait, now condescending, questioned not just the Sergeant's grammar but also his sanity.

Price too, for the first time took his gaze from the victim.

Peel realised how it had sounded. But he had to explain. "The officer on the scene states that he saw the…" Peel paused to make sure he didn't put his foot in his mouth. "…attacker, over the boy, writhing its head from side to side." He cringed at the fact he said 'its' not 'his'. He decided to spit it out to get it over with. "He said it was some kind of creature; hairy and vicious it was biting the boy's neck."

80

McConait threw up his hands in despair. "Oh, well done Peel, so we've thrown the towel in. Shall we join the space cadets down on the beach, or Tuthie and the inquisition at St.Oswin's?" McConait's voice turned to pleading. "For Christ's sake we've been through so much. This is what we're fighting against, this whole 'hocus pocus' nonsense. Listen to what you're saying man.

Peel made his first act of defence. "Well that copper was in a hell of a state, he was 100% sure what he saw; he's traumatised."

"Well there you go. He tried to help a boy in real trouble. He tried his best but it wasn't good enough, of course he's traumatised."

"But he was right here!" Peel pushed his hand passionately into the hedge.

"I saw his face; twigs scratching his eyes, adrenaline pumping, pitch black. You work it out. What about the woman in the house? Did she identify the killer?" McConait made perfect sense.

"She saw nothing." continued Peel defiantly.

"And the police helicopter, I heard that circling, the police on the beat, the neighbours?"

"Nothing." This time Peel was less confident in his argument.

"So nobody else saw a bloody great big murdering mythological monster; there's a surprise!" McConait turned, put his hands on his hips and shook his head.

Peel tried to save some face, "He's a good copper!" Peel didn't know him from Adam but he meant what he said, he had grown tired of the police being challenged over every action, instead of being trusted to get on with the job.

"Of course he is but the atmosphere's got to him, it was a tense night. All the same we can't afford this lack of clarity Peel."

"Of course you're right." With that, an irate if deflated Peel turned and went back in the house.

McConait looked at Price, "What now?"

Price was characteristically calm and reassuring. "Let's take a walk around the rest of the scene, staring at this poor kid's not doing any of us any good." Price was right; it wasn't just the

81

police officer that was succumbing to the atmosphere. This latest murder hit everyone hard.

They toured the street, down and back to the top of Queensway, then walked the school field, filled with blue overalled SOCOs searching every blade of grass. One overalled figure stopped and looked at McConait. As McConait joined the gaze the figure started to walk towards him. Even in the unbecoming blue overall McConait could make out the shapely figure of a woman. This was further enhanced when the figure removed her mask to reveal a beaming smile and then the hair net was pulled away and with a shake revealed a bounce of blonde hair.

McConait's heart was racing, he was strangely attracted to this woman and what's more this was not a new feeling, this was a face from his distant past. As she drew nearer she held out a hand, "Hiya Sylvester, remember me? Andrea, from school?"

Open mouthed McConait struggled to speak, " A..A..Andrea, of course. I mean of course I remember you, Andrea O'Neil, you haven't changed."

"Well the name is Andrea Swan now."

"Oh I see, you're the woman in forensics. I take it you're married then, what with the name change."

"Yes with two kids, but not for long, married that is, I hope to have the kids for ever. And you?"

"Me? No." McConait shook his head as if the very idea was preposterous. An uncomfortable silence was broken by Price, "Hello I'm Fr. Liam Price, I'm helping Dr.McConait, it's great when one runs into old pals, don't you think, Dr?" Price turned to the dazed McConait who was still staring at a girl who still sparkled as she had back in his school days.

This time Andrea broke the silence. She held out a card. "Here's my number. Give me a call if you want to talk…about the case or anything."

McConait took the card; a grunt was all he could muster in reply.

"Lovely to see you again… and nice to meet you Father, bye." Andrea turned and jogged back across the field.

82

Price snatched up the card and buried it into McConait's breast pocket. He grabbed McConait round the shoulder and whispered into his ear, "If you don't call her you're a bloody fool McConait." As he turned to the priest McConait could see the sparkle in his eye and a grin on his face.

*   *   *   *   *

As dawn arrived a car pulled up and the WPC who had interviewed the boys, got out escorting the fourth youth who had left the scene before the killing. The boy had not returned home, as was suspected, but was found on the beach in a distracted state. The police suspected solvent abuse; glue sniffing. Peel came out to meet them and Mcconait stayed a few yards away, observing.

"We found the boy on the beach Sarge, his Mum was beside herself when he didn't come home, she'd already put a call in to the station."

The young man ran his hands through a greasy mop of hair and revealed a pasty acne ridden face, with small eyes and gaunt cheeks. He sported the mandatory black garb of the Goth; quite a contrast from his Chav mates in their shell suits and baseball caps. The boy looked around shiftily; he didn't want to be questioned by the police.

Peel got the boy's attention, "Oy Sunshine!" McConait liked the irony of Peel's choice of phrase, this ghost faced Goth, exuded anything but sunshine. "What's your name then?"

The puny teenager, looked awkward as he muttered his name, "Adam."

"Adam what?"

This time the teenager looked right around him as if checking who was about; as his eyes met McConait he divulged his identity, "Adam Bates."

The reaction in McConait was immediate, the feeling returned for a third time. The feeling at the church, the feeling at the last murder scene, it hit him even stronger. Images began to dance before his eyes; the dead teenager, the traumatised policeman, the youth in front of him, running nail bitten fingers

83

through lank greasy hair, Maria's tear drenched face, his anger, his rage. It all made him sick to his stomach. The only thing he could do was to get away. As his head grew dizzy from the spinning carousel of disjointed images, he turned and staggered towards the school, with a worried Price at his heels. "Are you okay? Let's get you in, out of the cold and let's have a hot drink."

Chapter 14
What Makes Ten?

The sun rose over the sea behind the Priory. It was an ironically beautiful morning; uncharacteristically warm, the sun's rays gilding the North East Coast, a temporary gloss that would soon tarnish, once the morning editions hit the newsagents.

There was no school that morning. Price and McConait sat sipping coffee from polystyrene cups, looking out the window of the year two classroom; onto the school field. They were happy to avoid the situation for a few minutes at least.

McConait's thoughts returned to Andrea Swan. Why had she made him so uncomfortable? His ice cool academic facade had cracked. He had spent years eradicating his past: his accent; his humble beginnings; his family; anything that exposed him or made him vulnerable to feeling real emotion. But now his mind was unravelling distant memories that he had buried.

He pictured Andrea back in the science labs in High School. Tucking her hair behind her ears to concentrate on the chemistry experiment in which she was engrossed; she was always the most enthusiastic science student. It made perfect sense that she would end up in forensics, not a brilliant academic like McConait certainly not 'Ox-bridge' material, but a hard working scholar who always got the job done; however mundane.

McConait never had much success with girls at school; his brain was no match for the brawn of the football and rugby types who got the girls. His wiry hair, specs and teenage acne didn't help either. He was flattered that Andrea Swan remembered him at all. She wasn't one of the 'it' girls at school but her natural 'English Rose' qualities and her intelligence had always impressed the young Sly McConait, and from the strange way he was feeling, it clearly still did.

Although angry at letting his guard down, McConait still enjoyed the warmth that Andrea's eyes had made him feel, warmth that he had denied himself since Maria. McConait's feelings switched from warm to cold, the thought of Maria made his palms turn clammy and a chill ran down his spine; Price's voice pricked him from his trance.

85

"Well that makes you think."

Price seemed completely distracted by a children's maths display in front of the window. It consisted of ten green apples, separated into a group of '6 + 4'. There was a laminated card, blue tacked onto the glass above saying

'What makes ten?'

"Even for six year olds there are lots of ways at looking at the same problem."

Price picked up a piece of children's work, which had been mounted on green card, and bore a "Good work!" sticker at the bottom. Price read it out loud:

0+10, 1+9, 2+8, 3+7, 4+6, 5+5, 6+4, 7+3, 8+2, 9+1, 10+0

"And look they've even made the connection" the matching calculations highlighted in matching colours, 0+10 and 10+0 in red 1+9 and 9+1 in blue and so on.

They've seen that two separate solutions, although appearing different, are actually the same. "Ah from the mouths of babes..." he gave a knowing glance to his unlikely colleague. "I like the process this child..." he looked closer at the paper to read a name "...Molly, has used. All possibilities demonstrated... then connections made, no conclusions jumped to. Wonderful! Molly's got a bright future."

"It's hard to see a bright future round here." said McConait, forever the cynic.

It appeared that Price was going off in a tangent, but nothing was further from the truth, his mind had not left the case for a second. "Do you know the Ancient Greek philosopher, Aristotle." He took it for granted that McConait a Cambridge Don knew plenty about Aristotle. "He said that, logic dictates that a tomato of, say, 100g, dropped from a certain height would fall and hit the ground 10 times quicker than a tomato of 10g, dropped at the same time from the same height. Now the logic is clear, but it isn't actually true, he never actually bothered to try it. It wasn't until 1583 that Galileo actually conducted the experiment from the tower of Pisa where he found that they hit the ground at pretty much the same time."

McConait finally caught on to what Price was driving at. "So what you're saying is that the theories don't always pan out."

86

Price returned a look that hinted that McConait was part way there. "How does a mind like yours end up in a dog collar? Surely there are too many contradictions even for a science deist. How do you resolve the conflicts? "

"What do you mean exactly?" Price knew what he meant, but loving an intellectual challenge, he had lain down a gauntlet for McConait.

"OK then, here's one of my favourite bug-bares. The Immaculate Conception, Jesus conceived without sexual intercourse. The Catholic church's favourite bit of sexual mind control, where's the sense in it Father?"

"Oh what you mean is the Virgin Birth, the Immaculate Conception is a separate Doctrine, which states that Mary was born without sin, Jesus on the other hand is the Virgin Birth of which you speak, a common misconception if you'll pardon my pun."

"They both sound as preposterous as each other, but do enlighten me."

"Well it's back to those Greeks again." Price sat down again, making himself comfortable to answer a difficult question.

"It's all Greek to me Father, but pray continue." McConait was, even if sarcastically, intrigued.

"You said it's a favourite belief of the church, well it's actually a bit further down the pecking order than you suggest. There is a "hierarchy of truths". The central beliefs of the Church are one God, creator of everything, one Lord Jesus Christ the only son, totally man and totally God. He was born (of a virgin) suffered and died, but then rose again and that fulfilled Old Testament prophecy. He then ascended into heaven to join his Father. The Holy Spirit is also God, and an equal part, which works among us, Baptism to cleanse sins, Life after death in the next world."

"That sounds like the Creed." McConait still knew Creed off by heart, and the priest's description had followed, in essence, the structure of the prayer.

"More or less." Price nodded, "In that prayer it lays out the basic beliefs of the Church. And a great deal of deliberation went on to narrow it down to these core elements. You see, in a growing Church, a lot of things could be changed due to interpretation. So a group of all the Bishops got together to state once and for all what it was that the Gospels really tell us; that was the council of Chalcedon."

McConait screwed his face and nodded vaguely remembering hearing this before.

Price continued, "From that we got the Creed. Everything else stems from that; the core beliefs."

"And what about those who didn't agree, or thought there should be other things added?"

"Well that's what we call Heracy. It's a term we still use. I've been accused of it a few times myself."

"Don't they burn people for that?"

"Father Tuthie might want that practise returned, but no, I have been warned off with excommunication, but if I apologise quickly enough and take a couple of steps back, it means I can regroup and come back fighting from a different angle. That way I can work for change from within; the best place in my opinion. It is best to be in the tent peeing out rather than outside the tent..."

"I know that old adage but what has this got to do with the Greeks?" asked McConait impatiently.

"Well everything actually. At the time of Christ and the time of the writing of the Gospels, Greek was the language of intellectual discourse. Some of the Gospels were written in Greek, when the early church started Christianity was spread to Greek speaking nations; St.Paul's letters to the Corinthians, Ephesians, Collosions, this was where civilisation was. And the great thinkers of Ancient Greece, Socrates, Plato and yes Aristotle were the benchmark in how to forward an argument. Remember that the only evidence the church had were Gospels, any idea or detail of Jesus' life, they didn't know about, had to stem from the central beliefs... the ones in the Creed. And it was done with classic Greek logic."

McConait took a final swig of his coffee. He was yet to hear anything that would make him more sympathetic to the Virgin fascination, the worship of the goddess, but not a fertile sexual goddess like other decent religions had, but a sexless prim and proper girl who would be an example to females anywhere who should keep their sexuality (created by their God) under lock and key. He folded his arms, his contempt now becoming visible, "I'm all ears Father."

"If, as the council of Chalcedon decided, that Jesus was true God and true man, that is to say not half and half, not sometimes one sometimes the other, but man in every way and God in every way, then the human and divine would be present in all aspects of Christ's life. Well let's consider the birth. It says in the Gospels that Jesus was born of Mary. God was born of woman; he was a child, a human, a man. Well that certainly takes care of the human quality of Christ, but it follows logic (all be it Greek) that there should be something equally Divine about his coming into the world, so that must mean the conception." Price paused as if giving McConait a couple of seconds to digest then carried on, "If Mary had conceived the usual way, sex with a man…"

McConait couldn't resist butting in, "I think I still remember how it's done."

"Well if she had conceived that way then Jesus is just man, and that's not what it says in the Chalcedon Creed therefore it doesn't follow logic. So logically speaking, it must have been a Virgin Birth."

McConait had been bamboozled by the argument, and he wondered why Price hadn't been a lawyer instead of a priest. "If you say so Father." McConait's mouth turned up at the corners and his eyebrows raised; his smile congratulations to the eloquent Price.

"Well it's not my say so. The early theologians worked with the tried and tested techniques of their time. Greek logic was the accepted wisdom of their age. Remember Aristotle and the tomatoes? Remember how long before Galileo suggested a different way. Galileo marks the dawning of the modern age. Things not accepted because of pure logic but based on evidence." Price had a sudden flash of inspiration and again it came from the simple display of children's work. He grabbed a plastic bucket and emptied its contents onto a table. All manner of plastic creatures poured out: snakes, dolphins, spiders, fish. It was a Noah's ark of beasts for children to sort, count or simply

89

play with. Price then took a few of the green apples and put them into the bucket. He pulled one out and held it in front of McConaits face.

"It's green and it's shiny, what is it?"

McConait humoured him, playing the six year old, "It's an apple."

Price pulled out a second, "It's green and it's shiny, what is it?"

"It's another apple." McConait had more dissent in his voice.

"Yes, because it's green and …?" Price played the primary teacher with gusto.

McConait complied "Shiny!"

Out came the third apple, "What is it?" Price waited holding the apple. Eventually McConait replied.

"An apple!"

"Why?"

"Because it's green and shiny!"

Now Price lifted up the bucket excitedly in both hands. "So in my bucket there is something green and shiny, logically what must it be?"

"An apple." McConait was starting to get the point.

But Price's lesson was not over, "Now you made that judgement based on what you know about the apples. You have no conclusive proof you had to make a logical assumption."

"OK well done, but there was another famous group of Greek philosophers, the Cynics. I think I'm with the Greeks on that one." McConait's joke was based in truth.

Price gazed into the bucket," Well, you asked me before about the contradictions, the conflict I face, science and religion, well I believe we should use the methods of the modern world when examining the life of Christ, and yet I still respect how and why the church, through history, has used theirs. I can't expect the church to turn on a sixpence. It's like an oil tanker; it takes a long time to turn round because of its size. The church doesn't work in our time frame, year to year but century to century."

"So you may have to be patient Father."

90

"That's one truth I have learned from experience Doctor. You see for me being a Catholic is like this: imagine you find a junk shop, and in that junk shop was a treasure, the most precious thing you could imagine, your heart's desire. And you went to the owner and asked him if you could buy it. Then he turns round and says it's not for sale, however you can have it for nothing on one condition; if you take all the other rubbish that goes along with it. Sure you have to take a lot of rubbish on board wearing a collar like mine but the rewards are unimaginable."

The conversation was interrupted by an officer at the door of the classroom, "Sorry Father, if you have a minute. It's the mother of the boy; she says she'd like to talk to a priest."

Price was on his feet and at the door without thinking; McConait's respect for this kind of priest had grown. Here he was after a night of prayer, expounding on the wonder of children, science, Greek philosophy, religion, then off to console a bereaved mother. McConait did not envy Price's existence, but he admired it; Price was altogether a different man than he.

McConait knew it was time for him to get back to work, but thought it only right that he should leave the classroom as they found it. He picked the child's work and pressed it back on to the window. He then gathered the apples and put them back in the groups of 6+4. Then he picked up the bucket, and stopped in surprise. Inside the bucket was not as logic had dictated an apple, but a shiny green plastic frog.

"All is not what it seems."

Chapter 15
The Shaman

After consoling the distraught mother, Price only managed to steal a couple hours of sleep before his engine like mind drove him back out of bed and back to his desk. A package he had been waiting for had been delivered and he didn't want to waste any more time. He opened the package, which had been sent from America, and took out an old copy of Life magazine from the eighties. He looked at the index and flicked through the glossy pages until he found the story he was looking for. He rubbed his tired eyes and began to read.

...in 1987 after 109 years, the Little Shell Ojibwa/Chippewa were officially a tribe again.

The U.S. Interior Department signed an order granting federal recognition of the tribe, which had about 4,000 members. Until the mid-1800s, ancestors of the Little Shells lived in the western Great Lakes area. As European settlements encroached upon their territory in the 1800s, they moved west to hunt buffalo and found themselves living on the small Turtle Mountain reservation in North Dakota. Facing starvation as the buffalo herds disappeared, the tribe broke into factions in the 1870s, with some following Thomas Little Shell into Montana, some staying at Turtle Mountain and some going north to Canada.

Four generations later, his people finally recognised as a tribe, Josh Little Shell, for the first time, walked with authority and his head held high into the Abraham Lincoln Memorial High School, Billings, Montana. All his life Josh had suffered taunts and criticism because of his background. Nicknamed 'Red Trash', because of his heritage and low income background, Josh was very much a loner at school. His closest friend was his Grandfather who told him about his family history. Now his tribe had been recognised by the Government the Little Shells finally had the respect they deserved.

When Josh saw the wealth that the other kids at high school flaunted, the new cars, the clothes, the cell phones, he had never been jealous. He knew what he and his family had. The power of the Shaman had been given to them by a great god, and with it, power and knowledge that the other students would never understand.

The frustrations of his existence had changed into a sense of clarity and calm. Today Josh wore his jet-black hair down and it hung straight and shiny. Around it he wore the traditional headband of buffalo hide decorated with the tiny white shells, which gave the tribe its name.

His checked shirt was unfastened to reveal his thin toned torseau covered by a wampum necklace of turquoise, white shells and wolves teeth, which rattled with every step. He wore buckskin trousers and moccasins. Everyone in the corridor froze and stared, Josh's get up clashing with the Nike, Levis and occasional Gucci, which adorned the other students. The corridor fell into silence apart from the rattling of wampum, like a ghost from the distant past, Josh stepped proudly onwards.

"Get back to the reservation, Red Ass!" This spaghetti western quote was a favourite of Todd Ferber, the person more than any who liked to taunt and bully anyone who was different, and today Josh had gone out of his way to be different. Josh had stood up to Todd's bullying in the past, and could still recall the many bloody noses and humiliation he had received. On one particular occasion Todd and a group of boys hung Josh up by his underwear in the gym locker room and drew mock war paint on him with indelible markers. It took three weeks to come off. Josh turned and fixed him with a primal glare.

*   *   *   *   *

Three weeks earlier Josh sat with his ninety-year-old Grandfather, Tenskwatawa which means 'Open Door', like so many times in his life his Grandfather shared stories of his family ancestry but as Josh was approaching his sixteenth birthday he had become more fascinated than ever. He feared that if his Grandfather passed away without telling him something it would be lost forever. His mother had died giving birth to him, and his dad had nothing but contempt for ancient magic. "Grandfather

93

tell me about your mother again, tell me what she could do, and the legend how we became Shaman."

Tenskwatawa sat cross-legged in the dirt outside his trailer. The sun was setting behind the Rocky Mountains and the evening had cooled; it was Josh's favourite time of day. The old man, with eyes closed, breathed a lung full of night air and nodded, slowly conjuring up memories of his mother. "My mother was one of the Mediwiwin, a secret group of medicine people. When the white man had driven us from our land the tribe was divided, many of the ancient secrets were in danger of being lost. The old practices were not allowed, so messengers would travel between tribes and gather in secret, to enact the sacred rituals. If these traditions had died out the white man would have won and there would be no tribes left. It was their prayers and offerings that have guaranteed our survival, it may appear to the outsider, and indeed your own father, that it's politicians and governments that have kept the tribe alive, but they don't realise that the spirit of the great bear, buffalo and wolf still stalk this land, not just here in the mountains but even in the Whitehouse. White man can build roads, houses and fences on the land but the land is still there underneath and the spirits are ever present.

My mother, was a medicine woman, a Shaman. The power of the Shaman was given to our people in ancient times by the great spirit of the Otter. The knowledge was passed down to her by her father. She passed the knowledge to me, and because your father has lost the path and abandoned the old ways I must pass it on to you."

Josh looked into Tenskwatawa's wrinkled face with admiration. "I can't wait Grandfather."

"But wait you must, you can not be Shaman until your sixteenth birthday, then you will be given a new name; a tribal name. You will become one with the ancient spirit and you will have the power to use the medicine bag; the herbs and the sacred shells like I have shown you over the years."

Josh looked at the medicine bag, which went over his Grandfather's left shoulder and rested on his right leg. It was made from wolf skin. It contained small bushels of dried

94

aromatic plants; Josh had seen the old man waft these about when doing a ritual dance. He said it fended off evil spirits and could heal those sick in mind or body. Also in the bag were the small white shells. These were found in abundance along the waters edge of the Great Lakes where the tribe originated; a symbol of there livelihood, one of the many types of food the tribe would harvest for survival, now in the mountains away from the lakes they were of even more symbolic value. They symbolised the loss of their land and their way of life. They were a reminder of where they had come from and where one day they might return. In a sacred ceremony the shells were used to conjure up great strength and courage among braves, it protected them against their enemies and made them fearless warriors.

Josh knew the medicine bag would soon be his. He would have to keep it secret from his father who dismissed the old man's teachings as a waste of time and a distraction from Josh's school work.

Josh's father was an activist for tribal recognition and rights. He had worked tirelessly for years in pressure groups, in protest marches and filing petitions with the Federal Government. He believed that the tribe had to look to the future and not to the past, to embrace the white man's methods and use them against them. He had marched with Martin Luther King in the 1960s and related to the struggle of the African American but felt that the struggle of the Native American had been overlooked. One thing he felt very strongly about was that talking about ancient magic and spirits was not the way to take on a problem in the twentieth century.

"Grandfather, I will be sixteen in three weeks. We haven't talked about the ceremony. What happens? Where will it take place?"

Tenskwatawa looked up at the sky. "One hundred and ninety moons have passed since you were born and your mother died. The next moon will be the most important in your life. You will smoke the ancient pipe, and dance under the moon. It will then be revealed to you what your animal spirit is; you will run, or fly, or crawl as your animal spirit. When you return you will have the body of a man but the animal spirit will always be there

95

to guide you. Then my boy you shall be the Shaman of the Chippewa."

*   *   *   *   *

Two weeks later the full moon lit the Rocky Mountains, Josh's official birthday was still a week away but tonight was the celebration of his tribal birth, tonight he would be born again.

"Josh wake up, it's time." Tenskwatawa whispered in the darkness.

"What is it?"

"Shhh! Don't wake your father." Tenskwatawa turned and left the trailer where his family lived; Josh rubbed his eyes and looked at the open door. Tenskwatawa was already striding out into the night. In the full moonlight Josh could see that his Grandfather was in full tribal regalia: Moccasins, buck skin, wampum and a magnificent head dress of eagle and turkey feather, which flapped with his footsteps as if a giant bird was taking to the air. After twenty steps Josh saw his Grandfather bend down and place something he had been carrying under his arm on the ground, then the old man carried on walking.

As Josh walked forward he could see that it was clothing wrapped into a roll. Josh instinctively began to strip. He unrolled the bundle and naked in the moonlight placed the wampum neckpiece of a Chippewa warrior over his head. He then put on his buckskins and moccasins before finally tying his headband, and strode after his Grandfather who was disappearing behind some rocks up ahead.

When Josh rounded the corner the old man was silhouetted in front of a fire. He pointed to the ground in front of him and Josh sat cross-legged at his feet. Tenskwatawa put his hand in his medicine bag and pulled out a carved round wooden pot. He removed its lid and plunged two fingers deep inside. He pulled out his fingers now covered in a yellow paste and ran them across Josh's face leaving two horizontal stripes across each cheek.

Looking up at his Grandfather's face illuminated by the firelight he could see that he also bore these marks. Tenskwatawa

96

sank to his knees facing Josh and raised his arms up to the full moon. He began a slow, monotonous chant, which he repeated over and over; now and again he would throw dust from the floor into the air or onto the fire. Still half asleep, the chanting and the dancing of shadows around him had an almost hypnotic effect. He did not know what lay ahead but he knew he was ready.

Still chanting, Tenskwatawa plunged his hand into the medicine bag again, this time pulling out a long flute like wooden tube, he then produced some herbs. He squashed some of the aromatic bundle into a hole near one end of the tube. He then took a burning twig from the fire and ignited the herbs. A pungent smoke reeked from the pipe. He held one end of the pipe to Josh's left nostril, then put his mouth to the other end. The old man and the young boy's eyes locked together for a second then Tenskwatawa blew.

Burning smoke shot up Josh's nose into his head. His eyes rolled back and his head felt like it would explode, then the boy fell backwards unconscious on the ground. Tenskwatawa sat by the fire and waited.

Josh found himself running through the mountains, more powerfully than he had ever run before and he felt he would never tire. Then the rock beneath his feet turned to grass and fern. All about him was a forest of mighty trees which seemed as high as the night sky. The moonlight danced and flickered through the branches.

Josh came to a halt in a circular clearing. He looked up and could see the moon was directly above him. When he brought his gaze back to earth he saw a pair of eyes in front of him, he looked left and again another pair of eyes, then right then behind him still more pairs of eyes; he was surrounded. Slowly the eyes began to move towards him. It was a pack of wolves closing in on the boy. But Josh was not frightened; now he realised he was one of them, his animal spirit was the wolf. He raised his head skyward and let out a howl from his lungs that split the night, the pack of wolves followed suite.

Josh sat bolt up right and his Grandfather turned to him smiling, "Well?" he asked expectantly. The boy stood up, the firelight giving his skin a golden sheen, "My name is Honiahaka... Little Wolf."

*   *   *   *   *

Josh couldn't wait for school to finish the next day, his Grandfather was picking him up, he had told Josh's father that they were going to get a few hours fishing but they wouldn't be back too late. Of course it wasn't just a bit of fishing, Josh would be learning how to use the potions and chants of the Shaman. Josh got to the door and looked around; the front of the school was crowded, cars and bikes, boys and girls arranging dates, mothers lecturing their children, but where was the old man? Then Josh spotted a group of boys he always made a point of avoiding; Todd Ferber was the ring leader. They were in a circle, laughing and shouting. They whooped and jeered at someone in the middle; Josh's heart froze. He saw the long grey ponytail of his Grandfather and immediately Josh dashed towards the gang, as he drew closer he realised that his Grandfather was sitting on the floor struggling to get to his feet. The circle of boys put their hands to their mouths making hooting noises in a mock war dance, and shouting scornful and racist remarks to the poor old man.

Tenskwatawa panted for breath in distress then just as Josh broke through the circle, the old man clutched at his chest in pain. Josh held his grand father in his arms trying to comfort him.

Realising what was happening, the taunts of the gang faded then someone screamed "Get an ambulance!! Get an ambulance!!" which brought the whole crowd around Josh and his Grandfather.

Through the pounding in his chest, Tenskwatawa fought to speak. He pushed something into Josh's hand and looked into the young boys sobbing eyes. "It's in your hands now Honiahaka."

Josh opened his hand. It was a small white shell. As Tenskwatawa drew his final breath, Josh looked up to see the face of a boy he had come to hate... Todd Ferber.

98

*　　　*　　　　*　　　　*　　　　*

Josh waited until sun down then went under his bed and stretched his arm in deep, he pulled out the medicine bag, and thought about his Grandfather. He stiffened his lip and set off into the mountains. He lit the fire as Tenskwatawa had done and changed into his tribal dress. Tonight he would take the smoke again and evoke his wolf spirit; he as Honiahaka would run with the pack; he would need his wolf spirit for what he was about to do.

*　　　*　　　　*　　　　*　　　　*

As the sun rose Josh packed away the pipe and took out the wooden pot. He dipped his fingers and applied the yellow stripes to his face he then put the wolf skin bag over his shoulder and began walking into town.

*　　　*　　　　*　　　　*　　　　*

The television headlines that evening broke with the tag line:
ANOTHER HIGH SCHOOL KILLING

The anchorman Larry Sandeen looked seriously into the camera, " Good evening. A terrible murder took place today in a Montana High School. Josh Little Shell, son of Native American Activist, George Little Shell, today went on the rampage at his school 'The Abraham Lincoln Memorial High School' in Billings Montana. Today, on the day when George Little Shell's campaign to have his tribe recognised was finally ratified, his son, dressed as a tribal shaman, or medicine man, savagely attacked a fellow student.

Sixteen year old Todd Ferber, fellow student and captain of the football team, was attacked by Josh Little Shell as school started this morning. Early reports say that the crime may have been race related. After the killing, Josh Little Shell attempted to evade arrest by charging at a police officer who was quick on the scene; after a call was made by distraught student, Sarah Cunliffe.

99

The officer shot and killed the sixteen year old on the steps of the school entrance. We go over to Sally Freeman who is there at the scene...

"Thanks Larry, well I'm here at Abraham Lincoln Memorial High School, where this terrible attack took place. An attack, experts are putting down as a case of 'Spiritual Therianthropy', where a person believes their spirit transforms into an animal; common in the Shamanic practices of the Native American. I am here with Sarah Cunliffe who actually witnessed the attack this morning and made the call to the police.

The camera panned to the left and zoomed into the face of a mousy looking fifteen year old girl who had obviously been crying. "Sarah, tell us what you saw here today."

The girl shuffled uncomfortably and began, "Well it was horrible, Josh came down the corridor dressed... well kinda weird like an Indian warrior or medicine man or something. Well everyone was shocked at first, then Todd started mocking him. Josh stopped for about a minute not blinking or anything while Todd offloaded all this abuse about him being an Indian, and a Redskin and stuff, then I guess Josh snapped. He leapt at him which knocked Todd to the floor." The girl sniffled and tried to compose herself. The reporter stepped in.

"And what kind of weapon did he use?"

"Well, he never had a weapon, he stuck his thumbs in Todd's eyes until blood squirted out. Todd was screaming, and beating at Josh but Josh never budged. Then Josh started bighting Todd's face, first at his nose, tore whole chunks off, then his cheeks and chin. The blood was everywhere. While Todd tried to fend him off, Josh clawed his hands away, like scratchin' his arms and stuff. A couple of guys tried to pull him off but he was too strong, he lashed out at them and they flew across the corridor." The girl was finding it hard to continue but the reporter kept pushing.

"Sarah, could you tell us what happened next?"

"Well everyone was screaming. Todd was still pinned to the ground, wailing in pain. Josh sat up and looked around at everyone in the corridor, as if, like, we could be next; people started running. Josh's face was covered in Todd's blood. Then

100

he went for him again, this time for his throat. I don't know how he did it but he bit right into his throat...tore it out... it was so... so..." Sarah could no longer continue.

The interview was interrupted by the anchorman.

"Sorry Sally we're gonna have to stop you there we're going over to city hall where we believe the chief of police is about to make a statement." The screen changed to a view of a tall, white haired man in a splendid dark blue uniform standing at a podium.

"Our forensic team have reported back and we seem to have a clear indication of what caused these tragic events. The perpetrator, sixteen-year-old Josh Little Shell, was heavily under the influence of narcotics; tests clearly show a number of hallucinogens and opiates in his blood including mescaline and ergine, or natural LSD. We can confirm that Little Shell killed Todd Ferber without a weapon. Todd died from asphyxiation caused by restriction to the windpipe." The Chief paused and adjusted his stance ready to deliver a message, "The Little Shell family, in particular the boy's father, George, have long been involved in political events often causing unrest, it would appear that Josh, under the influence of drugs, and his family has taken political matters into his own hands."

George Little Shell was arrested for incitement to violence. Narcotics in the form of dried bundles were found in various hidden places in the trailer. George denied all knowledge, but was subsequently convicted for seven years, a huge set back for the civil rights movement of the Ojibwa/Chippewa.

Chapter 16
Price Goes To Rome

The issue with Father Tuthie had become a sensitive one in the higher echelons of the Catholic Church. The media circus in Tynemouth was at its peak and Tuthie's name was on TV and in newspapers throughout the developed world. Tuthie had towed the party line in so much as when confronted by a reporter he always said the standard phrase, "No comment." But parishioners were more than happy to share what Tuthie was preaching and the image of the nutty old priest looked great in the tabloids. Price received a call issuing him back to Rome to meet with some Vatican Lawyers to discuss how to proceed and to go over some "Worse case scenarios." With the hiatus in the investigation it was as good a time as any. There was some further research Price needed to do and in the Vatican he had access to everything he needed. His only reservation about leaving was his concerns for McConait. Price was aware of his delicate mental state. His strange turns were hard to explain, but Price had a feeling that the pills McConait was popping had something to do with a vulnerable mind under extreme stress.

Price decided to go and inform McConait of his impending departure but to his surprise he found it was McConait who had already started packing his bags.

"I came to tell you I've been called to Rome, but it would appear that you are not going to miss me. Is everything OK?"

McConait looked up from his suitcase with weary eyes. "I've seen so many killings now. It gets to a point where you can't close your eyes without seeing a mutilated corpse. And the worst thing is I'm becoming numb to it all. They've ceased to be people. It's the thrill of the chase for me now, and I think I've lost the scent."

"So what will you do?"

"I've got work to do back at Cambridge, at least I can feel of some value down there; God knows I'm bloody useless up here. It was a mistake to come back. I don't want people pointing the finger at me saying it's all my fault."

"You talk like it's you that's the killer."

"And do you know that I'm not? It could be anyone; every avenue we've investigated has turned out to be a blind alley. Nobody has a bloody clue, my profile is all conjecture, based on what? A few smart arsed judgements made by a Cambridge boffin."

"Well you know that I am not a fan of conjecture, we do need some concrete findings, but I think you do yourself a disservice. I won't try to talk you out of going my friend, you look like you need the rest." Price walked across McConait's room to a painting hanging above a dressing table. A copy of Monet's water Lilies. Not taking his eyes from the picture he continued to talk to McConait who was packing his case again. "Life's a bit like an impressionist painting." McConait said nothing; he was used to Price's pearls of wisdom by now. "If you get too close, you can see lots of detail, the brush strokes, the mixture of colours, but you've no idea what's going on in the picture, to do that you have to step back away from it. Once you have some distance you can then see how that detail fits into the whole picture, then you have understanding."

McConait stopped what he was doing and joined Price in gazing at the reproduction of the Monet. The two stood in silence for a second and then Price turned. "Good luck McConait, I hope you find what you need back in Cambridge, but I can't help but think that, when you get down there, you'll realise it was here all along." He patted McConait on the back as he left and returned to his own room to pack for Rome.

Chapter 17
Wolf Boy

The next morning Price awoke in the opulent room of his Vatican apartment. He knelt by the bed and said morning prayers. A knock at the door interrupted him. He blessed himself with a sign of the cross and pulled on his dressing gown before walking across the room furnished with antiques from the time of the Borgias. "Come in!"

The great oak door opened and a young, dapper looking Italian priest in full length black cassock swept in. "Buon journo, I hope you slept well." The young man placed a package on an ornate bureau and then with a flutter of his cassock walked the full length of the room. He pulled the curtain cord to the right of a great window, letting the Roman sunshine stream in. Turning round he gestured to the package on the bureau. "The book you asked for Father. Unusual subject matter, but we didn't have any problem tracking it down, our American brothers were only too happy to help the great Father Price."

Price walked over and ripped open the package, as the young priest got back to the door, Price remembered his manners, "Grazie mille."

The young priest was delighted with the thanks from the famous guest. "Prego!" and with that he swept subserviently out backwards; closing the door behind him.

Price sat in a chair bathed in sunlight and took out the contents of the package; a hard back American book: "Amazing tales of the Great Depression." He opened the sage green cover and scanned the index before flicking to the chapter he was looking for: chapter 7 Wolf Boy.

Price popped on a pair of reading glasses and began:

Julio Aceves was one on five children; son of Raul and Anna Lucia. He was born in Loreto's Town in Mexico in 1921. Like all his family he bore the genetic defect which made them outcast; a condition called Hypertrichosis, hirsutism or excessive body hair. Members of his family had suffered from the condition, to differing degrees, for generations. Julio's whole body had a covering of hair; lighter in some places, his stomach and legs, but his entire face, shoulders and back were covered in thick black hair.

His older brothers Luis and Emilio could pass for normal when clean-shaven and fully clothed. It was worst of course for Julio's two sisters who rarely ventured from the family home, which was a small farm in the hills, far away from scornful looks. When the family Aceves did venture into town, men would look disgustedly and spit on the ground as they passed. What Julio hated most was when women would cross themselves and pray to Santa Maria as if the devil himself was walking past; they averted their gaze and shielded their children's eyes so as not to be offended by such an abomination.

The family spent little time in their hometown, mainly the winter months when the rains came and the roads were turned into mud. The rest of the time they worked in Mario's which boldly proclaimed to be 'The greatest circus in Mexico'. His two sisters Beatrice and Consuella were famous as bearded ladies. Julio was part of the act by the time he was six. He would come into the ring on all fours wearing only a pair of shorts and a spiked dog collar. He was lead around by the ringmaster, where he would bark and pant, roll over and catch food in his mouth. Then the ringmaster would tell him to sit and Julio would run into the crowd and cheekily sit on a lady's lap giving her a kiss. Sometimes this was met with screams, but mostly with laughter. To finish the show Julio would sing while occasionally breaking into a howl (with comic effect) the rest of the family would then join him and sing a final number. As the youngest of the Aceves family (and also the most hirsute) Julio, as 'Wolf Boy', became the most popular member of the troupe.

Life was pretty good while the family were touring. The other people in the circus accepted them and they made good friends. As a popular act that drew the crowds the Aceves were making good money. But things were about to get even better; Mario's circus was going to tour the USA, a tour that took them through seven of the Southern States. Travelling in an anticlockwise direction they started in Texas, then to Louisiana, Mississippi, Arkansas, Oklahoma, and then they were to finish in New Mexico before returning home. They became a massive hit:

They were in Newspapers; they appeared on movie newsreels; film stars and politicians all wanted to meet the Aceves family. Songs by popular writers filled the music halls, with dances to go with them: 'The Moondog', 'The Mad dog' and 'Wolf Boy Boogie', to name but three, became smash hits. Julio even had his picture taken with Charlie Chaplin for the 'Review magazine'. Chaplin pointed down to Julio while he took a begging position, the caption said, "Bad doggy!"

The Aceves family were never going to be truly accepted, and were certainly not treated as well as other celebrities but their lifestyle was more comfortable than ever. A sponsorship deal with a hair products company was lucrative, as was a poster campaign for shaving soap. Life had never been better; people still pointed and talked as they walked past but now because of their celebrity not because they thought they were devils.

In October 1929 came the stock market crash and the Great Depression. Every member of American society was touched by it in some way; mass unemployment swept the nation.

By 1931 things had hit an all time low. Few professions or communities could avoid the effect. Millions were now out of work and people had no money for something as frivolous as Circus acts. Mario's was disbanded and the entire troupe was now homeless, the great Mario himself, bankrupt. The Aceves' spent what they had on lodgings, they hoped their celebrity might open some doors but after a short while they were broke and realised that they were better off back on their farm in Loreto's Town; unfortunately they were in Oklahoma and Mexico was a long way away.

The Aceves family started the long journey home. They drifted from town to town looking for any employment but they were rarely welcome. Luis and Emilio occasionally got some labouring work but it didn't go far enough to support seven people. When they could find affordable lodgings they would often be turned away; people were suspicious and very sceptical of anything that could be seen as a bad omen.

The Aceves family had spent practically all they had and were now forced to sleep rough; they were not the only ones. Many people were now migrants looking for work and along the

106

highways they set up small camps. When trying to join one of these groups of fellow travellers, the Aceves family were chased away with murderous intent, so they instead headed for some woods just outside Ardmore, Oklahoma.

That night, in the make shift camp of the migrant workers, a killer struck. No-one saw the killer. The bloodied body of an eighteen-year-old young man called Buck was found torn apart a short distance outside the camp. He had gone to relieve himself in the night and never returned. The body bore claw marks all over it, flesh had been chewed from his limbs, and his guts were spread in a six feet radius.

With people in such a state of desperation many were pushed to their wits end and often took solace in moonshine (grain alcohol), which was brewed illegally in stills all over the South. Violence was never far away and rather than jumping to the natural conclusion that the boy had stumbled across a pack of coyotes, they pointed the finger at the Aceves.

A group of men were easily stirred up by the talk of werewolves and demons, the general feeling was that even if it wasn't the poor Mexicans that had committed the crime then it would be a righteous act to rid the world of such an obvious effrontery to God's creation. These migrant people who had been in the gutter for so long now at last had someone to look down on and retribution for the injustice of their own existence would be dished out that evening, regardless of the small detail of who or what really killed the eighteen year old.

Fuelled by alcohol and rage the posse of men charged into the forest. It wasn't long before they came upon the Aceves' pathetic camp. Luis and Emilio, the two oldest brothers leapt to meet them. The father went to join them while the Mother, the two sisters and Julio huddled together by their meagre fire. The crowd of wild-eyed men in the posse gazed in amazement and obvious disgust at the strange looking Mexicans. The tallest of the gang stepped forward, "You God dam freaks o' nature, you ain't human, you're a pack o' werewolves, and you done killed my cousin Buck last night you sons o' bitches!" With the word bitches he pointed at the mother huddling with her children. The crowd laughed and began to shuffle forward. The Aceves men

107

stood tall ready for what lay ahead, they had lead tough lives that few people would understand and along the way they had learned how to fight. The acrobatics they performed as part of their circus routines had given them muscular frames. Luis turned to his mother, "Mamma, run, for God's sake run!"

In seconds, five of the posse lay on their backs at the hand of the Aceves men, the Mexicans waded into the crowd with wildness and passion as if everything they had suffered in their lives was coming to the boil. The women dragged Julio, almost lifting him off the ground, and swept him away into the forest, leaving the yells and groans of the battle behind. It wasn't long, however, before the Aceves men were over powered and were beaten senseless to the ground; the posse turned their attention to the women. The voices grew louder and the mother, sisters and Julio ran deeper into the forest. The sisters went one way and Julio and his mother went another. As the voices gained on the fleeing family, Julio's mother fell. Julio looked back at his mother who had injured herself badly and could not get up. Julio ran back and grabbed her hand, "Get up Mamma, get up…please!" The small boy could not get his mother to her feet, the voices were almost upon them, his mother looked up from the dirt, "Run Julio, save yourself." With tears in his eyes, Julio let go of his mother's hand and took to his heels, his heart raced as he heard the voices and footsteps reach his mother and stop. He heard her screams and the pounding of their fists and boots against her body until she screamed no more. Julio kept running deeper into the forest until out of breath he collapsed in the hollow of a tree stump and curled up in a ball.

That evening six bodies hung from the trees at the edge of the forest; the depression had claimed its latest victims, the famous Aceves', of the Mario Circus, were almost wiped out; one remained, concealed by the forest.

A great deal of moonshine was supped after the lynching, no-one cared that the youngest had escaped, and as the revelry continued by the camp fire a pair of tear filled eyes watched from the cover of the trees. The lifeless bodies of his family swung in the night breeze, silhouetted against the light from the fire in the camp. Julio had removed his clothes; the thick black hair of his body camouflaged him in the undergrowth. As the singing and dancing of the carousing drunks got louder, Julio slipped from the woods unseen into an empty tent. There was little inside: a mangy mattress; a bundle of clothes; a sepia photograph of a family in a wooden frame perched on an empty packing case. Seeing the picture made the rage at the loss of his own family swell in the newly orphaned young boy. He looked round the tent for something else, a weapon, anything, but there was only a large earthenware jug. Julio knelt down in front of it and pulled out the cork stopper. He froze; frightened the pop of the cork might give him away. But the noise from the celebrations outside was too loud. He placed his nose to the jug and sniffed, pulling his head away quickly in repulsion, Julio had received an eye-watering nose full of alcohol vapours; moonshine.

As hoots and laughter filled the air outside, Julio stiffened his resolve and, unable to lift it, began to drag the jar from the back of the tent. He stopped at a rolled up bundle of dungarees and tilted the weighty jar. Clear liquid lapped from the jar onto the clothes. Julio then righted the jar again and replaced the stopper. Into the darkness, he ventured once more, dragging the jar behind him. From tent to tent he crept. Some of the tents had sleeping children or those ailing from malnutrition, but Julio crept so silently that not one stirred. In every tent he poured the moonshine, the jug getting lighter as the volume inside decreased, until after ten or so tents the jug was practically empty.

As Julio snuck back into the forest he heard inebriated voices quarrelling about a jug of moonshine that had gone missing, the voices finally concluding that they'd probably already drank it, and were soon appeased when someone else produced another full jug.

The revelling continued for another half hour before the moonshine rendered most of them unconscious, and in the firelight Julio saw some men being carried by their wives to their tents, others slept where they had collapsed, within fifteen minutes the entire camp had fallen into silence, apart from the rattle of drunkards snoring. Now was the time for Julio to strike.

The small hirsute frame of 'Wolf Boy, Julio Aceves stalked the sleeping campsite. His ears pricked for any sign of movement, but there was none. He walked bare foot and silent to the fire, still naked but holding his shirt in his hand which was doused in the last of the moonshine. He lifted a long sturdy branch from the ground and wrapped his shirt around it, tying it in a knot with the sleeves. He held the branch into the flames and with a 'whoosh' it instantly caught fire. The flaming branch made an excellent torch and Julio could now see his way clearly around the camp and scurried with greater speed.

He revisited the tents one by one. Remembering exactly where he had let the moonshine spill out and putting his torch to it. One tent, then another, then another went up in flames. As screams rang out behind him Julio moved faster; now people were stirring as the boy entered their tent. For many the last thing they would ever see would be the vengeful face of a wolf like boy and then the blinding light of flames in their eyes. The camp was in a state of drunken panic. Julio was calm as he skipped from tent to tent, wreaking havoc on the bewildered workers.

People rolled in the dirt trying to put out the flames which lapped about their bodies. Mothers drenched children in what water was around, people were smothered in any blanket that was not ablaze. Some were too drunk to try to escape and were engulfed in their burning tents.

The fire lit the campsite like it was the middle of the day, Julio stood on the edge of the forest surveying his handy work, revelling in his destruction. As the survivors rallied together away from the blaze a young woman pointed a trembling finger towards the trees. Holding his blazing torch high above him, the hair covered figure of Julio Aceves looked down on them, his eyes were orange reflecting the flames before him; he let out a wicked cackle. He looked in every way like the devil himself, and the woman let out a scream of terror. Julio, satisfied that his work was done, turned and ran into the woods never to be seen again.

The forest was searched for three days but he was never found. How long a child could survive in the woods is unknown

110

but some people say he may have become feral, turned wild and lived with coyotes.

The legend of Ardmore Woods, Oklahoma was born, and when a howl is heard on a moonlit night, people keep their doors tightly locked and their children are told, 'Be good or the Wolf Boy will get ye!'"

Chapter 18
Andrea's Breakthrough

Andrea Swan had done every test imaginable on the samples from all three killings trying to find a connection; something that would link them together and to a common killer. The victims had common blood types, no unusually high or low iron or blood pressure no sickle cell anaemia, nothing uncommon. There were traces of drugs in the first two victims but only prescription, and the boy victim had a small amount of alcohol. All pretty predictable, she was frustrated but was not about to give up; the last test she ran on Mark Pembridge's blood had shown something different; an unusual viral strain. This really bothered her; she had no explanation for it, something out of her experience, strange enough to be perhaps from the animal world, as a result she had sought the advice of a top veterinary surgeon and was copying him in to her findings.

She had, of course, to get more samples from all the victims and it had taken her a while to gather all the materials together. In what seemed like typical police fashion, different people had worked on the different cases; people had gone on holiday, or samples were sent to a different lab because another was tied up. This meant that there wasn't one clear vision of all three cases and that was what was needed if the incidents were to be tied together in a useful way. Now at last she had the samples of all three victims and, although she thought it unlikely there would be a connection, she was going to look anyway. She brought a picture of the sample from the second victim, Mark Pembridge, up onto her computer screen; she had saved this image as it clearly showed the viral strain, like links of sausages coiling round and through the healthy cells. As a drug user and needle sharer Pembridge was prone to picking up all kinds of viruses, but the first victim was a middle-aged wife and mother.

She took the sample from Rose Stearman and prepared a slide; she slid it into a cartridge and placed it into a recess under the microscope. At once a blurred image appeared on the screen. Andrea began to type instructions via a key pad to the right of the microscope. The image was zoomed in then out, rotated

112

colorized filtered until Andrea saw it. With mastery she guided the sensitive lens of the microscope to the exact spot and with a click a digital image was taken. She clicked again and this time she had the new image side by side with the one from Pembridge. She sat back in her chair and cupped her face in her hands as if stopping her jaw from dropping.

There it was in front of her; the drug abusing Mark Pembridge shared the same unusual viral strain as the tormented housewife Rose Stearman. There was a link. Andrea had one more sample to check, the blood of Jamie Spence; the young boy slaughtered in the garden in Queensway.

This was the part of the job she loved the most; her heart raced. She prepared the final slide and her professional composure was all that kept her hands from trembling so much that the droplet of blood would have missed the wafer thin glass slide. It was still an outside chance, a rogue virus that she had spotted, by good fortune, from the sample of a drug abuser; it would have been missed by most forensics, but not Andrea Swan. She had only got to where she was today by being thorough. It would only be a matter of moments before she would discover if her theory would be borne out.

A blurred image appeared on the computer screen, a few seconds adjustments and there it was, a real 'Eureka' moment. She clicked and the image was recorded. Within minutes they hurtled through cyberspace via e-mail to Detective Sergeant Peel and Scotland Yard Forensics (to check against the London victims) then to another contact... a veterinary surgeon who awaited her findings.

Chapter 19
Return Of McConait

It had been a week since all three men had gone their separate ways. The trail had fallen cold once again. Price was still in Rome and McConait had been back at Cambridge, finishing a paper called, "Why Good People Kill?" He had enjoyed getting back in his comfort zone and was about to jack the Tynemouth investigation in, when Peel called. It was there first real conversation since the garden on Queensway, and both men were tentative with each other.

"Hello Doctor, sorry to disturb you but I thought you'd want to be the first to know. We've got something. It's only a small connection, but it may prove useful; you never know", Peel's tone was apologetic in case the esteemed Doctor ridiculed the latest piece of information.

"Oh of course, I'd love to hear whatever you've got." This wasn't strictly true. If Peel said they had the killer and McConait's profile had been right all along, then yes, he'd be glad to hear it, but he had the sneaking suspicion that wasn't the case and he could feel himself being dragged back to Tynemouth.

"It's your friend Andrea in forensics. It's taken her a while but she's found a link in the blood; between the murders. All three of the Tynemouth victims have something in common, in their blood. They all contain the same virus. It's very unusual, so it looks like all the victims have come in contact with the same source; the same killer. So, well done Andrea Swan; not just a pretty face eh."

Out of embarrassed politeness, McConait acted more impressed than he really was.

"Oh good, that's really great, so that's concrete evidence, it's the same killer. At least that confirms our suspicions anyway." Which was another way of saying, 'we already knew that'.

"No there's more than that, it matches the London killings too, it's the bloody same virus; Too much to be a coincidence. It's the same killer!"

There was a deathly silence. McConait's stomach flipped. "You mean we got the wrong man?" London had been really stressful, but at least McConait felt justice had been done, now there were flaws in his profiling, an innocent man had been put in prison, and there had been more killings as a result. He flopped dejectedly into an armchair.

Peel, however, was less concerned, "Listen Doc, don't get yourself in a state about the London case. That guy's done a few months in the clink; big deal. He was far from squeaky clean, and we could have got him on a number of charges. He can sit at Her Majesty's leisure until everything is sewn up. Who's to say he doesn't have the same virus and worked in tandem with the Tynemouth killer? A stretch I know but let's just work with what we've got. Andrea Swan has saved our bacon on this one, let's close the deal and get this killer once and for all."

McConait got back to his feet, here was a chance to rectify the mistakes of the past. He knew Andrea's findings were a real breakthrough; the killer's movement between London and Tynemouth would be key. "I thought there might have been a chance it could be the same killer, but I thought it was more likely to be copy cat." The thrill of the chase had at last returned, "So he's a traveller, a business man, he's got a reason to travel between the two scenes, not just to kill, he'd do that anywhere, he's been in London at least 5 times last year, and now he's in Tynemouth. Train tickets, air tickets; who's gone from London to Newcastle in the past Year? Which businesses have links to Tynemouth from London? That may be a slim one, but he would need digs, a change of address the electoral role, estate agents and landlords." McConait was now pacing up and down his Cambridge study, in excitement, the telephone in one hand, the other gesticulating every new idea that flashed in his mind. "And let's not rule out the family connections, London /Tynemouth, yes, he could be with relatives. So maybe he's not a loner after all, I know my profile hasn't turned up much so far but cross reference our suspects in light of what I just said, it could just come together."

"We're ahead of you on that one; we're looking into the London/Tynemouth connections already. Looks like you're back on board then. Look, I know I kind of went off message with the Queensway killing, I should have known better than that; won't

115

happen again. For a while I thought I'd cheesed you off for good."

The tone had lightened and the old partnership was back together which lifted their spirits, "Don't be daft; the power of suggestion can get to anyone." Replied McConait playfully, "I mean even I myself, believe it or not, believed in a fictional animal that appeared at certain times and then vanished again, you may have heard of it too…the Easter Bunny."

"Oh very bloody funny, just get yourself up here before I have you arrested for impersonating a bloody comedian."

"I'll be on the next train."

"Great give me a bell when you're back."

"Looking forward to seeing you Sarge."

"You too Doc!"

McConait hung up, and leapt into action. He'd left Tynemouth with his tail between his legs. The "local hero" had let the side down and ran off when things weren't going his way. Now he'd found out that the London case was a failure, but now was his chance to atone for his guilt.

Within a few moments of getting off the phone with Peel, there was another call, this time from Rome.

"Hello Doctor McConait, it's Father Price here, I know things haven't being going so well but I wondered if you'd had time to consider the talk we had; about looking at things from different perspectives?"

"That trick with the apples and the frog, and the Monet. It's never been off my mind actually. Why do you ask?"

"Well I have a theory which may need you to have an open mind, it's been playing on my mind for a while, and since I've been in Rome I've been able to do a bit of research. The Vatican's got fabulous resources."

"I bet." said McConait cynically. The Catholic Church's afluence, and the hypocrisy that entailed made McConait's blood boil.

"Anyway I'm flying back to Newcastle in a few days; are you going back?"

116

"Funny you should say that but yes, and this time I'm actually looking forward to going back; we're going to solve this thing, once and for all."

"My thoughts exactly, I'm glad to hear a more positive attitude McConait. See you soon, God Bless."

"Goodbye Father."

McConait packed quickly, and then made his excuses to the college secretary over the phone. He could make the 6pm train, it would be packed with commuters, but he'd probably get a place in first class. He picked up his keys and a bottle of prozac then grabbed his bags and headed for the door. Something made him stop. He had forgotten something. He put down his bags and dashed back to his bedroom and picked up two objects from his bedside table, and rammed them in his pocket. It was the card with Andrea Swan's number and a cross; the one that Father Tuthie had given him.

Chapter 20
In The Blood

McConait called Peel, as his train arrived at Newcastle Central. This time Peel himself picked him up in his Volvo. They talked excitedly the 10 miles up the Coast Road back to Tynemouth.

The spring had arrived in force, and the sea breeze, which dropped the temperature a good 4 degrees, was almost forgiven when the views of the Priory, King Edwards bay and the stretch of golden beach known simply as 'Longsands' swung into view. For McConait the view was to get a whole lot better, as they reached Percy Park, where the small police hut was now dwarfed by two huge police trailers; amongst a mellay of uniformed officers, stood with her nose buried in a file of papers, was Andrea Swan. A smart red overcoat and knee-high boots had replaced the blue SOCO outfit and McConait was pleased with the improvement.

Peel turned to McConait, "I thought if it got too technical Andrea would be useful."

"Oh of course... absolutely...she's essential..." replied the flustered doctor.

Peel gave a knowing wink, "Didn't think you'd mind Doc."

They got out Peel's police Volvo and Andrea lifted her head from the file and her grin made the sunny morning all the brighter.

"Morning Sarge, hiya Sylvester. I'm glad you're back. When I heard you'd left I thought it would be another thirty years before I'd see you again."

No one ever called him Sylvester but Andrea's informality was a breath of fresh air from the stuffy academic world that McConait had made his home.

"I have to say it's good to be back under the new circumstances, your findings might prove to be the solving of this case. Well done." McConait's praise made Andrea bristle and even brought a blush to her shiny cheek.

They proceeded into the hut and Peel clicked on the fire; rubbing and blowing his hands against the chill which filled the room. "Well you'd better fill the Doc in Andrea. I'll put the kettle on."

Andrea flicked through her file and pulled out three large glossy photographs and laid them on the table. "This image here is a sample of blood taken from Mark Pembridge, the second victim. These round cells are healthy blood, but look here; these longer shapes, they're a virus, and quite unusual."

McConait nodded and perused the strange image, "So Pembridge had a virus."

"Yes, and not surprising considering his background, needle sharing and all that, but here's the blood of Rose Stearman. A middle aged house wife, comfortably well off, and look the same virus."

McConait was ahead of the game and picked up the final image, "And this is the young lad on the school field."

Andrea drew in close and lent across McConait to point at the image, "And here again, the virus." She left out the London victims deliberately so as not to rub salt in McConait's wound.

McConait was warmed by the physical closeness and he had to step away to get his mind back on task. He walked across the room and pinned the images on the wall; he picked up a whiteboard pen and wrote quickly but no less neatly on the white board.

"The virus is a real breakthrough, this could be the way. The blood, it's in the blood. It runs deep, well hidden, it's in the very make up of the killer, we need to do what you've done Andrea, we need to look closer, within." McConait wrote as he talked:

VIRUS BLOOD DEEP HIDDEN KILLER CLOSER

McConait turned to Andrea, "Look more deeply, the blood. We may find the killer under the microscope, what else can the blood tell us, is he black, white, big, small, any congenital health problems, I don't know much about it but if it can give us anything, anything at all." He gesticulated with his dry wipe marker, "It's in the detail, it's in the blood."

Andrea swelled with pride and excitement. "I'll need access to all the materials from all the incidents. I know people have already tried but if I could isolate any material that is not from the victims, or find any more links…"

McConait and Andrea were on the same wavelength, he didn't wait for her to finish; he turned to Peel, "Can you sort it Sergeant."

Peel nodded, "I'll have to clear it with Andrew Boe, he's in charge of that side of things but I'll find a way of getting him to play ball." Peel was famous for 'finding ways'; that was what made him so effective.

An inspired McConait turned back to the board, "It's in the blood. It's in the DNA, the genes, the family, something about his mother or father, a history of abuse, neglect. The parent has the history; our killer is related to someone who has killed before. They've got the record, the history of violence. The killer is just following in their footsteps. A cycle, like the moon, it's coming round again."

GENES FAMILY MOTHER FATHER ABUSE
HISTORY FOOTSTEPS CYCLE MOON

"The suspects; cross reference any with relatives who have a record of violent crimes or any history of neglect or abuse."

Peel got to his feet and put out his hand, "Glad to have you back Doctor." McConait shook his hand and knew that his creativity had returned. "Oh, one other thing, the original list of suspects, we cross-referenced them; like you said. None of them are connected to London apart from this man." Peel slapped down a file onto the table and flicked open the cover.

"The Mexican; what was his name again?" McConait remembered what Peel had said to him, about not working on feelings, but all the same he had a feeling about this one.

"Rufus Infareño, he's got family in London, and word on the street says that he runs a bit of Cannabis from there and deals it up here. We found quite a stash in his house and in the surf shop, but no-one's talking, so all we can get him on is possession. We know he's been up and down the country over the past year but he says it was mostly surfing related, and as you'd imagine he's not been very forthcoming with information."

McConait, Peel and Swan looked at each other, with smug satisfaction. "I know we don't work on feelings but...I think I'll get Signor Infareño back in." With that Peel scooped the file

120

back up and swept out of the hut, leaving McConait and Andrea alone.

McConait didn't feel so bumbling now. He was in his element and in charge of the situation. In Andrea Swan he had found a woman who impressed and inspired him. She had appeared like an angel resurrecting his feelings and the case. She could be the diligent hand to McConait's creative mind. He held her in his gaze for a while before speaking. "I'm really glad we ran into each other after all this time. It'll be great working together, maybe we could meet later for a drink, I'm at the Grand, the restaurant there's first class if you fancy…"

Andrea beamed, "That would be lovely Sylvester, eight o'clock alright?"

"Absolutely, see you then."

Andrea gave a cute wave and swept out of the hut. McConait closed his eyes and inhaled the scent of her perfume that lingered.

Filled with life, McConait turned back to his board.

RUFUS INFAREÑO LONDON POSSESSION OF DRUGS

He knew that this could be the breakthrough; link the virus from the victims' bodies to Rufus Infareño and the job was done. He went through the information one more time and everything pointed to this suspect. Once Peel tracked him down and Andrea analysed his blood then his profile would be proved right and the warm rays of adulation would once again shine on the Doctor. For the first time in years everything was going right.

*   *   *   *   *

McConait readied himself in his room; he didn't put on anything special, he always wore the same kind of clothes: Chinos, a cotton shirt, this time pink and a brown corduroy jacket. All his shoes were brown suede. He'd decided years ago that this was a standard academic style; at times he still wore his university scarf to complete the look. With effort he ran a comb through his hair and he was ready to meet Andrea.

As Geordie girls do, Andrea knew how to dress up. And an evening out called for some glamour. Her blonde hair now

121

flicked out from her neck. A sparkling sequined top with an open back shimmered with every footstep. She wore trousers, which hugged her curves but kicked out at the ankle just covering what she would call 'killer heels'. Her makeup was subtle; a subtlety that took her ages to achieve and lip-gloss completed the look, a look that was a million miles from the blue overalls she wore at the crime scene.

The outfit had the desired effect and McConait nearly fell off his seat as she entered the restaurant. He was even more taken aback when she leant across the table and gave him a peck on the cheek. "Hiya Sylvester, hope you haven't been waiting long." McConait just shook his head; without stopping, Andrea continued her nervous chatter, "Well it's a long time since I've been anywhere posh like this. Pizza Hut's usually my limit, well the kids like it so that's a good thing, and what a lovely view."

McConait had his back to the window and took a look behind him in acknowledgement. "Red or White?" Andrea continued.

"Pardon?" McConait failed to see the connection to what she had previously said.

"Wine... Red or white?"

"Oh Red for me, actually I have a bit of a confession, I've developed a liking for the Shiraz, is that OK?"

"Well I won't argue with a connoisseur."

"Connoisseur? That's better than wino. I could do with a detox ... but not tonight." McConait knew he'd need a glass or two before he'd be relaxed enough to be himself in the presence of such an attractive woman. Until then Andrea would have to dictate the conversation.

"So Sylvester, it's been a long time, it must be weird coming back. Do you get home much?"

McConait toyed with his fork, "No not much at all, the last time before this was 25 years ago; my mother's funeral."

Andrea looked concerned, "Oh yes I heard about it, I'm sorry, are you sill in touch with anyone up here?"

"No, I guess I made a clean break. I wanted to move on, not stay tied down to my roots. Why would I? There's nothing in the North East, the people are friendly but so peroquial." McConait

122

realised how he sounded; a pompous snob. Here he was sat in front of a woman who had stayed in the North East, a woman who was friendly and perhaps peroquial, but she was still fabulous.

Andrea squirmed a little "Well we are none of us perfect."

McConait felt like a heel but he needed to let Andrea know that he didn't mean to be such an ass.

"On the contrary…"

Andrea recoiled it appeared McConait had a very high opinion of himself.

"I mean I think that you might just be… perfect that is. You didn't have to run away to reinvent yourself, because you are lovely the way you are. With all my acclaim, it's your discovery that may have cracked the case, you're an excellent forensic and you still managed to be a good mother and a wife."

"Well my husband might not agree with you, he seemed to think that lots of other younger women could do a better job."

"Then he's a bloody fool." McConait's blood was coursing through his veins, but then Maria came to mind, and his guilt swept over him, who was he to criticise another man's behaviour after his own past?

Andrea seemed to sense what he was feeling. "And you? Did you ever marry?"

"There was one girl that I thought was special, it turned out she was especially cruel, and it got …messy." The drinks arrived saving McConait from continuing. As the wine flowed and the evening continued, Andrea and Sylvester laughed about school days, and talked about cases they had worked on and as the night drew to a close, McConait fell deeper into Andrea's sparkling blue eyes.

McConait gallantly got the bill and arranged a taxi for Andrea, as he opened the taxi door, Andrea turned and looked at him, "Thanks for a lovely evening; I suppose we had better keep it professional." She gave him a quick but genuine hug and a peck on the cheek.

"Only until the case finishes and I have a feeling that won't be long."

123

The taxi drove off, and McConait stood feeling a foot taller. He breathed in the sea air and returned to the Grand Hotel.

Chapter 21
The Interview

The next few days were crucial; McConait knew if they <u>had</u> found the killer, they had to get him off the streets before the full moon. It would all be so simple, they would drag Infareño in, check his blood for the virus, it would match and that would be it. In one swoop they'd solve eight murders. He knew it to be vain, but he pictured the headlines of the national press, his prestige back in tact, but most of all he would love the local adulation, embraced once again into the arms of his hometown. He got the call he was looking forward to. "Hello Doc, Sergeant Peel here, we arrested him. We nabbed him as he was opening up the surf shop; we said it was on the grounds of dealing. We got a dope-head to grass him up, excuse the pun, it's a fit up job, this guy would sell his granny for a fiver, a little leaning on the witness but we won't go into that, the main thing is we've got Infareño and we can do what we want with him. I thought you might want to come down for the interrogation."

"You bet... Oh Peel."

"What?"

"Good work."

McConait was picked up by a squad car. The end was in sight and McConait had butterflies of excitement. The interview was being held at the North Shields police station. McConait wondered if it would actually have a two-way mirror, like on the films; it did.

Rufus Infareño was brought in by a uniformed officer. He was even more striking in the Spartan interview room. A tall well formed man, broad shoulders, built up from years spent in the sea, catching waves. His shoulder length hair brushed away from his face by a powerful hand, to reveal a golden complexion, rugged and swarthy. His features bore the characteristics of the Aztec. Deep-set brown-black eyes, which looked like they held the mysteries of ancient times, hid beneath a canopy of thick black eyebrows. Young but wise, innocent yet ruthless, he folded his arms, taking up a defensive position as he sat on a chair in

125

front of a solitary table. The pentacle tattoo, now exposed, twitched on a flexing bicep.

Peel came in, sat down, organised his notes and pressed record on the digital recorder on the table between him and Rufus Infareño. "9:15, Tuesday, 25th May. Detective Sergeant Peel, interviewing Rufus Infareño."

"Is your name Rufus Gonzales Jose Infareño?"

"Yes."

"Do you reside at 35a Percy Park, Tynemouth."

"Yes."

"Could you please tell us where you were at approximately, 3:55 am March 31st."

"3:55am? Asleep."

"Where?"

"At home, Percy Park, like I say before."

"Do you have anyone to corroborate that."

"No, I slept alone."

"Do you know anything about these?"

Peel laid out the pictures of the dead victims; starting with the most recent. It was like a demonic poker game, each time he placed one down, Peel looked at Infareño, seeing if he gave anything away.

Inferano recoiled silently at each picture, sometimes taking his eyes away in disgust, each time Peel said the same thing, "Could you please look at the picture in front of you Mr. Infareño." The most polite form of torture McConait could imagine.

"No, I don't know nothing about the pictures, what happened, any of it."

"When was the last time you were in London Mr. Infareño." Peel had made him vulnerable and now caught him off guard. Infareño shuffled uncomfortably. Peel had the reaction he wanted. "Could you answer the question please Mr. Infareño."

"I…I…I was there last year."

"What was the purpose of your visit?"

"Family, I have family…from Mexico. They live there, a long time." Infareño was definitely jittery.

126

"How many times did you visit London last year Mr. Infareño?"

"I don't know maybe... I don't know... a few."

"Possibly five?" Peel was moving in.

"Five...four maybe." Infareño instinctively felt that agreeing with the detective was not in his best interest.

"Can you give exact dates for these visits Mr. Infareño?"

"No, I just go when I want, it's family, family stuff."

Peel began to toy with him, "Family stuff? Oh birthdays, anniversaries that kind of thing, well Mr. Infareño, it should be easy to work out the dates then."

Infareño was easier to break than his tough surfer exterior led one to believe. "Please, leave my family out of this, they are good people, good simple Mexicans who want a better life. I just try to help. You got me for the weed, I admit that, just leave my family alone."

"Interview stopped 9:40 am" Peel thought one confession at a time was enough. Even though this wasn't the confession he really wanted.

Peel left the interview room to talk to McConait. "OK, he's wobbly on the whole London connection, he's guilty about something there and it's not the dope, he soon spat that out."

"He's got no alibis, he could have done it, what we need to establish is would he have done it? Links to the moon, the occult; delve into his childhood, I think there's something in his family."

"I think you're right Doc, he was very defensive when we mentioned his family."

In their peripheral vision a huge shadow loomed at high speed.

"BANG!!!"

Rufus Infareño was inches away snarling with rage. Only the reinforced glass of the two-way mirror separated them. Two of the largest policeman had been given the task of escorting Infareño back to his cell, they picked them selves up from the floor, where Infereno had dumped them, they each grabbed an arm and began wrestling him backwards, Infareño's crazed eyes never left the mirror. He couldn't see Peel but he sensed he was there. In a verbal torrent of Spanish rage, Infareño was beginning

127

to succumb to the police intervention, but only because now the two original coppers had been joined by three others.

Peel turned to McConait, "That's not the reaction of someone pulled for a bit of dope dealing. I'm going to check out the London connection."

Peel left the further questioning of Infareño, to the local CID, and set about organising his return to the big smoke. Whilst phoning Scotland Yard, a plain clothed officer thrust a piece of paper into his hand.

McConait realised he wasn't needed and began to leave the police station, as he was leaving Peel called after him, "Here Doc just got this, from Andrea."

"Has she checked Infareño's blood already?"

"No we've got to get through a lot of legal stuff before we can force him to give a sample, no that will have to wait, it depends on how much fuss his lawyer kicks up, anyway you asked her to look closer into the blood, I don't know what it means but I wrote this down, she says to go down to the lab and she'll explain everything, as I say it means nothing to me. Anyway see you when I get back I'm going to check out 'La Familia Infareño." And with a waving hand Peel ran back inside the station.

McConait looked at the paper which had scrawled on it words which meant nothing to him:

P.U.L Virus

McConait made his way through a maze of corridors and into a lift which took him down to a subterranean level. The dank atmosphere soon brightened when he entered the lab to see Andrea sat at a lap top.

"Hiya Sylvester." McConait found himself in a stare in Andrea's presence, once again. "I take it you want to know about the P.U.L. virus."

McConait snapped out of his daze, "Oh yes, what is it?"

"Well that's the thing we don't really know. *P.U.L... previously... undiscovered... latent*, means that we haven't come across it before."

"Is that significant?"

128

"Not really, there are always new strains of virus; there are hundred's for the common cold, so it's not unusual."

"What about the latent part? What does that mean?"

"Well that means that it lies dormant until triggered by something, a bit like a cold sore, the Herpes Symplex virus lies dormant until triggered by temperature swings, caused by a cold or the sun, then it blisters, producing a cold sore."

This struck a cord with McConait, "Or Lupus… inherent until triggered. Then the immune system attacks the healthy cells of the body, affecting the joints then attacking the organs." McConait's tone was bitter and distant.

"Yes very much like that Sylvester, you seem to know a lot about it." Andrea was taken aback by McConait's change in tone.

"So the virus tells us nothing interesting at all?" asked McConait snapping back on track.

"Well it is still unusual, the fact that all the victims have it. I still feel they all got it from the same source. The type of virus it is, is only passed by blood, saliva or sperm. Like the A.I.D.S virus in that respect, so it looks like it came from the killer."

"So would the killer display symptoms?"

"Only when the virus was triggered."

"Any idea what the symptoms would be?"

"No can't say and I've no idea what the trigger could be either. Sorry Sylvester."

"No not at all, thanks for your help. So what we do know is that we don't know."

"I'll keep at it. There are more samples I haven't checked, but the killer passed on the virus we're more certain of that fact at least."

"Well I'll let you get back to it, Peel's off to London to track down Infareño's family, but call me if there's anything else."

"Of course Sylvester." She gave a smile and McConait left the lab. Returning to the lift he stared at the piece of paper in his hand. It played on his mind all the way back to the police hut. When he got inside he went straight to the whiteboard and began writing.

PUL VIRUS DORMANT TRIGGER

129

McConait wasn't satisfied with the limited information, he knew many leading professors of medicine back at Cambridge. Could they throw any more light on the situation? He picked up his mobile phone. Then changed his mind, Andrea knew what she was doing, he felt he should have faith in her, somehow he knew this woman would not let him down.

Chapter 22
The London Flat

Scotland Yard took no time in tracing Infareño's contacts. In the whole of London, only one Infareño was listed, and it was the right one. Taking no chances, the Yard watched the house for 24 hours, to assess the situation. For a two bedroom flat, there was a lot of activity. A couple of flashy white guys in a BMW came and went with packages of different sizes. Five other males, who could have been Mexican, came but never left, with this number of people in the flat, the police decided to come tooled up; fifteen officers in total all armed and wearing body armour, accompanied by four plain clothes CID.

With every exit covered, the police team froze in silence as Peel went to the front door. He could almost smell the adrenaline; this case had been weird from the start, and Peel feared what might lie behind the front door.

Peel knocked. The team stood psyched. Peel heard a shuffle behind the door as someone pressed their face against the other side to look through the eye hole. Peel could only hear whispers but he ascertained it was in Spanish. He knocked again; this time not even the whispering. "Open up this is the police." again nothing. "Mr and Mrs Infareño, this is Detective Sergeant Peel of Scotland Yard, open the door or we will have to break it down." nothing. Peel took two steps back and grabbed his radio. He looked round at the team and clicked his radio, ready to give the signal to the officers at the rear of the flat.

"GO! GO! GO!"

The team were trained in exactly what to do and in what order to do it. The front and back doors were battering rammed simultaneously. The men with the rams stepped aside to let others in who secured the entrances. When they shouted "Clear!" more would pour in, room to room, again shouting "Clear!" as they went. Then the voices grew in number. "Nobody move! Hands on your head! Hit the floor! Nobody move! Nobody fuckin' move!!"

Twelve Mexicans, men and women, were pinned to the ground, their hands tied behind their backs with plastic ties;

131

police kneeling on their backs pressing gun barrels to their temples. Woman cried in terror, men pleaded in Spanish.

Peel radioed for the police van to pull up in front of the house and stood in the middle of the flat so he could be heard in every room. "Who's Infareño? Come on! Infareño, Signor Infareño?"

A voice muffled by a policeman's thigh answered, "Me, I am Infareño."

Peel nodded at the officer holding Signor Infareño, who stood up dragging the frightened Mexican with him.

"I'm Detective Sergeant Peel, I need to talk to you." Peel gestured to an adjoining bedroom and the man was shoved in it. "Get the rest in the van and down the nick, get them all processed; strip search and blood test. The Spanish translator's down there already. Good work everyone!" As the flat began to clear, Peel gazed around the dingy Victorian flat, big enough for a couple of people to live in, but not twelve.

Signor Infareño stood with his face against the bedroom wall. He wasn't what Peel expected: about fifty; short and squat; slightly balding with a paunch. Nothing like the hulk of a man they had in a cell up North.

Peel sat the Mexican down on a single bed. "Signor, can you tell me what relation you are to Rufus Infareño?"

Finding it difficult to take his terrified gaze from the big copper who had just been sat on him, he finally looked at Peel nervously, "I am his father. I am Gonzales Infareño. Rufus is my son; is he OK?"

"You are his father?" Peel was suspicious; there was no resemblance.

"He was adopted, when he was five we took him in. But he is my son. Is he OK?"

"When did you last see him Signor?"

"Last month, he comes down regular. Please sir is Rufus OK?"

"He is in no danger Signor? But we need to know what he was doing down here." Signor Infareño looked at his feet.

"He looks after his family, he is a good boy." Peel bent down to be face to face.

132

"We know about the dope, he's admitted that. Who were all the people in here tonight?"

"Sir they are just good Mexicans; they mean no harm, they want to work, make a new life, there's no crime in that. Rufus wants to help them, that's all, he helps them with money; gets them started."

Peel straightened back up. He realised that what he had come across was not a murderous cult, but a bunch of illegal immigrants. That's what Rufus was covering up. The drug dealing was a means to an end. He shook his head in disappointment. Normally disposing of immigrants would give Peel great pleasure, 'getting rid of foreign scum' was how it was put by the Sergeant. Now the foreigners were getting in the way of his investigation.

"Take him in, process him." The officer needed no further instruction, he grabbed Signor Infareño and frog marched him out of the flat.

Chapter 23
Mad Monk

Price arrived into Newcastle airport at 10:30 am. and jumped straight into a taxi. The driver sped off from the airport and in fifteen minutes Price had arrived at Bishop's House. He wasn't there to meet the Bishop but the Diocese archivist, Father Maxwell, a rotund balding old priest who was the font of all knowledge in all matters regarding the history of the diocese of Hexham and Newcastle. "Ah Father Price, glad to have you back. I managed to track down the document you asked for, if you'd like to step this way? The two priests stepped into a great library and walked through the records of over one thousand years of Christianity in the North East of England. The air was filtered and clean, kept at a constant temperature so as to preserve the books. Father Maxwell stopped at a door and turned to Price. He held out a pair of white gloves. "You'll have to use these of course." Price pulled on the white gloves worn to protect ancient scripts from human hands, and entered the room through the door held open by Maxwell. "I'll leave you to it Father, I hope it's of use." Maxwell headed back through the library leaving Price in the side room staring at a huge book on a stand: An ancient handmade text made from velum and illuminated by hand; it had been opened at the correct page.

Looking at the illuminated parchment in front of him Price smiled. "Well done Father Maxwell; just the thing." Price pulled up a chair and made himself comfortable.

In bold letters at the top left of the page it read 1538 Anno Domini. Following with a white-gloved finger Price continued translating from the Latin:

A chilling sea fret washed its way in along the North East coast, the journey from France had been blessed with sunshine but now as the ship neared its destination the land disappeared from view in grey mist as if a portent to what lay ahead.

The captain of the small vessel called for silence, as without visibility, their only guide would be their ears. All aboard held their tongues and strained their senses trying to find a bearing in the endless grey. The sea lapped and crashed against the hull and the creaking and straining of wood and rope added to the tension; any second that wood might be dashed against a rock.

A monk knelt on the deck and began to pray silently. His name was Brother Walfred of the Benedictine Order from the Abbey of San Hubert in Normandy. He had spent most of the journey with his head over the side of the boat being violently sick. This was his first overseas trip and he was already hoping it would be his last, and if they didn't find shore safely it may be just that.

With his eyes tight shut he prayed to St. Christopher, the patron saint of travellers, over and over in his mind until…there it was…yes there it definitely was, the peel of a bell, faint in the distance but it was definitely there. The Captain and crew knew this bell and a swarthy unkempt seaman let forth a yell, "The Priory Bell captain; portside."

"Hard to port!!" the captain called and the crew fell into action for a few moments and then held still at their station, to listen for the bell. It was getting louder, and the sound of the sea had changed. As well as the bell they heard the crashing of waves against rocks, they were closer but they were in danger. Then a gap in the mist one hundred feet above them, revealed a menacing building perched on a rugged cliff; black and dreary, weather beaten and worn, it glared down at the travellers like an angry giant.

"We're too close Cap'n!!" the voice of the seaman almost drowned by the crashing of a wave against the rocks which were now perilously near.

"Hard a starboard!! Hard a starboard!!" Again the captain's order sent the crew into frantic action. The wheel was spun and then tied with rope to stop it swinging back. More sail was set to the wind to drive the ship away from the rocks against the raging sea. A sickening scraping sound worked its way from bow to stern, and then breaking free from the rocks beneath, the ship lurched to one side almost capsizing then springing back to an upright position and drove forward through wave after wave away from the deadly rocks.

The test had been passed and as everyone breathed a sigh of salvation the mist began to break and sunlight filtered through.

At last they saw Priors Haven a small cove with a gentle curve of sand, filled with fishing boats. They had made it.

A welcoming committee of Brothers from the Priory were on the shore to meet the travel weary Walfred. He picked up a small chest, which was padlocked and clambered ashore. In the chest lay the Papal Bull, official orders, giving him power of Inquisition and granting him passage and safety on arrival.

An unusually tall monk with an ill fitting habit, which could have been for a man half his size stepped forward and grinned insipidly. "Ah welcome Brother Walfred, welcome to Tynemouth Priory. I am Brother Ralph. We are truly honoured and relieved that you are here. Prior Bothwick will receive you into the Priory and meet with you following evening prayer. I know you will be anxious to give thanks to God for delivering you safely here on our shores."

"Absolutely Brother, prayers and then down to work." Walfred wasn't too comfortable with the formalities and wanted to get on with the job he had been sent to do.

"Prayer and work, work and prayer, the way of the Benedictine. Please follow us, allow me to help you with your heavy things." The tall monk's version of help was clicking his fingers and two young monks stepped forward to relieve Walfred of his burden.

The tall monk spun about and then with long lanky strides walked up the beach towards the Priory.

After an hour of Latin prayers in a cold and dark chapel, Walfred stepped back outside and his eyes smarted in the light. As his eyes adjusted the tall monk appeared, and clapped his hands twice, on this signal all the brothers formed into neat rows behind him; all their eyes on Walfred. In a sycophantic tone Ralph began the formal welcome to the Priory. "Our esteemed, enlightened and gracious guest, welcome to our community. Your skills and learned wisdom are renowned throughout our order. And your very name is a by word for..."

Walfred had had enough, "With all respect and thanks to you Brother Ralph and indeed all of you brothers, I need no plaudit or praise. I am a simple monk who wishes only to serve the Lord Our God and help his brothers."

Ralph looked crest fallen and an embarrassing silence was broken by a booming voice from behind him. "Humilitas! Humilitas!" A fat figure stepped forward who was anything but an example of humility. "You are right brother Walfred, we need not talk of your achievements we must learn from your diligence and humility. Ah humility is such an important virtue in a Brother."

The fat monk moved forward and the sea of brothers parted and bowed their heads as he swept passed. His monk's habit was not a simple coarse garment; it looked made to measure from a finer material than the others. Beneath it was an under garment, a full length robe made from crisp white cotton. His rope belt was of golden silk and on every podgy finger was a jewelled ring, solid gold with rubies or emeralds. Only one was simpler than the rest, his ring of office, which was gold with a cross, embossed on it. Around his neck was a thick gold chain with a bejewelled cross, which must have weighed several pounds. His jowls wobbled as he spoke and he puffed and wheezed with every movement. Walfred thought to himself that this was not a humble monk; this was a vain man and a glutton. Walfred knew who this was.

"Prior Bothwick thank you for allowing me to enter your Priory, is there somewhere we can talk?"

"The Prior looked Walfred up and down and was visibly perturbed that Walfred was dictating affairs. Smiling falsely he fluttered round with a waft of lavender scent and waddled away beckoning with one of his chubby ringed fingers for Walfred to follow.

Walfred had not made a great first impression, but he had hated his trip and he did not want to be here a second longer than he needed to be.

Prior Bothwick's quarters were in every way as ostentatious as Walfred would have imagined. Carved oak panelling covered the walls floor to ceiling; dressed by intricately woven tapestries of scenes of local saints, Cuthbert, Aiden and Oswin. On the far wall were bookshelves filled with printed works which themselves were precious objects. The room smelt of incense and lavender. The fat Prior lumbered into a velvet covered chair

137

which looked in every way like a throne. The two young monks followed them in and with a nod from the Prior, placed the chest they had carried from the beach onto the huge desk, which dominated the middle of the room.

Walfred pulled a key on a piece of string from under his habit and opened the lock.

"Here are my credentials and my instructions, if you'd like to see them." The Prior waved a disinterested hand and then sat forward commanding the room.

"I'll give the instructions in my Priory Brother Walfred. Ralph will fill you in with the gory details, but as I'm sure you've already been informed some…shall we say, unfortunate events have taken place here, and the reputation of our Priory, indeed our whole order is in jeopardy. We must show that we can deal with our own problems in an efficient and open manner to regain the trust of the people of the area who, after all, we rely on to pay taxes and keep us in the manner to which we are accustomed."

Walfred was disgusted by the Pior's attitude but he had seen it before. Class existed within the walls of abbeys and priories just as much as outside. The people in charge were from rich backgrounds and took what they felt due to them because of their class as if it was a God given right. It was this corruption and abuse of their position that was the real danger to the Church's reputation. And the rising Protestantism on the continent was gaining support in England too.

Walfred said nothing, but the position of the two men was clear by the expressions of mistrust on their faces. Walfred took his documents from the chest, placed them on the desk and left.

Ralph was waiting for him. Before the lanky monk had a chance to begin another ingratiating speech Walfred raised a finger to silence him.

"Brother Ralph where is the perpetrator of the crimes?"

Ralph looked a little confused at first, "Oh you mean Brother Osgard. He is clapped in irons in the cellar."

"And how long has he been there?"

"Four weeks now; ever since the incident."

138

"So you caught him straight away. Are sure you got the right man?"

"Oh we didn't catch him, he offered himself up, practically begged us to chain him up, he was beside himself, terrified."

"Terrified of what?"

"Ask him yourself." Ralph pointed to a door to the right of where they were standing. It bore a heavy lock, and as they walked towards it Ralph produced a huge bunch of keys on a large metal ring. He went straight for the key amongst a load of others and held it up in front of Walfred.

"Prepare yourself Brother Walfred he's not a pretty sight."

The two Brothers entered and found themselves at the top of a spiral stone staircase lit by a single candle in a niche in the wall. Ralph picked up the candle and the two brothers began the descent into the bowels of the Priory.

It was damp and claustrophobic; Ralph had to bend uncomfortably to squeeze his tall frame into the small staircase. The stairs ended to the relief of Walfred who disliked confined spaces nearly as much as sailing.

The room now opened up into a rectangle twelve feet by eight. A shaft of light came in at an angle from the left where there was a grate in the ceiling, but Walfred could not see anyone in the room. A rattling of chains from the right hand corner broke the quiet of the cell and then the silhouette of Brother Osgard entered the shaft of light. In an excited and anxious voice he spoke. "Is it him? Is it Walfred the inquisitor?"

Walfred stepped forward into the middle of the room. "It is I. You were expecting me?"

"I requested they sent for you, you are the only one who can help me...save me...you will help me won't you?" pleaded Osgard.

"I'll do what I can in the service of God and no more."

"That's all I ask Brother; thank you for coming." Osgard sat on the floor in the pool of light and bathed his face in the rays cascading from the top of the room. He was pale and gaunt. He had a scruffy growth of beard and the hair had grown back in to fill his tonsure, the shaved crown worn by monks as an act of respect to God.

139

Ralph went to the corner of the room, picked up a wooden stool and placed it in front of Walfred. Walfred sat down and gazed at the sorry figure on the floor in front of him. Ralph remained standing, towering above them.

"Then let us begin. I, as inquisitor of the Holy Mother Church, am here to determine the truth in the recent occurrences of evil here at the Priory, to flush out Satan and his followers and to redeem the immortal souls of those under his wicked influence." Walfred made a sign of the cross in the air in front of him and the two other men followed suit by crossing themselves, "In the name of the Father, and of the Son, and of the Holy Spirit…" in unison the three Brothers spoke, "Amen."

Osgard took a deep breath and closed his eyes as if bracing himself. "Now I'll tell you everything, every word I will speak to you is the truth, so help me God."

Osgard braced himself and the chains that bound him became taught.

"It started a couple of months ago. I had been visiting a family to the north of here; the Delavals. They're a very important family and own a great deal of the land around here. I sometimes say Mass for them, they have a chapel on the grounds of Delaval Hall. I always take a shortcut through the woods at the South gate of the estate. It was later than usual and the sun was setting, I seemed to lose my way in spite of the fact I have walked that route a hundred times. Then I heard the sound of dogs, Master Deleval's dogs, then voices shouting. It was the hunt and it was coming towards me. I wondered what they were chasing, then I found out; a wolf, a great wolf, huge. It leapt twenty feet then it was on me." Osgard stopped and turned to face Walfred. He pulled his habit forward to reveal a huge scar, from his neck to his shoulder. "An inch further and it would have killed me. And better if it had. Then the hounds were on it, the Master lost twelve of his best dogs that night. The huntsmen threw spear and fired arrow yet the mighty beast still managed to kill two of them before disappearing into the forest."

Walfred leaned forward listening intently, "A lucky escape Brother Osgard."

140

"I thought that at the time, but not now. The wound healed miraculously quickly. At first I thought it was the prayers of my Brothers but it was the devils power racing through my veins. All was well for a couple of weeks, and then the full moon rose above the Priory. I was at evening prayer when I caught sight of it through the East window. I felt sick and feverish, I had to get out. Almost delirious I made my way back to my room and locked myself in. Then the shaking started I was bouncing from wall to wall. I ripped off my clothes. My skin felt like it was on fire. Then I saw I was covered in hair. I could hear my own bones cracking inside me, the pain was unbelievable, and I could feel my organs moving, changing. I felt my heart was going to burst. My mouth filled with blood as my jaw cracked and pushed forward splitting my lips. My teeth pushed down from my gums. I say my teeth but they were long and razor sharp. It was then I heard the bangs on the door. I had been yelling in agony the whole time and some of the brothers were banging on the door to help me. The banging got louder; they were breaking in, I was cornered. I didn't know what to do. As the door finally gave way, time seemed to go slowly. I can still see the expression on their faces..."

Osgard stopped and his body began to shake. "They could see what I had become; a monster." He sobbed uncontrollably unable to continue. Walfred got up from his seat, "Osgard you must go on, tell me what happened!" but no reply. Walfred jumped forward and grabbed Osgard by the shoulders and began to shake him. "I can't help you if you don't tell me what happened. Come on ...for the love of Christ speak, in the name of all that is Holy, SPEAK!!!"

Osgard came back to his senses and looked at Walfred with wide frightened eyes. "It was then I became the beast, I didn't think as a man but as an animal. I killed them, all three of them, when they tried to run I pounced on them, pinned them down, they were my friends but I ...I...ripped out their throats. The blood, the savagery, and it will happen again, the next full moon...please make it stop!!" Osgard curled up in a ball and began weeping again.

141

Walfred turned away and looked at Ralph; they stood stunned at the revelation. Walfred picked up the candle and headed back up the stairs. He took a gulp of fresh air and tried to make sense of what he had heard. He turned to Ralph who had followed him out. "Ralph you know him, what kind of man is he?"

"The best, he was one of our most devout and compassionate brothers. He showed kindness to all God's creatures."

"So not a killer then."

"Nothing of the sort, what has happened here is unbelievable. You saw him, you see how repentant he is." Ralph paused and placed a hand on Walfred's shoulder. "Brother can you save him?"

"Well I believe he truly wants to be saved."

"And what he said, changing into a beast, do you believe that?"

"I believe that he believes it; it is that belief that possesses his soul. The beast lies at the heart of all of us; it is only through diligence to the word of God that we can be free of it. What happened to him in the wood has left scars much deeper than the one he showed us." Walfred rubbed his chin, deep in thought. "Apart from the killings he mentioned have there been any other happenings?"

"No...apart from the suicide attempt."

"Suicide attempt?"

"Yes, Osgard tried to hang himself the night of the killings."

"Then he would be damned for taking his own life." The Benedictine held suicide as much a sin as murder.

"Yes but he did it because he says he will kill again, unless it is ended."

"So as he was damned anyway, by his act of bestial murder, the taking of his own life wouldn't make any difference. So how can I help him? What difference could I make?"

"I don't know but he believes you can save him. He was adamant that they send for you."

"But he must know that as inquisitor I can have him killed, his fate would be the same as with the local authorities." Then

142

Walfred's logical thinking, for which he was famed, began to find a path through the mystery. "He thinks I'll purify him with fire; his physical body would die but his soul would be redeemed by cleansing flame."

Ralph looked upset and turned away. "I'm sorry Brother Walfred, it's just I hoped...we hoped..."

"Hoped what?"

"We hoped there was another way, that you could somehow change him back."

"Change him back? You mean cure him?"

"Yes, we have all heard how learned and intelligent and..."

"Don't start that again."

"Please Brother Walfred is there no other way?"

Walfred stood still and gazed out to the sea, which splashed against the rocks sending foam high into the air. "I have heard of this kind of thing before, a condition called 'Lycanthropy'. Osgard believes he is a lycanthrope, a shapeshifter, a werewolf."

Ralph physically stiffened at the sound of the word 'werewolf'.

"In his mind, perhaps in his spirit, the sufferer changes into a beast. Triggered by a traumatic event, he develops an alternate personality, in the case of Lycanthropy, the persona of the wolf. It taps into our basest instincts; we return to the primitive savage, and when the mind is under the influence, the body will follow, and when cornered, a man in this state is capable of terrible savagery." The sea air cleared Walfred's head and he now thought freely and creatively, "We have a legend back in France that says a werewolf can be killed by a weapon blessed in the chapel of St.Hubert, now if the evil entered him by the infection of his blood, through a bite, then we must kill that infection, we must cleanse his blood. If his blood is cleansed then perhaps Brother Osgard will be saved."

Ralph clapped his hands together; at last a glimmer of hope, "Oh everything they say about you is right you are truly..." Walfred's raised eyebrows were all it took to stop Ralph.

"So you believe the legend Brother Ralph. Let's hope Osgard does too."

143

The two monks set to work preparing the strangest ritual ever performed at Tynemouth Priory. Walfred barged into the Prior's quarters to the disgust of several old monks who were Priory administrators. The Prior himself was nowhere to be seen. Walfred knew it would be the right thing to wait for the Bothwick's return, to seek permission for what he was about to do, but there was no time.

Walfred was well versed in blood-letting practises and in the chest he brought with him was a dagger blessed in San Hubert's chapel. He carried it mainly for opening documents but it had drawn blood before; it had been used more than once in defence against robbers. Dagger in hand, Walfred stood in front of Bothwick's bookshelf and scanned from left to right. "Eureka!"

Walfred pulled a black leather bound book from the shelf; the title read:

'The Sacred Rite of Exorcism'

Walfred turned and left, ignoring the still outraged administrators, flicking through the pages as he walked, reacquainting himself with the rite.

Back in Brother Osgard's makeshift prison, Ralph had already set up a table with a silver chalice, holy water and towels. As the light from the grate dwindled with the setting sun, Ralph brought the gloomy cell to life, with what must have been fifty candles. A smoking incense holder covered the smell of damp, sweat and urine. The scene was set.

Osgard did not have time for explanations. He knew he had to trust these men implicitly if his immortal soul was to be saved, but time was not on his side and he pleaded with them, "Quickly Brothers, the moon… it will be appearing in the grate soon, I don't want to be responsible for your deaths."

Ralph was visibly shaken by the words but Walfred was single minded about his task and began. "Ralph, hold his head still." Ralph, trembling, grabbed Osgard in his huge hands. A vice like hold from the big monk was just what Walfred needed.

In the candlelight Walfred read from the book.

"We are here in the name of the Lord Jesus Christ.

We are here to redeem the soul of our beloved Brother Osgard.

We are here to dispel the Unholy Spirit, which torments him.

Jesus Christ Prince of Peace, guide my word and steady my hand to slay the demon who offends thee."

Osgard held the dagger in front of him, a small glimmer of moonlight appeared from the grate. At this Osgard became transfixed. Taking some holy water Walfred poured it over the blade. "Bless this blade, make it straight and true, to do thy Holy Purpose." As the water dripped to the floor, Osgard began to convulse. He thrashed at his chains and began to wail in unworldly tones.

Ralph adjusted his stance to brace himself against the motion. "He's getting difficult to hold Brother Walfred. I don't know if I'll be able to…"

Interrupting once again, Walfred looked Ralph straight in the eye and snapped back, "You can and you will. Have faith Brother Ralph."

Osgard's face contorted, not just from the restraining fingers of Brother Ralph but from something inside him. The pathetic wretch they had talked to an hour ago was now a snarling fiend.

Walfred ripped open Osgard's habit, brought the dagger to his scarred shoulder and began to make a vertical incision, "Brother Osgard I bless you in the name of the Father …"

He then crossed the first incision horizontally.

"…and of the son…"

Osgard yelled and finally broke his head free of Ralph's grasp. Walfred leapt away from the snarling fiend before him.

"…and of the Holy Spirit, Amen!"

Blood began to ooze from the cross, etched into Osgard's shoulder. His eyes rolled back and were completely white. He bared his teeth and arched his back straining at the chains that bound him, then collapsed, exhausted on the floor.

145

Walfred grasped the chalice from the table. "Ralph, secure his head again."

The dazed and terrified Ralph did as requested, this time using his arms to lock Osgard in an inescapable embrace. Frothing at the mouth, Osgard wheezed and groaned; his energy seemingly spent. Walfred held the holy cup in front of him, and then began reading from the book again.

"Jesus Christ with this sacred cup we drink your blood,

and proclaim your death so that we too may join in your resurrection.

Satan with this sacred cup I cast thee out and proclaim your death, so that our Brother may live again."

Walfred pressed the cup to Osgard's shoulder so that his blood began to run into it.

"Satan I cast thee out. In the name of Our Lord Jesus Christ."

Osgard's strength returned and he threw himself backward on top of Ralph, who hit the floor hard but did not release his grip. Again Walfred returned with the chalice. He looked into Ralph's eyes, to steady the tall monk's nerve, "Join with me Brother Ralph." Now the two monks chanted in unison,

"Satan I cast thee out. In the name of Our Lord Jesus Christ."

As the blood trickled into the chalice the brothers kept repeating their chant,

"Satan I cast thee out. In the name of Our Lord Jesus Christ."

Every time the line was said, the struggling Osgard calmed a little, until with the chalice full, he lay peacefully on Ralph's lap.

Osgard returned the chalice carefully to the table, and turned the page in the book.

"We give thanks to the Lord Our God
for the redemption of our brother,
we praise your Son Jesus Christ,
the Prince of Peace
and his victory over evil.
Amen."

146

Walfred and Ralph sat watching the resting Osgard, gathering their thoughts and letting the adrenaline settle after the ordeal. Walfred stood first; he took one of the towels from the table and poured holy water on it. He then knelt over Osgard and cleaned and dressed his wound.

Ralph broke the eerie silence, "Do you think it has worked?"

"The question is, does Osgard think it has worked?" Walfred looked up at the grate where moonlight was streaming in, "There's one way of finding out. Unchain him."

Ralph was uneasy, "We can't release him without the Prior's permission, and what if it hasn't worked he could run through the Priory and the whole village and massacre…"

Walfred stopped Ralph who was getting himself into a state, "Have faith my brother; the key."

Ralph condescended and produced his ring of keys. With trembling fingers he unlocked Osgard from his chains.

Osgard lay limp; the snarling beast was gone and now here was the face of the calm and gentle man that Ralph had described. Walfred and Ralph began bundling Osgard up the tight staircase.

Osgard came to his senses as they reached the top of the stairs. The sea air of Tynemouth had never smelled sweeter and as he knelt down on the cool damp grass, he felt reborn. He slowly looked up and the silver light from the full moon illuminated his face.

Walfred and Ralph held their breath. Osgard turned his gaze towards the Brothers and slowly got to his feet. He smiled a kind and grateful smile; he knew that the moon had no power over him anymore.

The three brothers embraced in the moonlight. Osgard was saved.

After a good sleep Walfred rose to a sunny morning. Weather conditions were good and today he could sail home. As much as he dreaded the trip, he was desperate to get away from England and leave the strange occurrences behind him. It would soon be time for morning prayers and Walfred put his habit over his head, when an abrupt heavy bang came from the door. He opened it to find a frantic Ralph.

"Brother Walfred it's Osgard, the Prior has had him arrested. A group of the town militia came for him just now and dragged him away."

Walfred was confused and scared, had the exorcism failed after all, had Osgard struck again. "What has he done, why is he arrested?"

"That's the thing; he says he has done nothing this time he says he went to bed and slept all night."

"So they have taken him for the previous killings then. I am surprised that the Prior has sanctioned that, he wanted this kept within the Church, surely that's…" Now it was Ralph who interrupted Walfred.

"No, no, it's not about the killings. Brother Osgard is accused of rape!"

Of all the unbelievable goings on Walfred had experienced since his arrival, this accusation was the most far-fetched. The good and kind Osgard who was held dearly by his fellow brothers had admitted to the atrocities he had committed. It would be unlikely he would deny rape.

Walfred wasted no time, "I'm going to see Prior Bothwick. He must realise this is a mistake."

Walfred stormed off leaving Ralph behind. Again the Prior's administrators tried to rebuff him, but Walfred pulled rank and stormed into the fat monk's chambers. The Prior spun round infuriated by the interruption. "What is the meaning of this? This is my Priory, you are but a guest."

Walfred slammed his hand on the desk in the middle of the room. "I am here on the orders of the Pope, if you had taken time to read my credentials, you'll find that you must accommodate me in any way I see fit. I was brought here at your request to perform a function, which I have done, only to find that my work has been undone by a preposterous accusation. One, which as Prior you have the power to overthrow."

Bothwick was now puce with anger. "I have heard about your antics last night, which were undertaken without my

148

knowledge. And I am certainly not satisfied that you have fulfilled the duties for which I sent for you."

"What more would you have me do?"

"Osgard was a confessed murderer. He should have burned. That's what the people of the village would have expected. Now there is another crime on everyone's lips and this time justice will be done!"

"The rite of Exorcism is substantiated by the Church, are you questioning its validity? This was a matter of driving out evil from within the soul of a brother not his body."

"And cleansing fire would have performed that function perfectly." Bothwick rose and walked to the window. "Your vessel is waiting for you Brother Walfred, it's time you got ready to leave and let us take care of our own problems; in our own way."

Walfred knew that all his paperwork and credentials weren't going to influence the Prior. He left his quarters and took to his heels. He had to get to the bottom of this crime to clear Osgard's name. He ran into the village, grabbing people in the street until someone could tell him where the alleged rape had happened.

He was pointed in the direction of the inn. The victim was the Innkeeper's daughter, a girl of innocent beauty but of poor wit. She was backward and mute, all but her family referred to her as the 'idiot girl'. Her name was Lucy and at the age of sixteen was able enough to help out with menial tasks around the inn, but her upkeep had been a burden to the family. A beautiful daughter would normally have guaranteed a decent husband, perhaps with wealth, but as pretty as she was no one would have taken on this poor girl.

The inn was empty apart from Lucy's mother who sat weeping in the corner. She was not pleased with the sight of a monk entering the premises. "Get out! Have you lot not done enough damage?"

Walfred understood he was not welcome, but justice had to be done. "Good lady, I am sorry what has happened to your daughter, but I fear they may have got the wrong man."

"They've arrested a monk haven't they?" she spat back at him.

149

"Yes but I'm sure it couldn't have been brother Osgard."

"One monk is as good as another. You're all the same, preaching at us one minute, robbing us the next."

"But what makes you think it was a monk?" Reasoning to a woman in such a state was not going to be easy.

"Think? Think? I don't think I know. He was a regular visitor to our poor Lucy. He was praying that the curse of stupidity would be lifted from her. He said our sins as parents had cursed her and if we repented then Lucy could be spared. So he would come. And…" the woman paused to regain control of her trembling mouth, "…pay her a visit. Oh I wanted it to stop, but my husband said we needed the money."

"He paid you?" Walfred was taken aback; rape had now turned into prostitution.

"Oh he had plenty money alright. But now he's washed his hands of her, now she's in trouble."

"She's in trouble? What do you mean, what has she done?" It appeared that Osgard was not the only innocent party in peril.

The woman looked at the floor and took a deep resigned breath. "I'll tell you what she did, she went and got herself pregnant that's what, and now we're going to have a bastard as well as an imbecile to look after."

"Are you saying that it was Brother Osgard that did this?"

"I'm saying you're all a bunch of hypocrites and liars, posing as men of the cloth, wolves in sheep's clothing the lot of you. And I hope they burn the bastard… whoever he is?" it was clear from her demeanour that she knew exactly who it was, but she wasn't going to say. What was clear was it wasn't Osgard.

Walfred ran from the inn, he had to try to save Osgard. As he got into the street a crowd of people were heading towards the Priory. At the front of the crowd was Lucy being led by her father. Walfred tried to push through the crowd; he was jostled and derided, but unharmed, he was nearly at the front, he had to make them stop; somehow he had to get their attention.

In desperation he shouted, "Lucy stop!!"

It brought the whole crowd to a halt. Lucy turned and, seeing a man in a monk's habit, acted submissively as she had been taught to do. She smiled a pretty smile and made the sign of

150

the cross; on the index finger of her right hand was a golden ring with an emerald set in it. This was not the ring of an innkeeper's simpleton daughter. Walfred knew where he had seen the ring before. Yesterday morning on Bothwick's little finger. One of the many gifts that ensured the family stayed as silent as poor Lucy.

Walfred was glued to the spot. Lucy's father turned her back around and the crowd carried on, leaving Walfred wondering what to do. His mind was made up for him. A gang of four burly militiamen came from behind him and grabbed him. The oldest of them spoke. "Prior Bothwick has sent us to remind you that your vessel is waiting at the Haven." Walfred tried to interject but was silenced by a slap to the face. The man continued in sinister tone, "Don't worry Brother all your things have been taken aboard. And we shall escort you to make sure you catch the boat, safe and sound."

Walfred tried to resist but a punch to the jaw left him barely able to stay on his feet, as he was dragged through the street and down to the Haven. The militiamen dumped him onto the deck and the older one commanded the Captain to cast off.

Bleeding from the mouth Walfred managed to get to the front of the boat but they were already under way and the militiamen were still watching on the beach. As the boat pulled away from the shore a blood-curdling scream came from the Priory above. Then cheers from the crowd of villagers. It was a few more minutes when the boat was clear of the cliffs, that Walfred could make out the figure of a man limp and lifeless tied to a stake and smoke rising high into the air.

Osgard was dead and Prior Bothwick looked out to sea, watching Walfred's ship sail south.

A year later on January 12th, 1539, Tynemouth Priory was dissolved by order of Henry VIII and the Priory's wealth and status as a place of worship were taken. Prior Bothwick was dragged through the streets of Tynemouth and beaten by the villagers before being hung. The villagers continued to be taxed but now the money was paid to the King.

Price closed the book carefully and peeled off his white gloves. The pieces of the jigsaw had come together in his mind; he was now ready to reveal all to McConait.

Chapter 24
The Final Sample

Andrea Swan was about to finish for the day when a call came from Peel,

"Andrea, glad you're still there. I'm still down in London but I've just heard from Infareño's lawyers, he's happy to give a blood sample, apparently he'll do anything to clear his good name."

Andrea clenched her fist in excitement, "Great! So he must be unaware of the virus; that works out perfectly for us."

"Too bloody right! He's still in custody but he's due to be released in the morning. It would be prudent if we could get the sample tonight, then we won't have to go and lift him again. Can you do it?"

"Yes of course, I'll get the sample straight away; will you clear it with the sergeant on shift?"

"I've already taken that liberty. And Andrea…"

"Yeh?"

"Be careful, he's a dangerous customer and I'd hate for him to have a change of heart half way through."

"Will do Sarge, I'll let you know when I get the results."

In minutes Andrea Swan was at the front desk of the station where the three biggest officers were waiting to take her down to Infareño's cell. Her adrenaline was racing as they opened the door to the cell, not knowing what to expect, she was surprised to find such a dashing figure of manhood sitting calmly on the edge of his bed. Even more surprising was the fact that he was pleased to see her. And a white smile beamed from his swarthy complexion. "I'm so glad you are here, I hope that my blood sample will help clear up these horrible accusations about the killings. My lawyer says you will be able to help prove my innocence."

Andrea was amazed that the lawyer's advice was playing right into their hands.

"Mr. Infareño, if you could just roll up your sleeve." Infareño pulled back his sleeve to reveal the pentacle tattoo, it

152

was the first thing about him that unnerved Swan; it reminded her of who she was dealing with.

"Now you may feel a little scratch." She never expected for a second that the big man would have a problem with needles and she was right, his eyes never left her face as she drew the red liquid from his arm. "There we go, all done, thank you for your co-operation."

"No, thank <u>you</u> Signora, when will you have the results?"

"Very soon." And she meant it. She wasted no time getting back to her lab in the basement. Her heart was racing, this was it; Infareño's blood sample. The answer was minutes away; she began preparing the slide. It was running late again but this time she wasn't concerned about the time. She took a long pipette and drew a sample from the vial of blood. One tiny drop on the slide was all that would be needed to prove Infareño the killer.

She replaced the slide into the cartridge and inserted it into the microscope. She began the task of rotating and adjusting the image that appeared on the computer screen. She continued focusing and refocusing, but she couldn't see the strings of virus cells. Over and over she readjusted the image but she still couldn't see it.

She withdrew the cartridge and prepared another sample, she didn't know how but somehow she must have done something wrong. Again she drew the blood sample prepared the slide and put it into the cartridge. Surely this time she'd find the evidence. Again she clicked and manipulated the image… nothing.

She pulled away from the screen that had given forth nothing. "He hasn't got it…he hasn't got it…damn!"

She picked up her phone to give McConait the bad news; she felt she had let him down. With hands trembling she pressed the speed dial button, after three rings he picked up. "Hello Sylvester it's Andrea. I've got the results of Infareño's blood test."

"Wow that was quick work I thought we had a legal battle to fight."

"No he gave the sample voluntarily."

"That was foolish of him."

153

"Not at all, really it was rather savvy…" Andrea paused to build up courage," …sorry I've got bad news… it's Infareño's blood…it doesn't have the virus." There was a stunned silence on the other end of the phone. "I've checked and checked… he doesn't have it."

McConait slumped into a chair, "But everything pointed to him, this would have clinched it."

"Don't give up hope, perhaps he doesn't have it but it doesn't mean he didn't give them it." Andrea knew she was clutching at straws but she could sense the desperation from the silence on the other end of the phone.

McConait's bubble was burst again, and he found it hard to see any positives, "What do you mean?"

Andrea scrambled for answers, and tried to sound as convincing as possible, "Well he may have injected them, or something, we could look at the bodies again, see if there are any needle marks." Again there was silence, "I know it's a stretch but the victims have two things in common…they were all murdered and they all have the virus, it's got to mean something, and it may explain why he was so happy to give a blood sample."

There was some logic in this argument but it was little satisfaction, "Look Andrea I'll see what Peel thinks but we seem to be at a dead end. Look into the syringe theory but those bodies, what's left of them, have been well scrutinised. You can probably count Pembridge out of the equation, I bet he was riddled with needle tracks, and even if the others have got a needle mark it could mean they'd given blood or had a flue jab, or a number of things." McConait sounded exasperated.

"OK Sylvester… Sorry."

"Yes… me too."

Andrea hung her head in her hands, and wept. Her lap top pinged indicating an email. She was about to shut the computer down but she thought she might as well check, it was from an eminent veterinary surgeon from Edinburgh University. She opened the email and her spirits lifted, at last something more concrete on the virus.

154

Chapter 25
The New Profile

Infareño had just been released.

Price returned to Tynemouth to find McConait with his head in his hands, in front of his whiteboards. "Hello Doctor, why so glum? I thought we were on the up and up. Hasn't there been a breakthrough or something?"

"Oh there has. It turns out that all the victims, including those in London, had an unknown virus in their blood samples, which would indicate they contracted it from the murderer during the attack. My wonderful profile narrowed it down to one possible suspect; who indeed turned out to be a criminal, however the problem is, he doesn't have the virus so all the evidence is circumstantial rather than conclusive." McConait slammed the desk, "I was so bloody sure!"

"But you say he's a criminal?" Price sat down to get the whole story.

"Yes, Peel explained it all to me. You see we knew the murderer must have had connections in Tynemouth and London. The guy we suspected, Rufus Infareño, a Mexican, lives in Tynemouth and had some dodgy connections in London. It turns out, that he's got some deal with a couple of Russian gangsters that, if he can get Mexicans to smuggle themselves over as well as various narcotic substances, they, the Russians, can sort them out with fake IDs, jobs and a tidy bit of cash. Well seeing as the Mexicans were breaking the law, by being illegal aliens anyway, I guess they figured 'to be hung for a sheep as well as a lamb'. So my clear cut suspect, does not have the virus, the forensics which would have nailed him, and his alibi for being in London was committing a separate crime, with which the authorities in London are far too preoccupied with to worry about Tynemouth, so he's out until his trial in a month's time."

"I'm so sorry, you seemed so sure." Price was genuinely sympathetic.

"Well it's as you proved to me the other day, logic isn't always enough." McConait's voice had an air of resentment that

155

he had been proved wrong, and at the same time Price had been proved right.

McConait looked up at the whiteboards. An intricate web of words, facts, pictures; the whole case mapped out in an organic diagram. "It's this… it must be wrong. Everything's there but it's not. The proof's amongst all that but I can't see it."

Price knew that this was the perfect time to share his thoughts with the Doctor. McConait was on a low and more likely to be open to suggestion. "Doctor, you have proved that you are an excellent profiler, watching you work is impressive."

McConait was waiting for the 'but', "But this man you are profiling."

"Yes what about him?" McConait wondered where this was going, Price was usually more direct.

"Well maybe you shouldn't be writing the profile of a man." Price paused and looked McConait in the eye, as if bracing himself.

"Really Father I don't think this is the work of a woman." McConait didn't think the priest could have said anything more off the mark, but he was wrong.

"No not the profile of a woman, not the profile of a man but the profile of a werewolf." Price stood in front of McConait, the expression on his face meant that this couldn't be construed as a joke, a bit of horse play between two academics, no, to McConait's amazement and disappointment, Father Liam Price was deadly serious.

If anything was worth the label of heresy then this was it; the empirical scientist, turning full circle to betray his own beliefs and his colleague. McConait had been let down by Peel in the garden after the last killing and now Price, the voice of reason, had fallen too.

McConait stood up and turned his back on Price, everything seemed to be going from bad to worse and he saw no way out, the full moon was upon them, the man he was sure was the killer was loose and the person he had counted on for support had flipped.

Price had to call on all his powers of calm and diplomacy to keep McConait in the room. "Doctor, I know you think I'm

156

crazy, but you have nothing to lose by listening. You feel unsure right now, lacking certainty in yourself and your abilities, well if you listen to me and you find I am wrong, then it will only prove you to be more right, and more justified in believing in yourself, and your abilities." Price's deep blue eyes and sincerity of voice could work miracles. McConait did not walkout. "Go on, humour a daft Irishman, why don't ye?" Price laid on a clichéd thick Irish, 'top o' the morning, kissed the blarney stone', brogue. But there was nothing daft about this Irishman. He placed a hand on the shoulder of the stranger who had become a friend; McConait softened.

McConait sat and waited for another one of Price's diatribes, but Price was going to use McConait's methods to explain. "May I?" Price pointed to the remaining blank white board.

"Be my guest." said McConait sarcastically.

In the centre of the board where McConait wrote killer, Price wrote:

WEREWOLF

From there he branched off and added the words:

ERGOT POISONING/ DRUGS

"Ergot: a bacteria found in rye, wheat, barley and other cereals, a poison causing hallucination and violent erratic behaviour. Throughout history mistakenly thought to be possession by the devil. An ergot derivative, ergine, is one of the sources of LSD and other hallucinogenic drugs." He carried on adding to the board:

LYCANTHROPY/LUNACY

"Lycanthropy: a mental illness, a mania, where the affected person, believes he is a wolf, takes on the characteristics, and commits violent atrocities. Lunacy: an outdated word for madness, where people were said to be influenced by the moon, causing mania."

PORPHYRIA/WEREWOLF DISEASE

"Werewolf or vampire disease: also known as the royal disease. The symptoms are: waxiness of skin, receding gums, light phobia, disturbed behaviour, and hair growth on the face and body."

HYPERTRICHOSIS/BODYHAIR

157

"Excessive body hair: a condition from birth, the entire body, face, hands and feet, covered in hair like an animal. A genetic throw back to our ancestors; it effects whole families, often in freak shows and circuses in the past."

THERIANTHROPY

"Physical Therianthropy: the belief that the body can physically change to an animal. Spiritual Therianthropy: where the spirit can turn into that of an animal. Shamanism is a religion that believes this can be done, popular in the Americas, tribal Shamans would bring on a hypnotically induced state to engage with animal spirits. Some cultures also chemically induced this state by eating plants that drugged them. Once under the trance they would take on the characteristics of the animal perhaps even using the animal's skin, teeth or claws to dress as the creature."

McConait sat dumbstruck at the diagram with the five lines emanating from the centre.

Price clicked the lid back on the marker. "Let's consider, a violent killer, possessed by some form of mania, perhaps chemically induced, which manifests itself at the time of the full moon, causing animal, wolf like, savagery. Remember the policeman at Queensway; the only eyewitness? He talked of body hair like an animal. Imagine a brut of a man with excessive body hair with receded gums to expose teeth, fierce, animal like, who, like the Native Americans, believes he spiritually and physically becomes the wolf." Price spun back to the board, "None of this is fabrication, this is all fact, researched and investigated, this is a werewolf, a real thing, not mythical but real. Find someone with these characteristics, you find the killer."

McConait couldn't believe what he had just witnessed; Price more or less had proved the existence of werewolves.

"You see it may not be logical to say that werewolves exist, but you know the problem with logic."

McConait had learned his lesson well, "The tomato, the green frog?" McConait yet again bamboozled by the eloquent Irishman.

"Absolutely, you see the werewolf is part of human social history. Every culture in the world has their version of the man beast. In our culture it links to our life in the wild wood. At one

158

time the whole of Britain was covered by a great forest. The wolf would have been man's predator, so stories and legends were born; Little Red Riding Hood for example. People with mental illness would become wild, and people would relate their behaviour to that of the wolf. The werewolf was born. And the word 'werewolf' comes from that time, the Teutonic language of the Anglo Saxons, 'were' meaning man, and it continued when the Romans colonised Britain, the Latin word very similar to 'were' being 'vir'..."

McConait finished the language lesson, "And the Latin for wolf is Lupus."

Price turned from the board to congratulate McConait's Latin knowledge, but McConait was staring at the floor in a distant trance, "Systemic Lupus, my mother had it. She was fine until she had me; childbirth triggered the Lupus. The immune system attacks the healthy body. She got arthritis, debilitating when she was in a 'flare', that's what they call it when the illness, is at its strongest; alive, angry. The doctors controlled it with medication. Every now and then she'd have a flare and be laid up. Dad would have to dress her, bath her, but then they'd alter her medication, she'd get better. Anyway, when I was 19 she fell pregnant again. She had to come off all the medication. The lupus began attacking her organs, the doctors wanted her to get rid of the baby, but she wouldn't, they told her to go back on the medication, but she wouldn't. She wouldn't do anything to harm her baby; it was against her precious beliefs, her own life was at odds with Catholic doctrine. Anyway, one day I was called out of a lecture, I'd just started Cambridge... and they told me."

McConait sat looking at the board depicting the various forms of conditions that could be interpreted as 'werewolf' in nature, what a sick and twisted irony that his own mother had fallen victim to an illness that bore the name of 'lupus', the name of 'wolf'.

"I'm sorry to hear it Doctor. I've heard of the illness myself; it can be very hard on people." The priest sat down and leaned towards McConait ready to council. "You blame yourself."

159

McConait's eyes moistened,"It was childbirth, it was the strain of having me, I ruined her life. She told me enough times, when she was really down."

"Then it's clear to me that it's her that's ruined yours. Doctor, you are desperately seeking forgiveness for what you think you did to your mother. Forgiveness is a two way street and sometimes it is better to give than receive. You need to find it in your heart to forgive her."

"Oh, spare me the 'Oedipus Complex', I hope you're not charging for this session. Look, I'm fine with my mother; it's all in the past." McConait tried desperately not to sound too defensive… and failed.

"You are fine with your mother you say, but you reject everything about her. Was she a devout woman?"

"Like Mother Teresa on speed."

"Well you've turned your back on your faith, her faith, you cut ties with your home town, her home town, the Geordie accent gone, you've physically cut her out of your life. Doctor you'll have to let her back in, so you can forgive her, and move on."

Father Price slapped the dry wipe marker back in McConait's hand, "Look let's not give up, look how close the police were last time, seconds away, this time Peel will have Tynemouth under lock and key. This killer is psychologically damaged, medically unusual, he's thriving on the atmosphere that Tuthie, the Druids and the Media have conjured up, but he can't hide forever. These traits on the board, don't make someone anonymous, on the contrary, now we know what to look for he'll stand out like a sore thumb. Time to go to work Doctor."

"I'd better work fast, it's full moon, tonight." The two men froze at the thought, it wasn't a matter of if, or even a matter of when, it was a matter of where and worst of all who.

"Look Doctor, I've got to go, Tuthie's got another prayer vigil planned and I'm worried what effect it might have; he's been getting stranger and stranger." With that Price tapped McConait on the shoulder, "God Bless." and left the hut.

160

McConait took the lid from the marker, and with Price's words spinning round his head he stood up and walked to the whiteboard. Above the word

WEREWOLF

He wrote:

LUPUS VIR

Wolf man.

He turned to the computer in the corner of his room. Price had given him a whistle stop tour but McConait wanted more detail. He looked at the desktop and did the most obvious thing; he opened up Windows Explorer, opened the Google homepage and typed in:

ERGOT

There was a host of entries, but the first site said it all, as Price had outlined; the history of villages in Europe affected by ergot poisoning, exorcisms performed by Catholic priests, the links to LSD, links to Hippy websites that hailed Ergot as a sacred chemical. McConait moved on:

LYCANTHROPY

These websites were less helpful, they were full of horror genre analysis, films, conventions and the occult. McConait moved on:

PORPHYRIA

The search results here were more medical, one talked about the Madness of King George III, 'The Royal Disease' even the monarchy implicated.

HYPERTRICHOSIS

McConait looked down the list of entries; the third one down caught his eye.

HYPERTRICHOSIS Dog Boy. A Mexican family ...

The word Mexican was enough, McConait clicked.

Dog Boy is the oldest son in a Mexican family who all suffer from an unusual condition called Hypertrichosis. In Guada Lupe the Da Silva family are local celebrities. Dog Boy (Luis Da Silva) has appeared on local advertisements for hair products, and even opened shopping centres. The family have given up years of shame and shaving to celebrate their excessive hairiness. The full body hair is caused by an 'Atavistic' gene, which is a throw back

161

to our hairy ancestors. Click here to find out more 'Hair raising' facts about other hirsute families.

Subsequent links revealed other families with the same condition all from Mexico. McConait looked back at the diagram drawn by Price, one left, he typed in:

THERIANTHROPY

A host of sites appeared. McConait was going through what Price had told him and his eyes soon fixed on what he was looking for.

Spiritual Therianthropy, Shamanism and Native American Indians. Mescaline, Ergine ...

McConait clicked on:

The Shamans of Native American tribes would use a number of substances to make a spiritual link to the wolf. In Mexico the leaves of the Mescaline plant, famed for its hallucinogenic properties, world be ingested, by the shaman. Wearing the skin of a wolf, or using the teeth or claws, he would go into a trance like state. It is said that in the trance, his spirit would become that of the wolf, and he would see and feel himself running, and killing with the pack.

Yet again the trail turned in a familiar direction. The word Mexico had once more put the focus back on the main suspect; Rufus Infareño. And McConait was now cogitating on how the virus may have been spread and why Infareño never feared the blood test.

McConait looked at the whiteboards, now all full. Three differing profiles, coming from different points of view all led to the same conclusion. He snatched up the telephone. "Hello Peel, it's McConait. Are you still in contact with the Infareño family?"

"Well yes, the whole illegal immigrant case, but we've kind of closed down that avenue as far as the murders are concerned."

"Well open it again, I need to know if Infareño suffered from Hypertrichosis."

"Hyper what?" Peel, who had been jotting down notes, stopped at what was going to be a particularly tricky spelling.

"Hypertrichosis, it's a condition that causes excessive body hair. It's very rare, but there have been a few in Mexico. Also find out if he has anything to do with tribal shamans in Mexico."

162

"And where is this leading us Doc?"

"I could tell you but you wouldn't believe me, I'll leave that to Father Price. Can you get the information?"

"I'm interviewing the mother Tomorrow, as it happens, I'll see what I can get."

"No Tomorrow's too late, it's full moon tonight, look I know we've been down this road before but, I've got a new profile, and it's still pointing to Infareño. It can explain why he would do it. It could even be backed up by eyewitness evidence, the policeman in the garden."

"That's exactly what I want to hear, but I'll need more than that, can you explain what you've got?"

McConait took a deep breath and looked round at his white boards. "Well if we start at the beginning, he fits the profile of a strong single man, influenced by the occult, thus the pentacle tattoo, he lives yards away from the Tynemouth killings, he has no alibi for the murders. He could have done it."

McConait now turned his attention to the second board, "He has contacts in London and could easily have been there for the London killings. He has access to, and may be under the influence of, various narcotics, which may trigger hallucinogenic if not psychotic episodes. He could have done it.

Now turning to the third board, he knew that this information was conjecture, "If he, as do other Mexicans, suffers from excessive body hair, he could have been the figure the policeman saw, over the boy in the garden. If he is influenced by Mexican Indian tribal culture he may be using drugs to create the feeling of spiritual bonding with a wolf; he may even be using parts of the wolf's body to disguise himself as a wolf. If he suffered from Lycanthropy, a madness which makes sufferers think they are a werewolf, he would be under the influence of the moon, he would act like a wolf and as a result could and would kill tonight."

"A lot of ifs Doc, but any evidence at all, and I'm nailing this guy once and for all. And I won't risk not acting on it. We'll lift him, we'll find a reason, and if he's banged up and the killings continue then at least he's got an alibi and we know we've got the wrong man, if not, then it points even more strongly to our man.

163

I'll go and see the Infareño family right away. Keep your phone handy and I'll let you know what they say."

"Thank's Detective, third time lucky." McConait hung up the phone: the profile, like his mind, had been expanded by Liam Price, he needed the conversation to continue with him, there were still a lot of questions that he thought only a man like Price could answer. He decided to walk round to the presbytery to see if he was there.

Chapter 26
Price Controls Tuthie

The Priory stood alone and still against a brooding sky. The sea mist, which lay like a blanket over King Edward's Bay, wisped around its ancient stones, and in and out of its Gothic arches. Sometimes there, sometimes not, behind a grey cloak, the setting sun dissolving its sandstone into a deepening silhouette. An ancient centre of prayer, learning and government. The resting place of two kings of Northumbria and one king of Scotland; situated dramatically on the cliff, it existed between land and sea, between the physical and the spiritual, the present and the past, the living and the dead and perhaps, heaven and hell.

Where monks and kings had once entered, now only the police could access. Armed officers stood in defence of a once great castle. Its spiritual power still a threat 500 years after the reformation, which stripped it of its monks, and its riches, its status as a centre of political power and even as consecrated ground.

What Henry VIII had started the police of the 21st Century continued; there would be no acts of worship on the grounds of Tynemouth Priory tonight.

       *   *   *   *   *

The door of the surf shop was kicked open by a size 10 boot. Armed police flooded the shop from the rear door. The front of the shop was in darkness, the roller shutters pulled down, it had closed early; no one was out shopping in Tynemouth today. Torches crossed beams as police officers scanned the premises, curtains of empty changing rooms were thrown open, heavy feet thundered upstairs but only to find racks of gleaming polished surf boards. Rufus Infareño was not there.

165

At 35a Percy Park, two-man teams took each of the five flights of stairs up to the loft apartment. No answer came from the flat. Simultaneously police climbed the fire escape, trying to keep heavy boots from making a noise on the painted iron. As one they barged open the doors, front and back. From the fire escape two men took the kitchen, "Clear!"

Another man took a small room straight ahead of the entrance, "Clear".

From the main entrance police flew in to meet another set of stairs, which took them to an upper level which held the bedroom, "Clear!" a small bathroom "Clear!" Now there was just the lounge. Inside was a black leather sofa, a flat screen TV, a shelf which contained a number of surfing videos and on one wall a large painted canvas depicting an ocean scene of Acapulco; opposite the painting a dormer window offered spectacular views over Tynemouth, the sea to the east, and the top of the Priory to the south. Rufus Infareño was not there.

A Tyneside wide search flew into action. Road blocks were set around all the exits from Tynemouth. Pubs, restaurants, shops, banks, everything was checked. Photocopied pictures of Infareño were slapped on any available surface: Shop windows; lamp posts; sign posts; all giving instructions to "Steer clear of this man!" the police number printed in bold on the bottom of each poster.

Work mates and friends of Infareño were interrogated; no one had seen him for three days. He'd gone underground; no trace, no forwarding number. He didn't want to be found.

*   *   *   *   *

St.Oswin's Church had, many years ago taken over the Priory's right to say Mass, and stood only 20 yards from the Priory entrance at the end of Front Street. Father Tuthie still held the belief that the Priory was hallowed ground; consecrated by the Holy Catholic Church, and Kings, Councillors or Police could do nothing to change that fact. Father Liam Price turned to enter St.Oswin's just as Tuthie was locking the church door.

166

"Father, where are you going? I thought there was another prayer vigil."

"There is Father Price but not here." Out of his pocket he pulled a purple stole, the scarf like garment that priests must wear to say mass. He lifted it in both hands carefully, and kissed a small embroidered cross in the middle of it before placing it over his head and round his neck. "Join me Father Price, on sacred ground. You did well clearing the Priory of the heathen mob, and the pagans, now let's finish this, let's reclaim it for the true Faith, let's give Tynemouth back its soul, before it's too late."

Price was taken aback but wanted Tuthie's explanation, before he made a judgement. "Too late for what?"

"Before there's another killing. Evil is stirring, the devil walks among us tonight, only the power of God can protect us, and only the Lamb will overcome the wolf."

"But Father the police won't let…" Price's words were in vain, Tuthie was already off towards the Priory where a small congregation of devout followers, were gathering to the dismay of the two armed police officers at the entrance of the Priory.

"Tuthie strode over the path which crossed what was once the moat, and curved round the wall to the entrance, his followers snaked behind him. He walked up to the uniformed policemen expecting them to part like the Red Sea. Tuthie's faith however was not borne out. The more senior of the two policemen, Sergeant Sindas, put a hand on Tuthie's shoulder.

"Sorry Father, no entry. It's not safe tonight."

"I know officer," Tuthie replied sincerely, "That's why I'm here, only if we turn to God will we be saved."

"Sorry Father, but I can't make any exceptions, so you'd do well to get off home."

The small congregation gathered; they didn't look like they'd be any trouble but it would still be an awkward situation for the police if they didn't back down.

Tuthie put his hand in his inside pocket, had it been anyone else the police may have suspected a weapon and wrestled him to the ground, as it was, he revealed a crucifix, just like the one he had given to McConait.

167

"This is consecrated ground; a place of worship, now let me past!"

The two policemen looked at each other, they had been briefed at length on the importance of tonight's operation, the whole force was on a high state of alert, and adrenaline was racing through every officer. Grabbing an arm each, they dragged Father Tuthie backwards, his heels scuffing the ground trying to hold on.

Two middle aged respectable men, members of the St. Vincent De Paul society, who helped out in church tackled the policemen. In the grapple one of the officers let go of one of Tuthie's arms. It was enough for the old priest to squirm free and land in a heap on the floor. The police were surprised to find themselves grabbed by six parishioners. They brushed them aside and withdrew but only far enough to take out their nightsticks. Only one parishioner was still up for the fight and dashed forward. An efficient blow was dealt to the side of the head and the parishioner fell to the ground. Clouds of breath emanated like steam from the panting gathering. They paused looking at a bleeding man on the ground, and considered how far things had gone. Tuthie was on his feet again, shuffling as fast as his frail legs could go; towards the entrance. Sergeant Sindas was there in a couple of strides. "Right that's enough fun and games, now get out of here before someone else gets hurt!"

Tuthie tried again, his small elderly frame looking pathetic against the policeman who could have struck him down with a flick of his hand, or put him under his arm like a naughty child, but out of respect he allowed the weak old priest to flail helplessly against his broad chest.

"Agnus dei qui tolis pecata mundi miserere nobis!"

Calling on divine help Tuthie gave one more push, but the human wall would not submit. Tuthie turned round, desperation in his eyes and ran past the entrance; he began trying to scramble up a grassy bank to gain access to the Priory. A fit young man could do it, however, the aged Tuthie was a sad spectacle as he clawed at the earth on all fours, gaining a couple of feet and then sliding down. His knees grass stained and muddy, the old man raised his hands to heaven, and quoted Jesus' dying words, "Eli,

168

Eli sabachthani?" (My God, my God, why have you deserted me?). Father Tuthie wept.

The policemen went to grab him again, this time they were going to arrest him. A figure, which had been watching events from a distance, rushed round at the sight of the affray, he wrapped an arm around the old man's shoulders and held out the other to halt the policemen's progress. It was Father Price, who carried more influence than Tuthie. "Please we're all rather excited, and understandably nervy. I'm sorry you've been bothered officers, please let me take Father Tuthie home." Again Price's calming influence prevailed. He helped Tuthie to his feet and began escorting him and his flock away from the Priory. After a few yards Tuthie pulled away and addressed the two policemen, his eyes burned into them, "Forgive them Father, they know not what they do!" Finally accepting defeat he turned again and continued back towards Front Street.

Back at the presbytery Tuthie's housekeeper attended the man who had been struck by the policeman. Father Tuthie spoke to his followers, "I'll get changed out of these muddy clothes then I'll open up the church again." The gathered ensemble of Tuthie enthusiasts consoled each other as they shuffled back out the door. Tuthie left the kitchen where they were gathered but didn't head directly upstairs; he went into his living room and poured himself a large Scotch.

Price followed him. "Surely you're not carrying on with this madness Father?"

"So there's something wrong with prayer now, is there?" Tuthie had regained his fiery spirit.

"Not at all, but I think these people would be better off praying in the safety of their own homes."

"Divide and conquer, is that not the devil's way? Was that not what the serpent did to Adam and Eve? You saw how few turned out tonight compared to last time. The devil is already weakening the conviction of our parish. We must stand firm against the forces of evil!" Tuthie swigged down the whisky and promptly poured himself another.

Price adopted his most official tone, "Father Tuthie, you know why I am here. Your eccentric behaviour is showing this

169

Parish and the Catholic Church in a bad light, tonight's exhibition was the last straw, it ended in violence, something that cannot be tolerated. The declining numbers are nothing to do with the devil, it's you and your bizarre activities that are turning people away. The press will have a field day when they hear about tonight's transgressions and the Diocese of Hexham and Newcastle can ill afford this sort of publicity. The Bishop has made it clear that this problem must be addressed. I have been instructed to inform you, that under the circumstances, you shall be taking a sabbatical, effective right away. I shall take over the saying of Masses and the general running of this Parish forthwith. And I'll begin by cancelling tonight's vigil." The normally calm and affable Irishman was now cold and impassionate, fulfilling a role he did not enjoy, but one he knew must be carried out.

Tuthie was wounded and incensed by Price's accusations, "Oh for God's sake, is the church to turn on me now? Price are you a man of science or a man of the cloth? A priest is what we need now, not a 'head shrinker' and certainly not a politician. These are the roles you've been playing, and my Lord have you been distracted, distracted by what should be at the forefront of your mind."

"And what would that be?" Price was ready for the backlash.

"The battle against evil, the evil that is pervading this place, an ancient, timeless evil, and you are getting in the way of what must be done, you are complicit in the devil's work. The Bishop has sent you on a damage limitation exercise, saving face is all he's worried about, but there's much more to be saved. Look at what's happened. People slaughtered, an area crippled by fear, a town under police control and now people turned away from the church by...you. The police and the scientists have done their best and where has it gotten us, the full moon is upon us and all we can do is lock our doors and hope it's not our turn to be victim to the beast. It's time to face the truth!"

Tuthie was again driving himself too far, his blood pressure going through the roof; he slumped back into an armchair and clutched his chest.

170

Price lowered his tone but was not prepared to walk away: he sat down to make his body language less threatening, "Father I have spent my whole life searching for the truth. You may be threatened by my scientific methods but I would use any method to reveal the truth that is Jesus Christ, it's the 21st Century and the best methods are those of science, the truth of science. If we could scientifically prove the divinity of Christ what joy would fill the earth, every man woman and child on the planet would share in what we already know. We are lucky, you and I, we don't need to be shown, Christ has revealed himself to us, but our job is to share that revelation, with the world."

Price's argument as always was convincing, but to Tuthie was seriously flawed. He shuffled his body round to face Price and propped himself up on one elbow. "The truth of science you say. It is only one scientist's version of the truth against another."

"And what's that supposed to mean exactly?" It appeared that the old priest was just going to be obstinate for the sake of it; Price was wishing he had just left after he had lain the law down to Tuthie. But the old man had an argument of his own to put forward to the eminent Father Price.

"One scientist comes up with a theory, his theory, a theory that will establish him, forward his career, even make him famous. Well he has to prove that theory to be accepted."

"Absolutely that's exactly my point..." but Tuthie was not going to let Price dictate the conversation.

"So he sets about proving it. He does experiments, but..." he paused dramatically, like he did to such effect at the lectern in church, " ...only experiments that will prove him right, he closes his mind to what may prove him wrong, he does not seek the whole truth. And when he's proved his theory correct, and has reams of data, and publishes his work, then he is applauded by the scientific community. But only until another scientist comes along who seeks his own fame and fortune and he comes up with a theory, which rejects the first and goes about proving it with experiments. When he then proves his theory correct then he is hailed as the new voice of truth and the first scientist is discredited. And this game of supremacy of truth goes on. And yes you are right Doctor Price," Tuthie deliberately dropping the

Father, "this is the method of the modern age, and every government dances to this tune, and wars are waged, and famines still ravage the earth and diseases still spread, and the great theories of science have brought us closer to absolute destruction than ever before."

Price appreciated the validity in the argument, but he had a come back, "You are right that every scientists brings his own interests to a theory, he invests himself, immerses himself but what's wrong in that? That's dedication, and it's no different in religion."

Tuthie squirmed in indignation at the suggestion, Price continued, "Every man who reads the Gospels finds what he's looking for. To one man the resurrection is the proof of God's divinity, to another proof that the Gospels are pure fiction, so it all comes down to your definition of what is truth, that's why evidence can settle it once and for all."

Tuthie's expression changed as if a voice was calling him, the anger and upset had gone, his face conveyed sadness, sincerity and resignation. He put down his whisky glass, turned to Price and placed a hand on his. "I have to tell you something Price and this is something that I know, not a matter of faith, or belief, it's what I know to be true. What if I told you that I knew who killed the boy, who killed Rose Stearman, killed the other man? I know, I know!"

"Well Father, tell the police." Price tired of flattering an old man's foolishness, stood up to leave.

Tuthie was not yet done, "It's evil, it's a monster only it's also a man, he changes, he changes into a wolf, he's changing now, I can't stop him, the police can't stop him, the law is impotent…"

At this Price headed for the door "Goodnight Father Tuthie!"

Tuthie rallied himself one more time "He doesn't want to kill, he can't help it, he seeks forgiveness he wants reconciliation with God, we must pray for his soul before the devil takes possession once again."

Price stopped at the door and turned round, Tuthie hoped he had made an impression. "Father Tuthie I'll be saying the 8

172

o'clock Mass, it would be prudent for you not to attend, I'll arrange for a car to take you down to the Cathedral, where you can attend Mass…and of course the Bishop may want a word."

Tuthie realised that his plea had fallen on deaf ears, and like a scolded schoolboy his head dropped and his arms fell limp at his side.

Price, picking up a large set of church keys from a table, turned and headed out. The moon appeared over the Priory.

*   *   *   *   *

McConait arrived at the Presbytery ten minutes after Price's departure. The housekeeper had also left, so it was father Tuthie who opened the door. The old priest, bleary eyed from exhaustion and whisky, looked a sight in his mud and grass stained clothes.

"My God! Father are you alright?"

Tuthie said nothing, but turned and walked back down the hall leaving the door open, caring not whether McConait followed. McConait entered and closed the door behind him. He followed Tuthie to his living room and found him slumped in an armchair rocking back and forwards, his knuckles white as they clenched around a crucifix.

"I came to see Father Price, has he been here?"

"Oh he's been here alright, but now he's off into the night to carry on disassembling any traces of genuine faith that may still be clinging on." With that he gripped the crucifix even tighter as if trying to squeeze divine grace from the wood and metal. "The crusaders carried a piece of the true cross into battle, against the Saracen Armies. Even when the odds were against them they achieved amazing victories. Joan of Arc inspired French soldiers to triumph over the English by the power of prayer. Faith has inspired mankind to victory in the face of adversity. With that kind of faith we could save this town we could help these people, but that faith is systematically being pulled apart by the church that is supposed to uphold it. The devil has infiltrated it, corrupted it, I fear it's too late now."

173

McConait knelt by the old man's side; he looked desperate, and although McConait knew he didn't have time, he felt compelled to stay a while longer. "Look Father, you may not agree with Price's methods but they are not strictly at odds with yours, his methods come to the conclusion, that a man at the time of the full moon, changes and commits these horrendous murders, he may even have a condition which would make him appear as a beast, some kind of wolf perhaps, what's more Father, his work has helped me and the police confirm who the killer is. The police have probably arrested him already."

There was a change in Tuthie's expression, as if the weight of the world had been lifted from his shoulders. His eyes returned to life, maybe he'd been wrong about Price after all, maybe Price had been guided by the Holy Spirit to come to the correct conclusion, "So they know who it is? They're picking him up; I hope it's not too late." Tuthie paused; he curbed his enthusiasm, "Who do they say it is?"

"Rufus Infareño, a Mexican who lives on Percy Park."

The colour once again drained from Tuthie's face. "No…no…that's the wrong man, it's not him."

"Do you know Infareño?" asked a confused McConait.

"Yes, of course, the big Mexican lad, I have seen him at Mass a few times and I know it's not him!" Tuthie seemed possessed and agitated.

"How do you know?"

Tuthie paused as if it pained him to divulge the information, "The killer told me, he confessed, he told me in the confessional."

The very word confession made McConait's skin crawl. His mind flowed back to his childhood, the terror of making his first Confession, all the preparation, learning the prayers and rituals reflecting on his sins, he couldn't imagine what sins a six year old was capable of committing, but he remembered the guilt. He remembered that the act of confession, the final prayer of the ceremony, ended with '…and by the power of your grace I shall not sin again." He left to do his penance, a decade of the Rosary, 10 Hail Marys, and genuinely felt cleansed; it was probably relief. The next day at school he got in a fight. The fight with a fellow

174

six year old had not left any physical damage but he knew he had sinned again, and broken his promise he had made to God in front of the Priest. He cried all night. Finally his mother got out of him what had happened. She knew exactly how to solve the problem, another trip to Confession, and the cycle of guilt, confession, cleansing and more guilt continued for the next 10 years.

"So that's why you haven't gone to the police, because of your promise as a priest not to divulge what is shared in confession. Father, if you could have stopped this, and you haven't, then surely that is the greater sin, never mind bloody doctrine, what about the victims, and their families, it's not the dark ages you simply must…"

Two softly spoken words from Tuthie interrupted McConait's rant, "I did."

"You did…you did… what?" McConait's voice was still raised, but Tuthie was not able to answer. He clutched his chest in wincing pain. And pointed an arthritic finger to the corner of the room, McConait spun round wondering what it could be: a statue of Mary; a set of Rosary Beads; a framed picture of the old Pope; a vase of flowers on a table; the telephone? He turned again to see Tuthie gasping for breath still pointing, again he turned, this time taking two steps in the direction indicated by the finger, he went to the table and began shuffling things around, then he saw it, a brown bottle of tablets; now he realised. He turned again wrestling the lid from the bottle, and pouring some pills onto his open hand, which he shoved under Tuthie's nose. Tuthie put out his tongue, and McConait placed a white angina tablet on it. He picked up a glass beside Tuthie, held it to his mouth and the old man gulped down a mouthful of whisky to wash the tablet down.

In the same way Tuthie had given the bread of life in Communion so many times, he now received a lifesaving tablet from McConait, the symbolism was not lost on either of them. Tuthie did not speak but his eyes said thank you. At that moment the door opened, it was the housekeeper. She raced into the room, "What with everything that's been going on I forgot to make sure you had your medication father." He nodded and

175

slumped into his chair. She looked at McConait, who expected a flood of thanks for administering his angina pills; instead she had a suspicious glare. "I'll see you out Sylvester." she had known his mother, and had no doubt bounced McConait on her knee as a boy. At the door she stopped him, "Look Sylvester, I don't know what you wanted but that old man has had a hell of a night. Since this whole malarkey started he has worked tirelessly, prayer vigils, Masses, consoling families, not to mention funerals. He's not up to it; he should be retired. The Bishop said he would send help but what did he get? Father Price, who has humiliated him in front of his own parish, a good man shouldn't be treated in this way, so why don't you just leave him alone?" The door was slammed before McConait could answer; the housekeeper had burst into tears, and went to care for old Father Tuthie.

McConait stood for a while, not knowing what to do, he looked up at the foreboding full moon, and Tuthie's words went through his mind. "I did."

He began walking back to the hut and decided to go round the sea front past the Priory. Talking to himself he said, "I did... what? What did Tuthie do?" McConait paused and turned back towards the presbytery, considering whether it was worth, going back to tackle the housekeeper, and get Tuthie to explain, but a voice made him jump.

"Sorry sir, but you'll have to get along home now. It's really not safe." It was the two policemen who had the run in with Tuthie and his parishioners.

"Oh of course officer I'm off right away." Again the strange feeling was upon him, the world began spinning: the moon; the stones of the Priory; seagulls screeching; his hand against Maria's beautiful face; his mother ill in bed; Father Tuthie's open mouth; the hand gripping the crucifix; Latin words rang in his ears, which faded into the two words of English which had begun to haunt him, 'I did.'

"Are you alright sir?" asked Sergeant Sindas, but McConait took to his heels, mumbling, "I'd best be off, it's not safe." The two policemen looked at each other, now they had met both the men who were helping the police solve the case, on both occasions they had not been impressed.

McConait decided it best to go back to the Grand Hotel. He went to the bar, ordered a steak sandwich and a bottle of red wine, sat down and popped some pills; even more than usual. He ate his supper, and wished the meat had been rare like he'd ordered. He picked up his half finished bottle and retired to his room.

McConait kicked off his shoes, and took off his corduroy jacket. He was about to hang it up when he paused, he slid his hand into the inside pocket and removed Andrea's card and the crucifix. He looked at the circle of letters in the halo like ring around Christ's head. His thoughts were back to Tuthie and what he had said. McConait shook his head at the effects of aging on the body and the mind.

He placed the cross on the bedside table, and poured himself another glass of wine. He felt that tonight, he would sleep peacefully, safe in the knowledge they had the right man, but his complacency didn't last long. The phone rang, it was Peel. "Hello Doc I thought I'd keep you informed. I'm back from London; I've got some good news and some bad news.

"Go on."

"Your profile worked out. Infareño was adopted when he was five. His real parents were, as you suspected, Mexican Indians, from some ancient Aztec tribe or other, but what's more amazing is the Hyper… Hyper…"

McConait finished the word for him, "Hypertrichosis."

"Yeah the body hair thing, he has it. His real parent's had it, got really picked on in school apparently, so he took up body building and surfing, you've seen his build."

"Brilliant!" McConait was jubilant.

Peel continued, "Apparently he's had electrolysis for years to get rid of it, around the eyes and nose, where it's difficult to shave I suppose."

McConait pictured the surfer, "What about his body? On the photo he was hairless."

"Totally, not a one, that's because he gets waxed, a place on Front Street has him booked in the same time every month. So with all that and a few Bic razors…"

177

"This is a real breakthrough; looks like the folks of Tynemouth are safe tonight."

"Well that's the bad news. We can't find him."

"What? Why not?"

"Oh the lads up here are turning every stone. The people of Tynemouth might be safe but only because I think he's buggered off somewhere else. We're putting his picture out nationally, checking bus stations, trains, planes, all that. He could be back in Mexico by now."

"All the same, we get Infareño we stop the killings."

Chapter 27
The 4ᵗʰ Incident

Detective Peel walked the Streets of Tynemouth, going from place to place checking that all the officers were at their post. The briefing he had given for tonight's operation had been meticulous; everything would be done as to Peel's instructions. A rotation of armed officers would go on through the night. Each pair of officers was given a strict beat to cover, systematically checking areas that may provide cover for a killer; radioing in to the station every half hour. Anything suspicious was reported, any sighting of anyone out that night was called in. A hotline for the public was set up; the whole of Tynemouth held its breath and stayed vigilant.

Peel walked the streets, his leather souls cracking on the pavement, the only sound in a silent town. Tonight was going to be the crowning moment of a distinguished career. As he walked he reflected on the journey that had brought him to this moment. He'd worked up the ranks of the force quickly. He was the keenest officer in training, and awarded top recruit at the academy. He'd studied law at London University before joining the police; his only purpose in life was to fight for justice, to clean the streets of his beloved England. Those days were well behind him; the impotence of the police had frustrated him, snowed under by paper work and targets; speeding fines and traffic crime made him despair. It was the innocent people, just driving to work, the law abiding tax payer, who seemed to be the target these days, while the yob culture grew, wearing 'asbos' like medals; stealing, vandalising, mugging and protected by the laws Peel fought so hard to uphold. In his mind it was all back to front, the general public lived in fear of the teenage louts. Then there were the drug addicts and illegal immigrants, to Peel just an unending stream of filth; all the usual policing methods were coming to nothing, the law seemed to get in the way of justice. Peel sought other routes.

Infareño was a foreigner who peddled filthy drugs, he was now the lead suspect in the worst crime spree on Tyneside, if he had the chance, Peel would not let this go to trial; Infareño had

179

evaded conviction twice before. The Detective put his hand inside his jacket to feel his police pistol, tonight this was his instrument of justice, and he hoped he got a chance to use it. How the top recruit at the academy would have been disgusted at his present abuse of the law and cock-eyed view of justice. How a good man could change.

His police radio crackled into action, "Sarge, we've got something; we're at the zebra crossing at the bottom of Percy Park."

The pace of his shoe leather was already quickening. "I'm almost there. What is it?"

"We got a report of someone in a cave on the beach. A surfer spotted a fire and a figure moving around."

"OK all units stand by, block all the exits." Peel was there in two minutes flat. Already beams of torchlight flashed across the beach. "Did they get a look at him?"

"Not really, they said he's a big bugger, and scruffy looking, that's all."

Stand ready here. Man all the exits until I say otherwise, there's nowhere else for him to go except the sea."

Adrenaline pumping, Peel drew his weapon and headed towards the beach, "Do you want support Sarge?"

"No thanks. I'll keep radio contact." Peel wanted to find Infareño alone, with no one else around, he could dispense his justice and plead self defence. The tide was out and the wide expanse of Longsands stretched before him. His eyes adjusted to the dark and he found that the full moon afforded him good light and was casting long moon-light shadows across silvery sand. All his senses were working at maximum: the sand compacting under his feet; the sound of distant voices; the barking of police dogs; the smell and taste of salty sea air; shadows and torch beams dancing across the beach.

Something moved quickly at the extremes of his peripheral vision. He stopped and his eyes darted to where it came from. In the dunes was a figure, crouching, then leaping back into the shadows. Peel thrust his gun towards the darkness. "Right you piece of shit, the game's up. Come out with your hands on your

180

head." There was no response. "Come out with your hands on your head...Right I'm warning you I will shoot!"

Years of pent up angst were swelling like a great bubble to the surface. This time justice would be done; Peel would be judge, jury and executioner. He stepped forward into the shadowy sand dunes. Peel could hear breathing, the moment was upon him. He wasn't going to ask questions, he was going to let him have it; one more step. A piece of driftwood snapped under his foot, the split second distraction was all it took.

The creature flew out from the darkness, not from the front where Peel expected, but to the right and above, from the top of the dune. Its weight felled Peel. A shot rang out as he hit the sand, not touching the attacker but disappearing into the blackness. Peel tried to get up, his free hand trying to push, but disappearing into cold sand. A claw pressed into the back of his neck driving his face down, he gasped for breath but inhaled only sand. As the weight of the creature crushed his lungs the last breath of air was squeezed out, he felt the end was near. Suddenly he felt the weight of the creature lift away, he flipped over and coughed out a mouthful of sand, he drew a desperate breath, and as his sand filled eyes blinked open, he saw the full height of the beast loom up above him, demonic eyes burned into him, teeth snarled and snapped then fell upon his throat, ripping it out, exposing vertebrae. A great claw ripped at the policeman's chest, in a frenzy of violent savagery, the rib cage was writhed open and Peel's heart was uncovered, its final beat exposed to the moonlight.

From the Cullercoats end of the beach, police came rushing across the sand at the sound of the gunshot. But they didn't get very far, something darted from the darkness across the sand, dogs were unleashed and flew at the figure, snapping at his legs, the police were closing in. "Stop or we'll shoot!" The figure kept running, "Stop or we'll shoot!" The figure turned to look at the approaching army of policemen, terrified human eyes glared from a face covered in hair, a strong hirsute hand beat down onto the nose of a snarling Alsatian; the dog squealed in pain. With the sea at his back he looked at the tightening noose of men. With all his strength he drove his feet into the wet sand to

181

sprint in an arcing movement to the biggest gap in the circle of police.

An armed policeman took aim, hardly believing the sight that charged towards him, and fired.

The figure didn't fall but spun round with the force of the bullet, with no sense of direction, just the instinct to run, he zigzagged towards the sea. As he reached the icy cold water he slowed and splodged forward into the waves. The waves that had been his passion throughout his life, waves he had followed around the world. A final shot rang out that night and Rufus Infareño's lifeless body fell into the sea.

As the policeman hauled the dead body from the sea, Infareño's shirt pulled away to reveal a hulking body completely covered in hair.

Chapter 28
Infareño's Cave

A few minutes earlier Rufus Infareño sat in the dark, huddled up in a sleeping bag. It was cold and he was forced to light a fire; even though the light might give him away. He had been weeks in the cave and he was now unrecognisable. A covering of body hair gave him the look of a wild animal; some protection against the cold at least.

There were several caves at the Cullercoats end of Longsands beach. They were home to bats and sea birds, and the occasional glue sniffer. Infareño only ventured out in the dead of night, in his hirsute condition he would be easily spotted during the day.

He looked out the entrance to the cave and saw surfers riding the waves on a grey North East day. Infareño should have been with them. His life had been turned upside down. His life as a boy had been painful because of his condition; he'd grown to be resilient and independent. He needed those qualities now more than ever. He decided to sit it out and wait for the right moment.

A shuffling noise came from outside and a large shopping bag on the end of a rope was lowered down to the cave. Infareño rushed forward and untied the bag. It was full of food, provided by an unknown ally; an ally that wanted to help Infareño continue his hermitic existence of solitude and sacrifice.

Later as night fell, the surfers left the beach, and Infareño's only connection to his former life was gone. The full moon rose over the sea, and Infareño's senses tingled. He heard distant voices, and the barking of police dogs, lights flashed on the beach, then the crack of gunshot split the night. In terror Infareño dashed from the cave.

183

Chapter 29
Crime Solved

The naked body of Infareño lay out on the slab in the mortuary, covered in course black hair from head to foot, apart from a T-shaped area around the eyes and nose, which added even more to the strange spectacle. Images of the dead body were already on the Internet, and one had made it onto a couple of tabloid front pages. A cleaner at the mortuary, lost his job over the pictures, but had made thousands selling them on.

Andrea Swan and McConait looked down at the corpse of Rufus Infareño. Since disappearing he had been hiding out in a cave in Cullercoats at the end of Longsands. Police found a sleeping bag and a campfire, a bag of clothes, a surfboard, a wetsuit and a pile of family photos. Hanging down outside the cave entrance was a coarse piece of rope, attached to a lamppost up on the road above. It had been used to lower provisions down to the hidden Infareño. He'd had an accomplice but the police weren't going to go overboard in finding him now that they had the killer dead on a slab.

All that was left to tie up was the inquest where all the details could be laid out and the case finally closed. There was also the funeral of Detective Sergeant Peel. A huge procession was being prepared to take the body to St. Mary's Cathedral, where a service would be held before the body was taken back to London. The national press and TV networks were getting in on the action. Any misconduct of the once squeaky clean policeman (turned corrupt vigilante) was forgotten, the media focused on the bravery of a Cockney copper who died in the line of duty; defending the public of Tyneside against a vicious killer.

"Well Father Tuthie won't be able to argue with this," said McConait, still amazed at the sight before him. "He actually reckoned it wasn't Infareño."

"Oh I know, he had it down to poor Bob Stearman, the first victim's husband."

McConait was stunned. "How do you know that?

"He came and told the police right at the beginning of the investigation."

184

"What made him think it was Bob Stearman?"

"To be fair we all did at first. Apparently the poor bloke confessed to him, he thought he'd done it himself, you see. The thing is he was plastered the night of the killing, and couldn't account for where he'd been."

McConait put his psychologist's hat on; "The guilt of leaving his wife, to go and get drunk, and then her ending up dead must have got to him. I suppose he felt he should be punished. Why didn't you mention this before?"

"Well he was out of the area for all the other killings. He didn't fit any of the profiles anyway. It just wasn't him. Well that's what Peel reckoned. He had a bee in his bonnet about Infareño, he never really liked foreigners, and he turned out to be right."

Now Tuthie's words made sense, "I did." He did go to the police. Tuthie's shame was that he had broken his vow of confidentiality; the Catholic belief that anything shared in Confession could not be repeated.

"Poor old Father Tuthie, he really thought Bob Stearman did it. This thing has been too much for him. The old priest has been a thorn in the side of the police from the start, if Price hadn't been brought in, he might have been arrested himself."

As they came away from the morgue McConait had very little to say, he had lost his friend and although he was glad it was over it seemed to be unfair that Peel wasn't here after all his efforts. His methods had been unconventional, and in the end, were his undoing. At heart he wanted to catch the bad guys, McConait saw nothing wrong with that.

Andrea put her arm around McConait's shoulder and they walked away together. "I take it you got the email I forwarded from the Vet in Edinburgh. I don't know if it's of any particular help anymore."

"On the contrary it helps cement a theory I've been working on, it should really help in the inquest. If you have time I'll explain it to you over a drink later."

"Sounds lovely." Andrea was glad that the case was over; she wanted her and McConait to move on beyond their professional relationship.

185

Chapter 30
The Inquest

Tynemouth had blossomed back into life, the police presence dramatically reduced and the hustle and bustle of the seaside town returned. The werewolf phenomenon had not done the place any harm; on the contrary, people in the town were marketing the connection. The surf shop had adopted a wolf and pentacle as its new logo.

Surfboards and T-shirts now bore various werewolf designs and slogans. The council was discussing tourist walks at full moon. Family and friends of the victims were cashing in on newspaper and book sales and the real horror and tragedy of what had happened was being sanitised and glossed over.

The inquest, held at Newcastle Crown Court, was a long and drawn out affair; so many killings, so many witnesses and pieces of evidence. McConait had plenty of time to mull over what he was going to present to the judge. He expounded all his theories and profiles. He demonstrated eloquently how at every stage of the investigation, Rufus Infareño fitted the profile.

McConait showed that Infareño's involvement in various criminal activities meant that his character was, "…that of someone who had no respect for the law". He dealt a range of drugs to children as young as twelve; revealing a disregard for human life. He produced a timetable of events to which Infareño had no alibi. The court was satisfied by what they heard; only one question was yet to be explained.

The judge presiding, Lord Cornelius Halifax, sat straight backed and grim, taking off his glasses, he looked at McConait, "You have been a real help to the police, Doctor McConait and a real asset to this investigation. I have listened with real admiration at the analysis of, what has to be said to be, perhaps, the strangest case in British history. I wonder, can you shed any more light on this undisclosed virus, and also the manner in which the victims were brutalised, in such a bestial fashion?"

It was something that had bothered McConait for a long time, this viral connection between each killing, which was not

187

present in the killer, and the clawing and ripping of the body; not the work of a human hand.

McConait walked to a data projector, which had been used to show a timetable of events and images of the crime scenes. McConait clicked a laptop, flashed a slide of the original profile of the killer and highlighted the words:

Into the occult   lives alone   big powerful male   no alibis   intelligent clean meticulous psychopathic tendencies and finally, *tools*

"Well Your Honour, as has been shown all these things on my profile fit Infareño. And I have evidence that he also used a particular kind of tool in the killings. I have received some information tracked down by our forensic scientist Andrea Swan. She has been in contact with one Professor Douglas Henderson of Edinburgh University, School of Veterinary Medicine."

The word veterinary caused a few raised eyebrows around the room. "A vet you say?" interjected the judge." A doctor of animals?"

"The best in his field your honour. His conclusion is that this virus although unusual, bore a resemblance to a similar virus discovered in Alaska over 100 years ago. It appears that while digging for gold in the Klondike, many of the prospectors were attacked, or killed by wolves. The wolves passed on the virus."

The crowded courtroom broke out in whispers and mumbles at the word wolves. His Lordship asked for silence, "Please Doctor McConait, do explain how a 100 year old virus, from the Klondike, could be present in the victims in Tynemouth."

"As I showed earlier, Infareños tribal origins may have led him to Spiritual Therianthropic practice. That is to say he may have, like tribal Shaman, acted out a ritual to try to engage with a wolf spirit. Through research I have found that along with ingesting plants such as Ergine and Mescaline, that would contain hallucinogenic properties, the shaman would wear the skin of a wolf. The wolf's head perhaps, put on top of his own, with the animal hide down his back or wrapped around his waste. Often he would also hold the claws of the animal, fastened to carved wooden handles. In a ritualistic drug crazed dance the

188

shaman would growl and claw the air, hallucinating that he was actually a wolf on the attack."

McConait went back to the data projector, and clicked the laptop and a picture of Rose Stearman's dead body flashed onto a screen.

McConait pointed with a pencil to cast a shadow on the victim's back. "Here, these claw marks, indicative with the claw marks of a large dog or wolf." Again McConait clicked the laptop to reveal the same marks on all the victims. "I suggest that to make him more connected to the wolf spirit, Infareño used real wolf claws. He tore at the flesh of his victims, mutilating their bodies, leaving these tell-tale marks. These claws may also have contained traces of the animal's blood and thus contaminated the victims. As long as Infareño never broke his own skin there is no reason for him to contract the virus. In conclusion, the virus and claw marks fit the profile of Infareño being under the influence of spiritual therianthropy."

The judge sat back in his chair and considered the theory McConait had laid out, "And this claw of which you speak, was it ever found?"

"No your honour. If you recall the last victim, D.S. Peel was murdered on the beach, the claw was very likely washed away by the sea or buried in the sand."

Judge Halifax seemed satisfied with McConait's explanation, only one thing had not been revealed, his final question was for the police, "And the rope down to the cave, the work of an accomplice. Have you any leads to who that may be?"

A CID officer who had been left in charge after the demise of Peel jumped to attention, "No your honour, he was well known to the surf community, and a drug dealer to lots of people, so without an admission of guilt or eyewitness testimony, there's not a great deal of mileage in pursuing it. However officers on the beat are asking around and keeping their ears to the ground."

Halifax nodded sagely and accepted what the Sergeant had said and passed a verdict of guilty. Protestations from representatives of the Infareño family were quickly squashed, and the honourable Lord Halifax ruled that all the killings in

189

Tynemouth were the work of Rufus Infareño; however there was not enough evidence to categorically link the London killings to the Mexican.

McConait could live with that. All in all, a satisfactory outcome; reputations were restored and he was already looking forward to sealing a contract on the book about the investigation.

Outside the courtroom McConait met Andrea who threw her arms around his neck.

'All done and dusted.' As McConait's mother Mary would have said.

"You did it! Sylvester."

"We did it Andrea, and a lot of credit must go to Fr.Price not forgetting poor old Peel. Of course there was a sizable contribution made by a cute, blonde forensic scientist; all in all, a great team effort."

Andrea was beaming, "Maybe, but your performance in the inquest was inspirational; all that about the Klondike and the wolf claw, brilliant."

"So I guess the drinks are on me. Shall we go out tonight to celebrate?"

"You bet, I've got stuff to sort out back at the lab but tonight would be lovely."

"I'll meet you at the Grand about seven."

They embraced, excited about what lay ahead.

Chapter 31
McConait Is Still Haunted

Sly McConait walked along Grand Parade, the road that looked over the beach of Longsands, the sun was going down behind the houses and long shadows were being cast by people walking dogs or lads throwing rugby balls and frisbees. Couples young and old walked across the golden sand. And a few people, (the working day finished) hit the surf, for the hour of daylight that remained. He was meeting Andrea soon but he thought he'd stretch his legs before she arrived; at this moment everything in McConait's world was rosy.

He looked to the right where Peel had met his end, then left up to the cave where Rufus Infareño had spent his last weeks of life. For the first time since the killing he had a feeling that something didn't fit. Again he swept his gaze from right to left, over the quarter of a mile of sand; he began to feel increasingly more uncomfortable. McConait cast his mind back a few hours to the testimony given at the inquest by a Sergeant on the beach that night:

"We heard a shot then out from the dunes, a couple of yards away, ran Infareño from one of the caves in Cullercoats."

A frown now appeared on McConait's face, the distance from where Peel was killed, the dunes at the Tynemouth end of the beach, to the caves at the Cullercoats end, where Infareño was hiding, was just too far. It was clear that Peel's injuries were so severe he couldn't have lived on after the attack for more than a few seconds. How could the attacker be at the opposite end of the beach, so quickly? Not even an athlete could cover that distance. McConait walked down to the dunes where the body was found, and tried to picture the moment when the shot rang out. The bullet was never recovered but Peel's gun was fired. The policeman Peel had been talking to, up at the zebra crossing, said they saw the flash and heard the shot from this point. Yet Infareño was at the other end of the beach, apparently at exactly the same time.

McConait began walking down the beach in the direction of Cullercoats. A rugby ball flew through the air and landed at

191

McConait's feet. An 18 year old ran over to retrieve it. McConait had already picked it up and held out the ball. The young man smiled and said, "Cheers mate." As McConait and the youth made eye contact, a feeling returned, a feeling that McConait thought he had seen the back of.

The 18 year old smirked and jogged back to his friends. McConait teetered back and forth, the world began to spin: sand then sky; sand then sky; span round and round. He bent double trying to catch his breath and then vomited on the sand. The group of young men playing with the rugby ball laughed, assuming McConait was drunk.

McConait fought the dizziness, turned and headed towards the steps leading back up to the road. Grabbing the handrail he staggered upwards, images flashing through his brain: Infareño's body; the deserted cave; the body of Peel; the confessional; the crucifix in Tuthie's hands; Maria's face this time laughing; then his mother doing the same.

At the top of the stairs the spinning began to subside, McConait oriented himself and, when he was able to focus, his eyes rested upon the police hut. He found himself running towards it. He hadn't dismantled his boards yet, and still had the keys in his pocket. He threw open the door and stood gasping for breath in front of the webs he had created on the walls. The boards, which had led to the death of Rufus Infareño seemed different now. Before they had connected together and lead the way, now they appeared as a stream of disparate words, meaningless and redundant.

It was the feeling; he had put it down to some sort of anxiety attack due to the investigation, but now it was over and yet the feeling was even stronger. He was a rational atheist but he couldn't rationalise this; this feeling was something more than a physical reaction, this was beyond the realm of his experience, something was pulling him, drawing him into something, something he couldn't explain, something that chilled him... terrified him.

It didn't fit anymore; his explanations, Price's profile, all made sense, but it didn't *feel* right. His heart was pounding;

something didn't fit, could it be the police had killed the wrong man?

In a frantic state he tore down photographs, pictures of victims, suspects, maps, and diagrams. He grabbed a cloth and angrily began rubbing out words. He stepped back to look at the mess that remained. He looked at the boards, the first one was completely erased, but as he studied the second, he began to see things in a way he never had before. Certain words were standing out, calling to him.

VIRUS BLOOD DEEP...he rubbed out.

HIDDEN KILLER CLOSER...he kept.

These words all made sense, these words were leading him somewhere; he began rubbing out others, as if directed by an invisible hand:

GENES FAMILY MOTHER FATHER ABUSE

Were all rubbed away:

HISTORY FOOTSTEPS CYCLE MOON

Were left.

DORMANT TRIGGER

Rubbed out:

P.U.L. VIRUS

Remained.

He looked at his remaining list of words scattered across the second board. There was something there, he'd always felt it but he had tried so hard not to work on feeling, Price's empirical ways, and Peels evidence driven investigation, had steered McConait away from what he felt in his guts.

Again he thought of the feeling that had haunted him since returning to Tynemouth, there had to be an explanation why he had these sporadic attacks. He thought of the times he had felt it, and began writing on the first board:

Church service when Tuthie gave that emotive Homily
Crime scene after the attack on Mark Pembridge
The school field when the boys were getting interviewed
Front Street with the policeman
The beach when handing over the rugby ball

The more he stared at the boards the more he realised the list of names and places meant nothing, but one suddenly stood out; the policeman. He took his rubber and rubbed out:

Front Street with

Which left:

The policeman

McConait scrambled through documents until he found the incident sheet recalling the altercation with Tuthie at the Priory:

SERGEANT SINDAS

This sparked something inside him, it was not Front Street or the moon, or the snub from Tuthie's housekeeper that night, it was the policeman. He looked at the rest of the board. At the church he'd been fine, he'd listened to the whole ceremony no problem, why did he start feeling so strange? When did he start feeling so strange? Then it came to him, the exact second the feeling struck him for the first time, it was when he first laid eyes on him. He rubbed out his first line and replaced it with:

ROBERT STEARMAN

Next on the list was the crime scene at he back of the care home, he struggled to pinpoint the exact moment of the strange feeling he put down to anxiety, then he had it, it was when he turned back to the forensic officer:

ANDREW BOE

Then the school field that was obviously something to do with the boys, he immediately scrawled a name:

ADAM BATES

But the boy on the beach was the person, who triggered his latest attack, and he didn't know his name, he could run back out and find him, he would surely be still on the beach. McConait ventured back out, but even a few yards towards the beach sent him reeling with nausea and fear, as if the feeling was warning him; protecting him.

He was back in the hut; he slammed the door with his back and caught his breath. He suddenly felt desperately alone, a feeling he recognised from the time his mother died. He looked at his watch it was gone seven o'clock, Andrea would be at the Grand. He dashed out the hut and ran to the Grand Hotel.

194

Andrea stood on the Hotel steps waiting. Her face turned from joy to concern when she saw McConait's distressed and dishevelled state.

"Sylvester what's wrong you look like you've seen a ghost."

"I can't explain it but something's not right."

Andrea was confused and concerned, "Not right… with us?"

"No the case, Infareño, I don't think it was him, I don't think it's possible. I think we got the wrong man."

Andrea drew close and placed a compassionate hand on his clammy cheek. "Sylvester, don't be silly love, you've worked so hard, we all have, proving it had to be him. What about the profile?"

"No it's deeper than that. The profile's too simplistic, it suggests everything but it says nothing. I see that now. I should have followed the signs the warnings." McConait was beginning to sound crazed.

"What warnings?" Andrea screwed up her face, beginning to realise that Sylvester was sinking into a behaviour that distressed her as much as him.

"People, certain people when I see them they trigger this reaction, the world spins, I feel nauseous, I get flash backs, horrible flash backs, my Mother's cruelty, I see the blood on my hands, I see me hitting Maria, it all comes back, all of it."

Andrea withdrew her hand and stepped back, "Look I don't know who Maria is or what this is about but I think you need help, to deal with whatever it is lurking in your past." With that she turned to leave.

The manic McConait grabbed her arm, which gave her a start. "Where are you going? Don't you see this isn't finished!"

Shaken and angry Andrea pulled her arm away, "It is finished as far as I'm concerned!" she descended the stairs and flagged a taxi.

McConait was distraught, "Andrea please! You're the only one who can help!"

Andrea turned back from the taxi door now with tears in her eyes, "The help you need I can't give."

The taxi pulled away and McConait was now alone. His love, his inspiration had deserted him. Who could he turn to?

The case was closed, Peel was gone and the police were packing up for good. Price, the priest who had become his friend was with the Bishop discussing what to do with Tuthie, who was now under some kind of ecclesiastical house arrest.

That was it... Tuthie.

Tuthie knew it wasn't right, the Infareño connection, he'd warned McConait and tried to help him, but he hadn't listened, no one had listened to the old man. Was Tuthie wise rather than delusional? McConait thrust his hand into his inside pocket and pulled out the crucifix with the circle of letters. Something told him he had to work out the letters. What did they mean? What power did they hold? He ran to the presbytery clutching the crucifix.

The Presbytry was locked; McConait found Tuthie alone in the church. The old man knelt in the front pew like one of the congregation; which effectively he had become. He now had to creep back and forth from the presbytery to the church, his life had become almost monastic: his Faith as unshaken as ever.

McConait walked to the front of the church, Tuthie didn't even turn round, his eyes pressed tightly shut, his lips whispering in Latin. McConait knelt beside him and looked at the ornate altar in front of him. Behind the altar were wooden carvings of six local saints, which showed the Church's place in local religious history. There were three panels on the front of the altar, depicting, 'the Annunciation' (Gabriel announcing to Mary that she was to have a son), 'the Nativity' (Jesus born in a manger with a host of angels around him and Mary), and 'the Adoration of the Magi' (the three wise men kneeling in worship at the new born child). Underneath ran the words:

INTROIBO AD ALTARE DEI

"So at last you have come into the altar of God, my son." Tuthie hadn't even opened his eyes yet he knew it was McConait; as if he had been expecting him. Tuthie opened his eyes and turned to McConait who was still staring straight ahead. The priest saw a look in the academic's face that he hadn't seen since

196

the Requiem mass for Mary McConait, but it pleased him to see that, in his hands, McConait held the crucifix.

McConait took his gaze away from the altar, and realised that he and Tuthie were both looking at the cross, gripped in his hand. "This cross you gave me, it's unusual, I want... no I need, to know what the letters on the disc behind Jesus' head mean."

Tuthie put his hand in his pocket and pulled out a well-thumbed, tattered paper booklet and handed it to McConait. On the cover was a picture of an old monk, behind his head was a halo, which meant he must be a saint. He held a bishop's crosier, the shepherd's staff that was a symbol of his authority and a reference to Jesus being the 'Good Shepherd'. In the same hand, held horizontally, was a book which McConait presumed must be the Bible. Balanced on top of the book was a chalice which he, at first, thought must have contained the Communion wine which Catholics believe to be the Blood of Christ, however looking more closely, he noticed a snake curling out from the inside. The monk's eyes looked down at the snake and with a raised right hand appeared to be blessing it. Above the picture was a title in capital letters:

SAN BENEDETTO

Tuthie finished his prayers, and stood up, "I'll be in the presbytery when you're ready." McConait let the priest out of the pew and then returned to his kneeling position. He turned the delicate page and began reading.

...St. Benedict (San Benedetto) was from Umbria in Italy and died at his monastery in Montecassino in 547. When he was 18 he went to university but was sickened by the vices of his fellow students... McConait's thoughts flashed back to Cambridge and some of the antics many students, including himself, got up to... Benedict, as well educated as he was, realised his knowledge was restricted to the ways of man, the physical world, he felt ignorant in the ways of God... again this rang a bell with McConait. All his knowledge and acclaim, had led him in the wrong direction; there was more he had to learn.

...Benedict withdrew to adopt the life of a hermit, living alone in a cave in Subiaco in upper Lazio. There a good man named Romano helped him. At the ringing of a bell he would lower a basket with food and drink down to the cave from the top of the cliff, by means of a rope...

It was now clear who had been helping Infareño; Tuthie had played down his knowledge of the Mexican and tried to protect him, until the real killer could be stopped, but the activities on the beach that night must have flushed Infareño out of his sanctuary and into the arms of death.

McConait read on... in the cave the devil attempted to weaken the holy man's resolve, his bell was broken and Benedict was tempted with obscene fantasies and terrible doubts regarding faith, hope and charity and was driven to despair... McConait knew the feeling.

...Benedict resisted: he threw himself naked, into a thorny juniper bush, although scratched and bleeding, his spirit was healed...

For the first time since his childhood, McConait felt inspired by a religious figure. He had never seen the connections between the stories he heard at church, school or from his mother, to the reality of modern day life. Now he could see that the examples of the saints could actually be a guide.

McConait turned another page to find a short account of a particular episode in Benedict's life... The monk rose through the ranks to be chosen as abbot in a place called Vicovoro, but the monks who elected him changed their mind when Benedict insisted on a return to strict monastic rule. The monks then tried to poison him. They put the poison in a chalice of wine and offered it to him. Benedict realised the evil presence in those that gave it to him and drew the sign of the cross on the side of the chalice with his finger. The chalice broke into a hundred pieces as if hit by a stone. Then Benedict left and returned to a life of solitude...

As was illustrated on the cover of the booklet, Benedict had overcome the devil, represented by a snake... His example spread across Europe and his followers of solitude and strict monastic ways became known as the Benedictine monks...

This was all food for thought but it was the letters, McConait had to understand the letters. He flicked through a

198

couple more pages about the life of St. Benedict, until he found a page with a diagram of the disc on the crucifix.

A circular band surrounding a cross with letters arranged around it. In the four quadrants between the arms of the cross and the circular band were four letters:

C S
P B

On the vertical section of the cross from top to bottom ran the letters:

C
S
S
M
L

Along the horizontal intersecting at S ran the letters:

N   D   S   M   D

Around the circular band in a clockwise direction starting at 1 o'clock were the letters:

VRSNSMVSMQLIVB

Mcconait had looked at these letters countless times, and every connotation he had thought of came to nothing; flicking to the next page revealed all.

Each group of letters were the first letters of Latin words; the English translations were written alongside.

C S
P B

Crux Sancti Patris Benedicti (Cross of St. Father Benedict)

C
S
S
M
L

Crux Sancta Sit Mihi Lux (Be the Holy Cross my light)

N   D   S   M   D

Non Draco Sit Mihi Dux (Be not the devil my master)

VRS

Vade Retro Satana (Back Satan!)

NSMV

Numquam Saude Mihi Vana (Do not tempt me with wicked deeds)

SMQL

Sunt Mala Quae Libas (What you offer me is evil)

IVB

Ipae Venena Bibas (Drink you yourself your poison)

So that was why Tuthie gave him this crucifix. This Cross of St.Benedict was to ward off evil, to overpower Satan, to keep the wolf from the door.

The chanting outside the house of Rose Stearman was Tuthie's attempt to drive out the evil that had taken up residence.

The story of St. Benedict and his prayer contained parallels to McConait's present situation. It was a life changing revelation, McConait's world was being turned upside down; the myth he had come to Tynemouth to dispel was growing more powerful. Could it actually be true? Was the devil present in this town? Was it pure evil that was the root of the killings? Could a man be possessed by a demon and change into a beast? Did werewolves really exist?

McConait's heart was pounding, his rational atheist brain desperately trying to fight what he was starting to believe. If the impossible had become reality, if myth was in fact truth, his strategies and psychological profiles counted for nothing, his research and his public acclaim were of no use to him now. He was stripped naked of the intellectual armour he had built up over years of study. He was like a child who had discovered that Santa Claus wasn't real but the bogie man was. He could only think of one possible strategy left at hand.

Still on his knees he held the book with his thumbs while his hands came together to pray. He looked at a statue of Mary on the right hand of the altar and remembered his own mother Mary, and thought "If she could see me now."

His eyes returned to the book and in his best scholar's Latin read aloud the prayer of St.Benedict.

Back at the presbytery McConait was met by a sceptical housekeeper, who condescended to allow him access to old Father Tuthie. He was busy packing an old brown leather case opened on top of a single bed. Into it Tuthie placed one item of

200

black clothing after another. Next to his case, was a beautifully finished, oak box. Carved into the lid, in an ornate script and then gilded, was the inscription:

L'eglise de San Hubert (The Church of St.Hubert)

McConait assumed the box to contain religious artefacts, perhaps Holy oils for the Sacraments like Baptism or Confirmation.

McConait didn't ask where he was going; he knew that the Bishop and Price had conspired to sweep the old priest under a very expensive Diocesan carpet, where he could sit out his retirement. An ecclesiastical gagging order was put on him, but no one was interested in what the discredited Tuthie had to say; no one except McConait. The sight of the suitcase panicked him.

"You're not going right away are you?" McConait couldn't bare the thought of being left alone with his new found belief.

"No I'll stay in Tynemouth tonight. I must be here tonight." Tuthie had a resigned look of trepidation on his face.

"What's happening tonight?" Tuthie didn't have to answer the question; he could see on McConait's face that the unpleasant answer was draining the colour from his face.

McConait answered it himself, "The full moon. My God it's going to happen again, we have to warn people, tell the police." McConait himself realised the futility in what he was saying.

"My son, the time for warnings are over, the devil has closed the ears, and hearts of the believers. The devil must be driven out by action, and by the power of God."

"What do you mean? How can you do that? This thing's a beast!"

"It has taken me too long to realise, all my prayers have been in vain up until now, but Jesus gave his disciples the power to drive out demons. The killer must be confronted when he is in a state of possession."

"You mean when he's..." McConait couldn't bare to finish his sentence, so Tuthie did.

"A wolf."

"But how will you find him, track him down?"

"He will come to me, he wants to be healed, he seeks forgiveness, and reconciliation with God."

201

McConait was taken aback, "How? Who? Where? When?"

"Bob Stearman came to me at the beginning, in confession. He told me how he had no memory of that night, except flashing memories of running with a wolf pack, of hunting, killing, savagery, but he was convinced he'd murdered his wife. I didn't help him; I committed a terrible sin by telling the police as I am telling you. Instead of helping him I broke his trust and abused his genuine attempt of reconciliation. He's back in Tynemouth and tonight, I'll be with him when he walks with Satan."

"And then what?"

"Then I'll perform the rite of exorcism, and drive out the demon within him." Tuthie's eyes were full of fire, his jaw clenched and his bottom lip gave a faint tremble. Tuthie's conviction was as strong as St.Benedict, but his body was frail. McConait looked down into Tuthie's suitcase, and saw the bottle of angina tablets; over exersion could kill him.

"Father, if Bob Stearman is the killer then this is too dangerous, you can't do this alone."

Tuthie turned excitedly and grasped McConait's arm, "Then come with me."

McConait felt sick at the thought of confronting the beast, it was the realisation that everything he stood for was worthless, that the life he had known was a sham. "What help would I be?"

"You are the only one here, in the end you found the truth, you didn't give up. You have your mother's faith; her spirit is with you. Will you come? Will you meet with Robert Stearman?"

McConait clenched his fists. He knew that the rational thing would be to turn around and walk out. If an old man wanted to commit suicide then let him. But he couldn't, something had awoken in him he could no longer resist, he knew that what he wanted to do was irrelevant. It was what he must do that mattered, and something in his heart wanted to believe that faith and faith alone could overcome the beast.

"When and where?"

"At sunset… at the Priory." There was no police barrier now, and if they sneaked in after it closed they would be alone. Tuthie hoped the spiritual power of this holy place would help to drive out the evil, but there was another reason why this location

202

was useful. If everything went wrong, no one else would be there to get hurt.

"Is there anything you need me to do Father?"

"Yes my son…you must be pure when we meet the beast, I must hear your confession."

McConait's loathing of this sacrament was swallowed, he was now stumbling in the dark, his reality had become a living nightmare. Tuthie's way was the only avenue available and he placed himself into the hands of the old priest. He fell to his knees, and made the sign of the cross. Over the next few minutes McConait gushed forth, like an erupting oil well, all the blackness that filled his soul: about his relationship with his mother; the guilt he felt about her death; how he turned his back on his faith; his family; his friends and his home; how he thought himself better than others because of his position, and finally, his violent act towards his lover and the subsequent bribery to buy her silence.

Tuthie absolved him "…in the name of the Father, and of the Son and of the Holy Spirit, Amen." He didn't need to give McConait a penance; they both knew the task ahead would be enough.

McConait left the presbytery emotionally drained. Today was like the first day of a new life, and like a new born foal, he was weak and struggling to find his feet, he needed to gain strength to stand up to what lay ahead. He headed back to the Grand Hotel to get some rest.

Chapter 32
Revelation

After a short and troubled sleep, McConait devoured a steak sandwich and washed it down with large scotch, at this moment Dutch courage seemed as good as any. He picked up his bottle of pills and considered taking one, but now he felt he was seeing things clearly he didn't want it clouded by his dependence on prozac.

He mulled over the events of the day: the strange feeling; the words on the white board, and the letters on the crucifix. He took a final bite of his lunch and paused, mid chew. "...the letters..."

The letters, once revealed, helped him and gave him strength, there was something in the letters; a hidden truth. He polished off his whisky and left for the police hut.

Inside he looked at the list of names and words that remained. All that was left of months of work, the fog was lifting and a sharpening of understanding, an emerging clarity was beginning to appear. He stared wide eyed at the boards. In the centre of one was:

WEREWOLF

It was in Price's handwriting; that word had taken on a new meaning today. He looked at his own writing below, the Latin version:

LUPUS VIR

Latin words had also taken on a new significance, he now saw a hidden strength, a truth in this ancient language, and then it struck him. His head turned back to the adjacent white board, and back again; he shook his head in disbelief as the letters twisted in his mind.

LUPUS VIR was an anagram of PUL VIRUS.

Could it be the words were telling him that the virus that had been passed on to the victims was in fact the curse of the werewolf? It surely must be a coincidence. McConait flailed around and grabbed at some papers, until he found a file for Bob Stearman. If he was the killer, perhaps he might have some medical history, a strange virus the police had missed. If so, he

204

could get the police involved again, and help Tuthie. He slapped the file on the desk and opened it:

ROBERT STEARMAN

Once again the letters began to spin in his mind. He snatched up the dry wipe marker and went to his board. He rearranged the letters underneath.

ROBERT STEARMAN
MAN BEAST TERROR

There it was; unbelievable. Words, names, were leading him to the killer. Could it be some kind of freaky coincidence? It seemed that today anything was possible. Saints could be an example, confession could purify the soul, anagrams held hidden messages and werewolves really existed. He took his marker pen and began joining the words that surrounded with a trembling hand:

WEREWOLF

Starting at the top middle with the words,

ERGOT POISONING/ DRUGS

He went diagonally bottom left:

LYCANTHROPY/LUNACY

He again went diagonally this time up to the right:

PORPHYRIA/WEREWOLF DISEASE

He then went horizontally across to the left:

HYPERTRICHOSIS/BODYHAIR

And then diagonally down to the bottom right:

THERIANTHROPY

And back, once again, to the top middle.

Standing back he realised that he had drawn a huge pentacle.

McConait still had an ounce of rationality left; he shook his head as if shaking off a coating of dust that had fallen on him rendering him ridiculously gullible. He picked up his board rubber and was about to erase the whole lot from the whiteboard, when he checked himself. It was one of the other names on the board. Adam Bates, it made his stomach flip; the letters

ADAM BATES when rearranged spelt

A MAD BEAST

With hand shaking he wrote down the new words, and looked at the other names, terrified at what they might reveal. His fears were realised:

ANDREW BOE

He could immediately spot the word:

BEWARE which left three letters:

'NDO' confused McConait at first, but he became terrified as he changed the letters round to:

DON,

a reference to his Cambridge position, an actual reference to him.

One remained on the board:

SERGEANT SINDAS, which came to him at once

IN GREAT SADNESS.

All the names unravelled seemed to make a sentence. McConait toyed with the connotations until he came up with:

DON IN GREAT SADNESS, BEWARE A MAD BEAST; LUPUS VIR MAN BEAST TERROR!

Now McConait was convinced, 'Don in great sadness' must surely mean him, a Cambridge professor with a history of depression, furthermore the sentence suggested that he might be the next victim. It seemed like a definite warning to clear off. McConait felt all his survival instincts driving him to quit. In an hour he could be packed and on the next train heading south, but what about Tuthie? Things had now got decidedly worse. The revelation that the name of Robert Stearman was an anagram identifying him as a werewolf meant the other anagrams surely had the same purpose. Each of the names he had unscrambled were also the names of killers. Not one single murderer, but four, all carrying an unknown virus which actually was the curse of the werewolf; passed on from victim to victim. They had been lucky enough to survive a werewolf attack but their life meant death to others as long as the werewolf curse carried on. That was why Stearman hadn't been around for the other killings. They were different people, but they all became the same killer, they transformed at the full moon into a savage creature; half man, half wolf.

206

In a whirlwind of panic-stricken terror, McConait ran out of the hut, and onto the road, a boy racer in a silver Renault Clio, narrowly missed him and hurled a torrent of abuse at the crazed psychologist. Trying to regain some sort of control, McConait put both hands on his face and yelled like a madman, "NO!!" He tore at his clothes and his hair trying to drag himself physically out of the nightmare all about him.

People crossed over the road at the sight of the dishevelled McConait who charged round the sea front like a lunatic.

Regaining his senses slightly, McConait took out his mobile phone. If he could believe it, then Price must too. Price was a stronger man than Tuthie; he was a devout man and well connected. McConait needed him now more than ever before. The phone connected and he heard Price's voice; it was only his voice mail, McConait was devastated but for the moment it was all he had.

With desperation in his voice, almost at the point of break down, he spoke, "Price, it's McConait, please come and help. The werewolves, there's more than one there's four, Stearman, Boe, the young lad Bates, and even the policeman Sindas, they're all beasts, possessed. It's real, I know it now, it's all real, like the folk tales say, they transform from men to werewolves. Please help us, I'm meeting Tuthie at the Priory at sunset, please come quickly, before it's too late!"

As McConait looked round, every face he saw seemed to bare a look of evil. Maybe the whole of Tynemouth was infected. Perhaps he and Tuthie were all that was left of normal humanity. The eyes of strangers seemed to be burning into him. As his paranoia grew, people walking their dogs became a potent symbol of man and beast, held in a satanic bond. He trusted no one, feared everyone and everything, he ran as fast as he could, heading for sanctuary, heading for the Priory.

As he rounded the corner of the sea front, the striking ruins of the Priory came into view as it loomed above King Edward's Bay. The road rose up hill and the run got more difficult. McConait's legs burned from the lactic acid that was building up. His fitness levels were low from his sedentary lifestyle and diet of steak sandwiches and red wine. He drove on, his chest tightening, his heart pounding from the exertion. He grew light headed as his brain became starved of oxygen. Finally he reached the path that led to the Priory entrance. He stopped and bent double, gasping for air, and feeling nauseous. He looked up at the solid entrance of the Priory. Tourists, streamed out from the portcullis; it was closing time, and soon it would be sunset. Once the crowd dissipated and the English Heritage staff locked up, it would be a matter of sneaking up the hill at the south side and scrambling over a wall. He remembered doing it as a young boy. The wall had seemed huge at the time, but now, as a man, McConait knew he would manage it no problem; he wasn't too sure about Tuthie.

As he regained his breath, McConait hoped above hope that Price had got his message, and was making his way to the Priory, armed with Holy Water, Crucifix, an array of weaponry, silver bullets or whatever the hell else might be needed, to put an end to this madness.

As the tourists disappeared and the sun set behind him, McConait was left alone in front of the Priory which grew gloomier and gloomier. Where was Tuthie? Perhaps if he told him about the number of killers he would call it off, perhaps, with McConait's support, people might listen to him and come to his aid.

The sun was almost gone and soon the full moon would rule the skies over Tynemouth once again. Waves crashed against the rocks below the Priory, waves too wild for surfing, waves that bore the full fury of the North Sea. Where was Tuthie?

Perhaps the old priest had decided not to come out, but there were no lights on in the church or Presbytery. Then a thought occurred to McConait, what if Tuthie was already inside, waiting for him? The old man could never manage the scramble up the steep sides of the hill and then the climb over the wall. He must have gone in with the tourists, Tuthie more than anyone would know a good place to hide amongst the ruins and graves of this ancient building. He was in there alone.

McConait breathed hard then ventured round the side and began the scramble into the Priory. The wall was indeed smaller than he imagined but the drop on the other side was not. He

208

landed hard jarring his ankles and knees, before falling forward onto his hands, which scraped against ancient stone. He got to his feet and limped forward into the increasing darkness. He strained his eyes and ears, but saw only silhouettes and shadows and heard nothing but the pounding of his own heart and the crashing of the waves. As he edged forward he became aware of a presence, he could hear breathing coming from an archway and as he strained his eyes, a figure stepped out from the shadows. The silhouette was vaguely familiar. It was Robert Stearman.

McConait's fear was superseded by his concern for Tuthie.

Stearman withdrew into the shadows again. "You shouldn't have come McConait, only a man of God can help me."

"Where's Father Tuthie, what have you done with him?"

"You'd better run while you have the chance," replied Stearman, pleading as much as warning.

*   *   *   *   *

Tuthie sat slumped in a thicket, which was growing wild in a far corner of the Priory wall. He was damp and shivering, with cold and fear. He had been there for the best part of an hour, repeating the prayer of St.Benedict over and over. As the evening grew darker, his anxiety increased, and now a familiar pain, stabbed inside his chest. Unable to get to his feet he had stayed there in his hiding place, trying to relieve his anxiety through prayer. He knew a severe attack might mean that he would never leave the Priory alive. He heard muffled voices in the distance and prayed for strength.

*   *   *   *   *

Price left the Bishop and walked from a palatial drawing room, clad in ancient oak, down a long corridor, lined with paintings of former Bishops of Hexham and Newcastle going back over the ages. His footsteps rang out on the parquet

209

flooring and echoed along the corridor. He heard the beep of his mobile phone, which indicated he had an awaiting voice message. He flipped open his phone and saw it was from McConait. He pressed a button and held the phone to his ear. He quickened his pace.

* * * * *

The moon was now visible from where they stood in the Priory. And its effect was instant. Stearman's eyes bulged from their sockets and in the bright moonlight McConait could see the whites had turned a mixture of blood red and bile yellow. Stearman clutched himself in pain and yelled, "Go!!!"

McConait felt like doing just that, but couldn't help gazing, transfixed by what was happening before him.

* * * * *

Fr. Price dashed down the Coast Road towards Tynemouth in a black BMW. The words on the phone had un-nerved him and he needed to get to McConait and Tuthie quick.

* * * * *

The muffled voices had turned into a roar of absolute agony. It was happening. Tuthie knew he had to act. He rolled onto all fours and then, with his hands, raised himself up; using the wall he had hid against. The branches of the thicket conspired to hold him back. Wheezing and holding his chest, Tuthie stepped free of the branches into the moonlight; under his right arm was a wooden box.

* * * * *

Stearman was on his knees and tore at his clothes as if they were ablaze, until he was naked in the moonlight. He was shaking with a force that McConait could scarcely believe. There was a sound of splitting and popping and Stearman's skin began to rip apart under pressure from a force expanding within. Large

210

gaping wounds ripped open, at first revealing a mucous which, in turn, split to reveal blood matted hair. Flesh was flapping down from every part of his body. A large section of his face, around the mouth, dropped to the ground as a snarling snout forced its way out. A rancid stench emanated from the emerging monster. McConait gagged at the smell, but worse was to come. The creature began snapping up the pieces of fallen flesh that now lay scattered around its haunches. It was getting energy from the feast of its own remains. One piece of flesh, which had covered a hand, flapped like a leather glove before being swallowed whole. The beast stood a full eight feet tall, in front of McConait. The remnants of the man were devoured and the wolf was born.

*   *   *   *   *

Price slammed on the brakes and brought the raging BMW to rest. The lights were still on in the police hut. He got out the car and paced towards the door, clicking the central locking on his key fob. When he got there he could see the door was ajar; in his haste McConait had left it unlocked, he pushed the door and it creaked as it swung open.

*   *   *   *   *

Tuthie was now shuffling closer to where the screams came from; clinging to the box under his right arm. The noise had died down and the crashing of the waves now filled his ears. But as he turned a corner towards a giant stone arch he detected another sound; a deep and heavy rhythmic breathing.

The beast inhaled and exhaled heavily, the transformation had been physically exhausting, and it was not at full strength. The wolf's face was hideous. It had a long snout with curling lips, which exposed yellow fangs drooling and dripping with the blood of its own flesh. The yellow-red eyes of Stearman were all that McConait recognised. Long shaggy ears flicked and twitched as it gathered its bearings. It began to sniff the air. Its appetite

211

had been wetted, now it craved fresh meat. Slowly it turned its huge matted head towards the trembling McConait.

* * * * *

Price stood in front of the white boards with files, photographs and papers at his feet. He scanned the names and the anagrams with a disapproving frown, seeing the hidden connections that McConait had revealed. He shook his head in disgust as he looked at the large pentacle on the white board he himself had used to bring clarity to the investigation. He stepped back out of the door and looked up at the full moon above. McConait's words on the voice mail were heart felt; it appeared that he and Tuthie had indeed gone to the Priory. Price ran back to his BMW and sped off around the sea front.

* * * * *

Tuthie saw McConait first, but McConait's gaze pointed him towards the direction of the creature that was once Robert Stearman. The old priest edged forward until he was half way between the two figures.

* * * * *

McConait caught sight of something moving to his right. It was frail old Father Tuthie drawing closer then stopping. McConait recognised the box he had seen earlier on the bed; he watched as the old man placed it on the grass in front of him and gingerly lifted the engraved lid.

The beast still breathed heavily from its exertions it would only be a matter of time before the new born werewolf became fully alert and ready to feed. It was aware of the scent of two men very close, but it waited for the right time to pounce. It licked the last remaining smatterings of blood and tissue from its great paws.

* * * * *

212

Price pulled up outside, what appeared to be, a deserted Priory. The wind blew and angry waves dashed against rock. Mountainous peaks fell to cavernous troughs as the tide advanced towards the shore. Price pricked his ears but was only aware of the sounds of the elements, yet still he sensed there were people beyond the thick stone walls of the ancient building. He did not need to scramble up the side to make an entrance, he had Tuthie's key and opened the portcullis. It gave a bone-chilling creak as metal rubbed against metal; the ruins beyond were but a silhouette against a backdrop of moonlit sky.

* * * * *

Tuthie was close enough to talk to McConait, even in hushed tones. "Thank you for coming my son." Looking at what had once been Stearman, Tuthie continued "We arrived and hid together, but as the sunlight lessened, he became more agitated and ran off. We may have caught him just in time. Have you your cross?"

McConait produced it and held out a trembling hand. "Try to angle the cross so the moon reflects off the disc with the letters, and see if you can flash it at Stearman." McConait rotated the cross back and forth as if trying to signal to the beast in semaphore. "You read the prayer of St.Benedict didn't you?" McConait nodded.

"I want you to look into his eyes and say Crux Sancta Sit Mihi Lux (Be the Holy Cross my light)." McConait did so. "Keep repeating it, say it with conviction, your life may depend on it." McConait did so. The beast turned its huge hairy mass towards McConait, as if oblivious to Tuthie's presence. It took a step forward. In panic McConait stopped his prayer. "Don't stop!" commanded Tuthie, you are evoking the power of the cross and of your faith." McConait continued, his voice wavering and increasing in pace as the beast took another step.

Tuthie drew something from the box and fumbled with it on the ground. "Now say the next part, Non Draco Sit Mihi Dux (Be not the devil my master), keep repeating it don't stop!" Tuthie held the object he had taken from the box in one hand,

213

with the other he raised his own Cross of St.Benedict, and joined in the chant with McConait; "Non Draco Sit Mihi Dux! Non Draco Sit Mihi Dux!"

*   *   *   *   *

Price walked towards the voices in the distance, he winced as he heard the chanting of ancient, outdated Latin words floating on the icy wind. What an anathema this was to him; how he despised it. He had more important things to do than waste his time with Father Tuthie and his sideshow, but now McConait was on his side; this was dangerous.

*   *   *   *   *

The creature now turned towards Tuthie. His cross thrust forward to repulse the beast as he carried on the chant. "Non Draco Sit Mihi Dux!" But the werewolf drew nearer. Any second now the beast would be at full strength and attack.

Tuthie started up the next line of the prayer, "Vade Retro Satana (Back Satan!)" The beast crept forward, "Vade Retro Satana!" the wolf was inches away, but Tuthie stood his ground, and yelled with burning eyes, "Vade Retro Satana!" The beast stopped.

Tuthie's last outburst was more than he could take; his heart cramped and spasmed inside his chest; he sank to his knees. His left hand still managed to hold the cross aloft, the other went to his chest and dropped the object he'd been holding. Sensing the moment of weakness the beast pounced. A 180-degree swipe of its claw sent the aged priest tumbling to the ground a good 5 yards away.

McConait filled with a new born conviction, leapt forward to where the old man had stood and scrambled on the ground until his hand made contact with cold steel. The object from the box was a pistol, at least 60 years old; McConait gripped the textured wooden handle and rose to his feet.

The wolf sank its filthy fangs into Tuthie's leg and dragged him closer. Tuthie whimpered in pain. McConait held out the gun, "Vade Retro Satana !" The wolf paused, its jaws open, over the cowering priest. McConait shouted again, "Vade Retro Satana!" He moved forward and the mighty beast backed away, the greater McConait's conviction, the greater the wolf's retreat. A few more yards away was the cliff edge, and as the werewolf backed away, Mcconait's ears were filled with the sound of the sea. The beast was entirely in shadow only a faint glow of its demonic eyes still visible. The great Eastern wall of the Priory towered above. It still bore the shape of its windows and McConait could see the moon through the gaps in the stone but the wolf was hidden by the darkness.

*   *   *   *   *

Price stopped; he found Tuthie bleeding on the ground, and McConait pointing a World War II pistol into the darkness. "McConait I know things have been difficult, but think about what you're doing. Put the gun down before someone gets killed!" The groaning at his feet made Price acutely aware of Father Tuthie's distress and turned away from McConait to attend the wounded old man.

McConait looked at the gun in his hand and at the bleeding leg of Tuthie, and could see how it must look. "No you've got it wrong it's a ..." the second's distraction was enough, and a snarling shape with devilish eyes emerged from the darkness. This time McConait yelled in panic, "Vade Retro Satana!" but the werewolf was already on the attack. McConait cocked the firing pin and emptied four barrels of the pistol into the oncoming monster. The creature reeled backwards, flailing its huge claws wildly in the air and returned into the blackness.

Price had seen nothing, but the gun fire made him jump out of his skin, "In God's name McConait what are you shooting at? Who have you got in there? Put down the gun I beg you!"

Tuthie was sat up in Price's arms and wielding his cross once again. Eyes closed, he summoned all his strength to drive the wolf back by the power of his faith. McConait did likewise, now the two voices spoke in unison, the prayer of St.Benedict rang around the ancient site of worship, which once would have been

215

filled with voices of monks in prayer. McConait felt the strength of the history of this place and strode forward towards the reeling beast, and joined it in the shadows. Invisible to Price and Tuthie the creature edged further back, away from the approaching McConait, who now looked directly into its eyes. Lifting the gun one more time he spoke the final line of the prayer, "Ipae Venena Bibas (Drink you yourself your poison)"

The final shot sent the evil creature over the cliff edge. It plunged headlong into the tempestuous seas and was swallowed in an explosion of white froth.

Price raced forward, "Have you gone mad? Who were you shooting at? Are you the executioner now?" He pointed to the injured Tuthie, "Look what you've done!"

"Yes look what he's done. He's rid the world of a demon." Tuthie bore a look of relief despite his wounds. He beckoned McConait to him. "Sylvester, my son you are a man of true faith and courage."

"But there are others father, there was more than one. The werewolf passed on the curse, the virus by …" McConait paused; the reality of the situation had become clear. Tuthie had been bitten by the wolf, and survived; he too would carry the curse, he too, by the light of the next full moon would transform into a beast.

"Help me up." McConait and Price grabbed an arm each and raised the old man to his feet. Once upright, Tuthie stood on his own. "You're right of course Sylvester, the fight against evil is never over. One must be vigilant against the power of the devil. But now we know how to fight it. The demon cannot be exorcised and leave the host alive. The werewolves must be identified and killed. There is no hope for the victims of the curse." Tuthie shuffled forward and talked as he went. He took back the gun from McConait. "This gun was blessed in the chapel of St.Hubert in France. St.Hubert is the patron saint of hunters. Only a weapon blessed in a chapel of St.Hubert can kill the werewolf." He looked at Price, "I'm sure you are aware of that Price?"

"I am aware of the legend Father," said price dismissively.

216

"I fear you are aware of much more than you let on." Tuthie stood on the edge and looked down at the sea that had taken the beast. "God bless you Sylvester, keep the faith." He looked up towards heaven, "God forgive me." Tuthie committed his final sin; he put the gun to his head and pulled the trigger.

The two men raced to Tuthie's body, which lay limp and lifeless on the cliff edge. They could see a scorched hole on his right temple, and a pool of blood, black in the moonlight, oozing from behind his head.

Price pulled something from his pocket; it was his purple priest's stole. He raced through a series of prayers, giving Tuthie the last rights before his immortal soul left his body. Price's normally unruffled persona gave way; in a mixture of tears and rage, he spoke as if Tuthie could still hear him. "So now more killing, more death… It was all over, it was proved but you had to carry on with this fantasy, about monsters and devils." Looking pitifully at McConait he continued, "And he dragged you into it all. I blame myself; I should have looked out for you. I knew you were popping pills. You were vulnerable, this is the church's fault, not yours, this mad man sparked what faith you had left and turned you into a…"

In disbelief McConait completed the sentence for him, "A killer? Is that what you think's going on here. Didn't you see it, didn't you see the beast."

"I saw you shoot into the shadows, and a figure tumbling into the sea. Then I saw a deranged old priest commit suicide. Are you saying that didn't happen?"

Desperate and disappointed McConait pointed at Tuthie's shoulder, where he had received the sideswipe from the wolf, "Look at that claw mark, look familiar?"

Price could see the four parallel score marks which went an inch deep into Tuthie's flesh. He was unimpressed, "It looks exactly how you explained it at the inquest. A wound made by the claw of a wolf, used by a madman in some shamanistic trance. The weapon was never discovered, and now we know why, the guy you blasted into oblivion must have got hold of it

217

and decided to have a go himself. And now it's crashing about at the bottom of the cliffs, it may never be recovered."

McConait stood and turned away from Price, wounded by his friend's lack of trust. "You think what you want Price. But I've learned something that you may never learn. There is more to this world than can be explained away or justified. Some things are beyond comprehension. They can only be addressed by one thing... faith. Faith, you hear me!" McConait's voice raised in volume. Looking at Tuthie's corpse he continued, "He knew it. He knew it from the start, we should have listened, we could have saved a lot of people. And this thing's not over, more may die, there are others out there ready to change."

Price got to his feet, "You mean the names on your board, the names you mentioned on the voicemail?"

McConait saw a ray of hope, "Yes, so you've seen the board, the anagrams, it proves it, you must see it now!"

But Price didn't see it. "Anagrams? You base your theory on anagrams? God is an anagram of dog. Does it make God an animal? Devil is an anagram of lived; it proves nothing! The people on your board are innocent people, they were involved in the investigation but then so were we, what if we made anagrams of our own names, what would that prove?"

"And what about Bob Stearman; he confessed. I saw him change into a werewolf in front of me. It was him that went over the cliff!"

"Then the tragedy and guilt at the loss of his wife surely drove him too far. He must have convinced himself of his guilt and then went about proving he did it."

*　　　*　　　*　　　*　　　*

The shots that had been fired had not gone unnoticed. Three squad cars and a riot vehicle with an armed unit hurtled along the sea front, their blaring sirens audible from inside the Priory.

*　　　*　　　*　　　*　　　*

218

McConait began to implore Price to listen to the events he had been involved in, but Price didn't want to know.

*　　　*　　　　*　　　　*　　　　*

Blue lights illuminated the entrance of the Priory. Officers streamed from the vehicles and through the entrance.

*　　　*　　　　*　　　　*　　　　*

Price turned one last time to McConait, as the sound of the voices of the police officers and the thumping of their boots on the damp grass grew louder. "Tell it to the police McConait; I want nothing more to do with it."

*　　　*　　　　*　　　　*　　　　*

A circle of armed officers pointed weapons at the two men standing in the Priory. They raised their hands in the air.

Chapter 33
Mad Doc McConait

McConait and Price were questioned all night. The police eventually pinned the death of Stearman to an act of self-defence, and the death of Tuthie down to suicide. The weapon was unlicensed but it was in Tuthie's possession. The wounds on Tuthie's body certainly favoured Price's version of events, as for McConait's testimony they put down to a man overworked and under severe mental stress. This blatant dismissal infuriated McConait and he flipped. In the end the police were forced to lock him in a cell and call for a psychiatrist. Throughout the night McConait refused to retract his statement about the events. His tale of wolf men, anagrams, Latin prayers and blessed guns all led the psychiatrist to conclude that McConait was experiencing some form of psychosis, brought on by severely traumatic events and a predilection for drugs, prescribed or otherwise.

McConait, desperate to reveal the truth lunged at the psychiatrist only to find himself pinned to the ground by two large policemen. Quoting section eight of the mental health act, the psychiatrist had the raging McConait certified and taken to a psychiatric hospital. There he was heavily sedated and diagnosed as suffering from possible schizophrenia.

* * * * *

A few days later Price walked along a quiet sea front. There was someone in the police hut, picking up and sorting out pieces of paper. It was Andrea Swan; she had been called to the case because of the latest incident. There was the threat of a copycat killer.

"Didn't expect to see you here." Price was pleased to see a friendly face.

"Me neither. They still haven't found the body of Stearman and the events of that night obviously have a connection to the Infareño case. So I'll be around until they tie things up. Speaking of which, I might pop in to see Mad Doc McConait later." She

220

turned her head away, her jest failing to cover up her feelings. "He's in a bad way I think."

"Yes I'm afraid he's seriously disturbed. You see these names." He pointed to the whiteboard baring the pentacle. "He reckoned that the anagrams he produced from the letters were clues to the killers. Even one of the police is implicated."

Andrea tutted at the suggestion, "So why the pentacle?"

"Well I suppose it's because there are five points to the star. There were five causes on the profile," Price pointed around the board at the five definitions he had written all those weeks ago, "and there are five incidents where McConait had his strange feeling, you remember the one outside the care home?" Andrea raised her eyebrows and nodded, "I think they might have been the onset of his schyzophrenia, you know hearing voices that kind of thing. He reckoned that the feeling was brought on in the presence of these people."

Andrea's analytical mind spotted the anomaly, "Five instances only four names. Who's the one the beach?"

"I suppose we'll never know." replied Price.

"Oh and there were five attacks in five months, in London." chipped in Andrea.

"And five attacks in five months here now. You can see why McConait, in his unstable state of mind, would start to make connections. And of course the pentacle, the five pointed star, is the symbol of devil worship, werewolves and all that kind of thing."

"It's a shame about McConait, I really cared for him; I guess he's just not cut out for this kind of work." Andrea wiped a tear from her eye, and continued sorting through Sylvester McConait's things.

$$* \qquad * \qquad * \qquad * \qquad *$$

McConait was in his pyjamas, dressing gown and slippers. He took his medication, from Peter the nurse on shift and shuffled back to his room. He placed the pills down on a small bedside cabinet. He knelt at the side of his bed and slid his hand under his pillow. He pulled out the Cross of St.Benedict that

221

Tuthie had given him and the tattered paper booklet. He opened it and began reciting the prayer he knew would protect him.

After his prayers, he returned the cross and booklet under his pillow. These were his prize possessions, along with a picture of Andrea she'd given him on one of her regular visits; they were the only things that mattered to him now. They were his protection against the forces of evil and the despair of loneliness, which he knew, from his experiences, were frighteningly real. He got to his feet and lifted the pot of tranquillising, anti-psychotic pills and swallowed them down with a gulp of water. He was glad to take them; it was the only thing that could take away the images of that night, the only thing that obscured the horror that was reality.

   *   *   *   *   *

A group of boys tossed a rugby ball on Tynemouth Longsands. One lad with shaggy blonde hair and a Newcastle Falcon's rugby top picked up the ball and began a teasing run towards his mates. He shimmied past one boy before being tackled by another. With whoops of enjoyment they wrestled in the sand before the boy in the Falcon's top got to his feet and clapped his hands in appreciation. It was the boy McConait had seen that day. His name was...

WILLIAM CARESS...

...I WILL MASSACRE

Biography

Martin Clephane was born in Perth, Scotland in 1970. He has spent most of his life in the North East of England and now lives in Tynemouth.

A fine arts graduate of The Duncan of Jordanstone College of Art, Dundee, he worked as an artist and exhibited in UK and also Cyprus (whilst living there for a year studying painting) before going into teaching.

He is a Headteacher of a Catholic Primary School and religious themes and beliefs play an integral part in his writing. He was awarded an Oxford Fellowship to research the teaching of RE and from this has created a series of books with resources which use religious philosophy in the classroom.